She had never kept secrets from her adopted tribe.

Glancing around to make sure no curious eyes were watching, Moon Hawk lifted the skin flap that covered the entrance to her lodge and dragged the travois inside. She had no wish to answer questions now. They would discover the white man soon enough.

If he survived the night.

The stranger stirred on the travois, his body straining against the rawhide thongs. Tugging aside the buffalo robe, she stared down at his face. His eyelids lay closed, the thick golden lashes frozen once more to his cheeks. His beautifully sculpted lips were blue with cold, his tawny hair and beard beaded with ice. There would be no rest for her tonight. And no peace, Moon Hawk sensed. She had brought home a load of trouble.

* * *

Wyoming Wildcat
Harlequin Historical #676—October 2003

Acclaim for Elizabeth Lane's latest books

Bride on the Run

"Enjoyable and satisfying all around,
Bride on the Run is an excellent Western romance
you won't want to miss!"
—*Romance Reviews Today* (romrevtoday.com)

Shawnee Bride

"A fascinating, realistic story."
—*Rendezvous*

Apache Fire

"Enemies, lovers, raw passion,
taut sexual tension, murder and revenge—
Indian romance fans are in for a treat
with Elizabeth Lane's sizzling tale of forbidden love
that will hook you until the last moment."
—*Romantic Times*

ELIZABETH LANE

Wyoming Wildcat

HARLEQUIN®

TORONTO • NEW YORK • LONDON
AMSTERDAM • PARIS • SYDNEY • HAMBURG
STOCKHOLM • ATHENS • TOKYO • MILAN • MADRID
PRAGUE • WARSAW • BUDAPEST • AUCKLAND

ISBN 0-373-29276-7

WYOMING WILDCAT

This edition published by arrangement with Harlequin Books S.A.

® and TM are trademarks of the publisher. Trademarks indicated with
® are registered in the United States Patent and Trademark Office, the
Canadian Trade Marks Office and in other countries.

Visit us at www.eHarlequin.com

Printed in U.S.A.

Please address questions and book requests to:
Harlequin Reader Service
U.S.: 3010 Walden Ave., P.O. Box 1325, Buffalo, NY 14269
Canadian: P.O. Box 609, Fort Erie, Ont. L2A 5X3

For Dad
You will always be my hero.

Chapter One

Wyoming Territory
June 12, 1866

Molly Ivins darted through the tall prairie grass, her seven-year-old legs pumping beneath the folds of her faded calico skirt. The two coyote pups scampered ahead of her, stumbling on their oversize paws. There was no sign of fear in their playful yelps. They seemed to know, as Molly did, that the chase was only a game.

Her white-gold pigtails flew behind her as she ran. It felt so good to be out of the dusty, lurching prairie schooner, even for a short time. Molly knew she should be sorry that one of the rear wagon wheels had lost a felly, loosening the spokes and forcing her family to fall behind the wagon train while her father replaced the broken wheel. She knew they would have to travel well into darkness, alone on the prairie, to reach the safety of the camp. But the day was so bright and sunny, the prairie such a glorious carpet of sunflowers, mallow, Indian paintbrush and blue-eyed grass that Molly could not muster so much a twinge of regret. She felt as if she could run forever, all the way to Oregon!

The two coyote pups had escaped. Molly stopped and prodded the grass for them, but succeeded only in startling a locust into buzzing flight. She sighed, feeling damp and sweaty in the summer heat. The pups were probably watching her right now, their little pink tongues lolling as they laughed at her in their doggish way. She hadn't meant them any harm. She had only wanted to play with them. But never mind. It was time she headed back to the wagon before her parents started to worry.

Dragging her feet a little, she turned around and began to walk. She would watch for buffalo chips along the way, she resolved. Maybe if she returned with her apron full, her mother wouldn't scold her.

She trudged through the long grass, zigzagging a bit as her eyes scanned the ground for dried buffalo dung to fuel the cooking fire. When she finally glanced up, expecting to see the wagon ahead, she discovered that it was nowhere in sight.

Molly blinked and rubbed her eyes. She was so sure she had come this way. But never mind, she would just retrace her steps to the spot where she'd lost the pups. From there she would have no trouble finding her way back.

With a growing sense of unease, she searched for her own footprints. But it was as if the bent grass had sprung back into place with the passing of her feet. Only the blazing sun overhead looked familiar.

Heart pounding, she stood in one place and turned herself in a slow, full circle. The prairie stretched in all directions, like an endless, rippling sea. And she, Molly Ivins, was no more than a dot on its vast surface—no more than a rabbit or a bird or an insect. Even when she shouted at the top of her lungs, her voice was lost in the huge emptiness of it, like the squeal of a prairie dog.

"Mamaaaa… Papaaaaa…"

She shouted until her voice gave out. Only then did she hear it, off to her right—the unmistakable pop and whine of gunfire.

Molly's heart jumped as she wheeled and raced toward the sound. It was all right. Her father knew she was lost. He was firing his rifle to guide her back to the wagon.

But as she ran, the fear grew that something was wrong. There were too many shots, and the difference in their tone and pitch told her they were coming from more than one gun.

Indians?

Sick with dread, she plunged forward, stumbling now over the hem of her long skirt. The gunfire had ceased, and a terrible stillness had fallen over the prairie. Even the birds were quiet. Molly tried to shout past the knot in her throat but could manage no more than a gasp. Each swish of her skirt against the sharp-edged grass seemed to split the silence like the crack of a whip.

Her foot sank into a badger hole. With a little cry, she pitched onto her hands and knees. Before she could clamber to her feet again, she heard the sound of voices. Men's voices. Laughing.

Did Indians laugh? Heart pounding, she crept forward. Through a blur of sunlit grass she could make out the faded canvas cover of the wagon. Dark shapes moved around it—men, four or five of them, dismounting, with their pistols still drawn. And they weren't Indians, she realized as she flattened herself against the earth and bellied closer. They wore long pants and cowboy hats, and their horses were saddled. They were white men.

Molly bit back the sickness in her stomach as a man emerged from the wagon with her mother's trunk. Laughing, he dumped the dresses and underclothes on the ground and pawed through them, pocketing the few treasures he found. Someone in the wagon train had mentioned there were bandits in these parts who preyed on lone travelers. But why would they bother her family? John and Florence Ivins were good people, and they had so little to steal.

Where were her parents? As the thought slammed into Molly's brain, she heard her mother's rending scream and the sound of rough laughter from the far side of the wagon. The screams and laughter went on and on, like echoes from a nightmare. Molly shoved her hands against her ears and pressed her face against the cool prairie earth. *Please make it stop…please make it stop…please—*

A shot rang out, and the screams abruptly ceased.

"Let's get the hell out of here!" The tallest bandit had unhitched the team of horses and tied lead ropes to their collars. The others loaded whatever they could carry—flour, coffee, bacon, blankets and a few odds and ends of clothing—into bags behind their saddles. One of the men had taken her father's rifle. Another, Molly noticed, was wearing his old felt hat. Her father had looked so handsome in that hat, with his blue eyes twinkling below the broad rim. The knot of rage that tightened in Molly's throat threatened to choke off her breath.

The bandits swung into their saddles. The one nearest the wagon crumpled some pages from the discarded family Bible, touched them with a match and tossed the burning paper into the wagon bed. Within seconds, the wagon was ablaze.

As gray smoke curled skyward, they spurred their horses and galloped away in a cloud of dust. Molly lay perfectly still, scarcely daring to breathe, until the riders had vanished over the horizon. Then, slowly, she rose to her feet and forced herself to walk toward the wagon. Left foot, right foot; each step was an act of will. She knew what she would find. But she had to see for herself. She could not leave this place of horror until she knew what had happened to her parents.

The acrid smell of burning canvas stung her wind-dried eyes. Through the smoke, she could see her father sprawled on his back beneath the burning wagon, his shirt stained dark red where the bullet had struck his chest. Florence Ivins's body, lying spread-eagled on open ground, was little more than a heap of bloodied, tattered petticoats, bare legs thrusting at odd angles from beneath them. Crouching beside her, Molly touched the sole of one trail-worn boot. She could not bring herself to look at what remained of her mother's beautiful face.

Her stomach had begun to heave. Clutching her belly, Molly stumbled back into the grass, bent double and retched until there was nothing left inside her. She wanted to cry. But crying was for babies. Mama and Papa were watching her from heaven now, and they would want her to be brave.

Straightening, she wiped her mouth on her sleeve and turned toward the wagon trail. By now the other families would be far ahead. But if she kept moving, she might be able to reach the campsite before dawn. There she would find Mr. Campbell, the wagon master, tell him what had happened and ask him to send someone back up the trail to bury her parents.

Walking was easier at the side of the trail than in the knee-deep wheel ruts. Blinded by unshed tears, Molly trudged along in the blazing midday heat. When her fair skin began to burn, she hiked up the back of her skirt and put it over her head, like the hood of a cloak. It crossed her mind that Mama would scold her for leaving her sunbonnet in the wagon—but no. The wagon was ashes, and her mother would never scold her again.

The sun crawled across the blinding sky, its heat blistering even through the fabric of the calico skirt. Molly had brought no water, and thirst raked her small body. The heat waves that swam before her eyes began to take on images—the flaming wagon, the blurred, vulturine bodies of men dancing around it. From the edges of her vision, a red-tailed hawk swooped on a rabbit. The rabbit's death scream joined with the screams that reverberated in her head.

Hour after hour, Molly forced her feet to keep moving. She did not even notice when her dragging steps left the trail side and began to wander across the prairie. The sun had dropped low in the sky. Its glare dazzled her eyes. Sick, dizzy and no longer able to see her way, she stumbled on. She had to keep going, had to reach the camp before…

The thought evaporated as her legs crumpled beneath her. Her body pitched forward into the grass. For an instant the aroma of sweet earth filled her senses. Then darkness closed around her like a gentle hand.

Molly whimpered and stirred, struggling against the bonds of sleep. She was dimly aware of a cool wetness on the back of her neck, a wetness that soothed her skin and dampened her sweat-encrusted hair. Was it raining? Was some curious animal licking the salt from her skin? Or was she only dreaming?

With a moan, she rolled onto her back and lay staring upward. The blazing sun was gone, and she saw that the sky was the deep, dusky blue of evening. A rasping chorus of crickets quivered around her, their song a soothing chant in the cool twilight.

The presence beside her was silent. Only when Molly heard the nicker of a nearby pony did her eyes move in the direction of the sound. Her cracked lips parted as she saw a figure crouched next to her in the grass.

At first her blurred gaze could only make out a dark shape. Then a face swam into focus—a man's face, as brown and wrinkled as a walnut, with fierce, aquiline features and birdlike eyes that peered at her from deep sockets. Two long braids, twined with otter fur and bright glass trade beads, hung over a beaded buckskin shirt. He looked of an age to be her grandfather, and when he spoke, his voice was like the rustle of wind passing through long-bladed marsh grass.

Molly's mouth worked in an effort to speak, but only a feeble croak emerged from her parched throat. The man's fingers, dripping moisture, moved toward her face, brushing her burning cheeks, her painfully cracked lips. His words took on a cautionary tone as he lifted her head and tipped the corner of a water-swollen skin bag to her mouth. Molly sensed that he was warning her not to drink too fast or she would be sick, the same thing her father had once told her. She willed herself to take small sips, even though the water was so fresh and cold that it was all she could do to keep from gulping it. The man rewarded her with an approving nod.

He spoke to her again, in a low murmur, as if he were soothing a frightened animal. His hands slid carefully beneath her legs and shoulders, arms lifting her, cradling her against his broad chest as he strode toward his tethered pony. He smelled of wood smoke and horseflesh and prairie grass.

Too exhausted to be frightened, Molly pressed her face into his soft buckskin shirt and closed her eyes.

Chapter Two

Absaroka Mountains, Wyoming
November, 1882

Ryan Tolliver cursed as he struggled to make out the markings on the faded, crumpled map. Wet flakes of snow splattered his face, driven by a howling wind that threatened to snatch the paper from his hands. What was the use? He had clearly followed the wrong fork of the canyon, and now he was lost. There was nothing to do but find shelter, wait out this miserable storm and try to get his bearings when the sky cleared.

With a snort of disgust, he folded the map and thrust it back into the pocket of his heavy sheepskin coat. He must have been out of his mind when he'd agreed to Horace Mannington's crazy scheme! The long-standing five-thousand-dollar reward the old man had offered for the recovery of his lost granddaughter had sounded like a fortune back in St. Louis. But no amount of money was worth freezing to death in a Wyoming blizzard!

The horse snorted beneath him, shaking the snow from its shaggy hide as Ryan guided it along the treacherous canyon slope. Far below, a narrow creek, overgrown by willows, gushed down the canyon like a tangled silver ribbon. Hellfire, he could have sworn he knew this country like the back of his hand! But in this blizzard, he couldn't have named the creek or the blasted canyon for all the fine liquor and pretty women in Laramie!

He'd give his eyeteeth to be back in Laramie right now, Ryan thought, imagining himself with a glass of fine bourbon in one hand, a royal flush in the other, and a voluptuous, perfumed woman hanging over his shoulder. Or better yet, to be back on the Tolliver family ranch, with his half brother Morgan, Morgan's spunky redheaded wife Cassandra, and their three lively children. Winter evenings in the big, rambling house were always filled with warmth, laughter, and the best biscuits and apple pie in the territory.

But he wasn't at the ranch. And he wasn't in Laramie. He was out here in the godforsaken middle of nowhere searching for a will-o'-the-wisp—a fair-haired young woman some wandering trapper had glimpsed with a band of renegade Cheyenne who hadn't come in when the rest of the tribe was herded onto reservations.

Word of the sighting had gotten back to Ryan, who knew that Horace Mannington, a wealthy St. Louis land speculator, had offered a generous reward for the return of his missing granddaughter. Ryan, who knew the mountain country and spoke passable Cheyenne, had contacted Mannington, and the two of them had agreed on the terms—five hundred dollars if his search failed after three months; five *thousand* dollars if he brought Molly Ivins home alive.

Mannington, stout and balding, had told the story with tears in his eyes. Florence, his only offspring, had been a beauty, with every wealthy bachelor in St. Louis at her feet. Spurning them all, she'd eloped with John Ivins, a schoolmaster with scarcely a penny to his name. The outraged Mannington had cut her out of his will and closed his door to the young couple.

Undaunted, the newlyweds had moved to Kentucky, where Florence had given birth to a daughter. Seven years later they had set out for a better life in Oregon, only to be murdered on the trail. A party of men from the wagon train had found the bodies of Florence and John beside their burned-out wagon. But young Molly had vanished without a trace.

Ryan thought of the small silver-framed portrait Mannington had lent him, now carefully wrapped in a red bandanna and sewn inside the lining of his coat. Florence Mannington had been a golden-haired fairy-tale princess, with finely chiseled features and vulnerable fawn eyes. If Molly Ivins had survived to grow up, there was a fair chance she would resemble her mother now—except for one thing, Ryan reminded himself. He had seen white women who'd lived among the Indians. The raw conditions and backbreaking labor turned most of them into crones by the time they were thirty, especially if they were unlucky enough to bear children.

Women rescued from captivity had a broken, haunted quality about them. Even if their families accepted them, few were able to fully return to life in the white world. He would be doing Horace Mannington no great favor by bringing his granddaughter back to St. Louis. The poor creature would probably be an embarrassment and a burden for the rest of her life.

But never mind. Five thousand dollars would buy a lot of dreams. *His* dreams.

London, Paris, Rome, Egypt, Africa…Ryan had burned to see those places from the time he was old enough to hold a book on his lap and gaze at the pictures. But the wealth of the Tolliver family was in land and livestock, not in cash. Profits from the cattle were always reinvested in the ranch, to pay the hands, buy more stock, keep the corrals and buildings in good repair and to expand the ranch's boundaries when any land came up for sale. For such a frivolous pursuit as travel, Ryan knew he would have to come up with the money on his own.

Molly Ivins, if he could find her, would be his ticket to the wonders of the world.

The snow was coming down harder now, slicking the already treacherous slope. Aspens moaned in the biting wind, their trunks showing ghost-white through the swirling mist of flakes. Ryan grimaced as a sharp gust penetrated his coat. No wonder the Cheyenne called November *He koneneese he,* the time of the hard-faced moon. It was a merciless time, the beginning of the long winter when people and animals went hungry and only the strong survived.

From the looks of it, the storm was going to get worse. He needed to find shelter now, while he could see his way.

Ahead, glimpsed through blinding snow, was a deadfall, where fallen timber had piled against a clump of standing aspens to make a tangle of limbs and trunks. With luck there would be enough space to crawl beneath it. It wasn't as substantial as Ryan had hoped, but right now he couldn't afford to be choosy.

Far below, the creek rushed and tumbled over its rocky bed. It was a long way to the bottom of the canyon, Ryan reminded himself as he guided the horse along the narrow game trail. A man who was careless enough to fall would be lucky to survive with a few broken bones. Even then, he'd probably freeze to death.

He could see the deadfall clearly now—a forbidding tangle already covered with snow. Before he tried to get beneath it, he would need to find a secure spot to tie the horse so it wouldn't wander off in the storm.

He was searching for a patch of level ground when a startled owl exploded out of the deadfall. Dazzled by the whiteness, the big bird flew straight toward the horse's face.

The horse screamed, jumped and lost its footing. Ryan sawed at the reins in a frantic effort to bring the animal under control, but it was no use. The white, whirling world of the blizzard seemed to cave in upon itself as horse and rider pitched down the slope.

Trapped in a flurry of kicking limbs, Ryan fought to free his feet from the stirrups before the tumbling horse could roll and crush him. Straining his tortured joints, he managed to work one boot loose. But it was too late for the other. The pitching motion of the horse flung him out of the saddle. Caught by one leg, Ryan found himself being dragged down the rocky slope.

Still conscious, he used his bloodied hands to push himself away from the worst of the rocks and brush. But the weight and momentum of the shrieking horse threatened to tear his leg from its socket. Twisting desperately, he grabbed for a passing boulder. He could only maintain his hold for an instant, but the brief resistance was enough to dislodge his heel from the inside of the boot. As the horse careened downward, Ryan wrenched his foot free, leaving his boot in the stirrup.

But it was too late to stop his own downward plunge. Rolling, sliding and bouncing, he shot down the side of the canyon. He heard the death scream of the horse as it struck the sharp rocks. A heartbeat later, Ryan's own body followed, tumbling past the horse and careening toward a line of jutting boulders that rimmed the creek. As he struck the first rock, something seemed to rip through the back of his head. He moaned, quivered and lay still.

As daylight passed into darkness, the snow fell around and over him, covering him like a feathery white blanket.

Moon Hawk had brought down a yearling buck high in the canyon. She had lashed it to a makeshift travois and was dragging it along the creek bed, toward the winter camp, when she came across the ravens.

The noisy black birds were pecking at a large mound—some kind of animal, covered with snow from yesterday's storm. Whatever it was, the ravens had managed to uncover a patch of dark brown hide and were tearing at it with their beaks. But the carcass was still fresh, the skin firm and tough. The birds had not made much progress on their meal.

Laying the travois beside the trail, Moon Hawk moved closer to investigate. In the hard season ahead, any source of meat would be of value to the small band of Tse Tse Stus she called her family. If the animal had perished cleanly, and the cold had kept its meat from spoiling, it might be worth sending some of the women back here to butcher it.

At her approach, the ravens flapped away to perch in the gnarled branches of an ancient pine tree. They scolded impatiently as Moon Hawk bent to brush away more of the snow with her otter-skin gloves. The snow crunched beneath the fat-rubbed soles of her moccasins.

She had expected to find a moose or an elk beneath the layer of white. When her hand touched the hard, smooth edge of a saddle, she froze, her blue eyes widening with shock.

A horse had died here—a horse ridden by one of the *ve hoe*—the spider people. It had most likely fallen from one of the higher trails. But its manner of death was the least of Moon Hawk's concerns now. Where there was a saddled horse, there would be a rider. And where there was one rider, there would likely be more. Perhaps many more.

Soldiers? Heart pounding, Moon Hawk brushed away more of the snow. Had the bluecoats found them at last? Would her little band be rounded up and force-marched to the reservation on the Tongue River, where even the bravest of the Tse Tse Stus— the people—had been sent? She thought of the great chiefs—Dull Knife, Little Wolf, American Horse and so many others—who now lived like penned cattle. She knew that, if forced to do the same, the members of her own weak little band would not survive.

Worst of all, perhaps, would be her own fate.

When the soldiers saw her pale hair and blue eyes, they would send her back to the world of the *ve hoe*. She would never see her beloved people again.

Moon Hawk brushed away more snow, uncovering the saddle, the thick striped blanket beneath, and the rifle in its tooled leather scabbard. She felt her tense breathing ease as she realized neither the saddle nor the gun were like those used by the bluecoats. But the rifle…

She slid it from the scabbard, biting back a whoop of elation. It was a fine weapon, vastly better than the bow and arrows she used for hunting. Once she taught herself to shoot, she would be able to bring down bigger and faster game, even buffalo! No one in the band would go hungry this winter!

Bullets—she would need them. They had to be here, maybe in the saddlebags. She was rummaging deeper when something caught her eye. Something brown, sticking out of the snow, just below the horse's belly. Reaching down, she twisted it loose.

It was a man's boot, designed for riding, with a thick heel that would hold to the stirrup. The boot was worn but finely made, the stitching small and exquisitely neat, the inside lined with the softest leather. Balancing it in her hands, Moon Hawk was struck by a strange awareness. Her senses prickled as she examined the boot, touching the scuff marks, noticing the way the damp leather had shaped itself to the bones of the narrow foot. The boot's size told her its owner had been long of limb. The even wear on the sole told her he had walked with his feet in a straight line like the Tse Tse Stus. But had he been young or old? Friend or enemy? The boot told her none of these things.

Moon Hawk shivered beneath her warm buffalo robe. A moment ago she had been gloating over the fine rifle, already counting it hers. But now the thought of the missing life, even the life of a *ve hoe*—

A sound from the creek side brought her sharply around, one gloved hand touching the hilt of her skinning knife. Holding her breath, she listened. Had she only heard the wind stirring the trees in its rush down the canyon? Could the ghost of the boot's owner be playing tricks on her mind? Laying the boot aside, Moon Hawk crept toward the spot from which the sound had come.

She heard it again as she neared the creek, a low but unmistakable groan. The sound of a human creature in pain.

Knife ready, she moved closer. A wounded man could be as dangerous as a wounded animal. She could not let herself be taken by surprise.

A drift of snow lay between two high boulders. Moon Hawk's sharp eyes caught a slight rise and fall, like the motion of breathing. Something was there. Something long and large.

Without taking her eyes off the drift, she picked up a bare branch that had fallen from a tree. Still keeping her distance, she jabbed the pointed end of the branch into the snow.

There was a convulsive movement and a sound that could have been a weak snarl. She jumped back, clutching the knife.

"Who are you?" Moon Hawk's English was still fluent, thanks to a well-read mountain man who'd married into her tribe and remained for three winters before dying of the coughing sickness when she was fourteen. He had urged her to practice the language, so that one day she might be able to speak for her people. That day had yet to come.

"Answer me! Who are you?" she demanded again.

No response came from the coldly glittering snow.

She repeated the question in Cheyenne, but the silence was broken only by the mocking *chuk* of a raven. Her eyes could detect no motion under the drift. Even a cautious jab with the limb failed to rouse the life that lay beneath the snow.

A slow dread uncoiled in her stomach, rising up into her throat, exploding in an urgency that drove her to action.

Her gloved hands pawed at the snow in a flurry of desperation. A shoulder emerged, clad in a heavy skin coat that was frozen almost stiff. One bare hand lay across the breast of the coat, a long-fingered, very masculine hand, the back of it frosted with a mat of pale gold hair. The fingers were scraped and battered, the blood congealed by cold.

Sheathing her knife, Moon Hawk bent and laid her cheek against the hand. The flesh was almost as cold as the snow that had covered it.

Leave him alone, the voice of caution whispered. *He is one of the* ve hoe. *Whatever reason brought him here can't be good. Better that he die and leave your people in peace.*

But even as the thoughts plucked at her mind, Moon Hawk was brushing away the snow from the stranger's face. The features that emerged beneath her glove were strong and fine—the golden eyelashes frozen to the pale cheeks, the lips blue with cold. Tendrils of tawny hair clung to his forehead, their color matching the scruffy ice-coated whiskers that covered his jaw.

He was young and strong and handsome, and so very cold.

Leave him for the ravens. The man is a ve hoe. *And even if he means no harm, you've arrived too late to save him.*

Ignoring the warnings in her head, Moon Hawk ripped open the front of the coat and pressed her ear to his chest. At first she heard nothing, and her heart sank. Then, straining against him, she felt a tiny flutter beneath the thick woolen shirt. It was so faint that at first she thought she might be mistaken. But no, there it was again. He was alive, but unless she could get him back to the camp, he would not be alive for long.

Frantically she scraped the snow from his limbs

and body. Although she felt no broken bones, he
could still be badly hurt. Moving him would be risky,
but she had no choice. The stranger was already too
weak to last much longer in the cold. If she left him
here, wedged between the rocks, he would die.

Wouldn't that be for the best? the voice shrilled
in her mind. *Look at him—he was meant to die! Why
should you interfere? Why should you risk the safety
of your people to save one who can do you nothing
but harm?*

Again Moon Hawk closed her ears to the warning.
Her people looked to her for protection. But she had
never killed a fellow human being nor willingly
watched one die, not even a *ve hoe*. Now she had
crossed an invisible line, and she knew there could
be no turning back. Somehow the life of this half-
frozen stranger had taken on value, as if, in that first
moment of discovery, he had become hers to save.

One of his feet was protected by the mate to the
boot she had found. But the other, clad only in a
dark stocking, could already be frostbitten. She
would do what she could to get the blood moving.
Then she would try to get him onto the travois.

Lifting the exposed foot, she peeled off the snow-
encrusted stocking. The skin beneath was icy, dotted
with the waxen grayish-white patches that indicated
the flesh had already begun to freeze. Heart sinking,
she pulled off her gloves and tucked them beneath
her buffalo robe. Then she cradled the stranger's foot
between her warm, bare palms.

Gently at first, she began to massage the foot, kneading the long, high arch, flexing the frigid toes. The strangely intimate contact triggered whorls of sensation in the depths of her body. Five winters ago, after the death of the warrior who had been her husband, Moon Hawk had knotted the leather chastity string between her thighs and given up her life as a woman. Her people had honored her decision and she had few regrets, except on those rare dark nights when she lay awake on her buffalo robes, staring restlessly into the darkness, aching for what she had barely known.

Now, in the blinding light of a cold winter day, she felt that same raw ache.

Her damp breath condensed in the frigid air, rising in silvery puffs as she rubbed the foot more vigorously. Slowly the chilled flesh began to soften and warm, but the stranger's pulse was feeble beneath her fingertips. She needed to get him warm, get him moving.

The hoarse groan that quivered in his throat startled her. She glanced up to see his face twitching with the effort of coming back to the world. Shifting her ministrations to his head, she rubbed his cheeks and forehead, carefully freeing the frozen moisture from his eyelashes. His face worked as, with an effort that seemed to take all the strength he possessed, his eyelids blinked, crinkled shut, then fully opened.

He stared up into Moon Hawk's face, but with no sign that he truly saw her. His irises were the fierce green-gold of a cougar's, the pupils shrunken to tiny dots in the sudden glare of sun on snow. If she could rouse him, it would be easier to get him onto the travois. But even with his eyes open, he seemed to be drifting in a darkness she could not reach.

"Who are you?" she demanded in English. "Can you hear me?"

As she spoke, his eyelids closed and he slipped away again, like a fish gliding through her fingers into black water.

Moving with urgency now, Moon Hawk shoved the buck's carcass off the travois and piled snow over it to discourage the ravens. Then she dragged the travois to the rocks and braced it below the cleft where the injured man lay. To get him down, she would have to lift him. His body would be dead-weight, and if he had serious injuries, the change in position could kill him. But delay would only worsen his chances. She had little choice except to try.

A rivulet of nervous sweat trickled between her shoulder blades as she worked her arms under his shoulders. "Wake up!" she muttered in Cheyenne, her teeth clenched with effort. "Wake up and help me!"

The tawny-haired stranger did not respond. Except for the thready pulse against her wrist, Moon Hawk would have believed he was already with the dead—which he might well be very soon if his spine proved to be broken.

Bracing herself against the rock, she cradled his

head against her breasts, worked her hands beneath his arms and lifted his shoulders. There was no sudden change—no separation of bone from bone, no gush of blood, no departure of life. Little by little, she felt herself begin to breathe again. Her worst fear was over. But the solidly muscled body was a deadweight in her arms. It would take all her strength to ease him onto the travois and drag him the long distance back to camp.

Grunting with effort, Moon Hawk hefted his upper body and staggered backward. His torso was clear of the boulders now, but the rough ground, slick with fresh-fallen snow, sloped downward behind her all the way to the creek. She fought to keep her footing as she maneuvered his legs between the rocks. She had not discovered any fractured bones, but one incautious move could turn a hairline crack into a bad break.

It's not too late. Leave him. He will die here, as he was meant to.

Yet again, Moon Hawk struggled to ignore the warning. She had brought the stranger this far, and she could not abandon him now.

His head rolled sideways against the hollow of her shoulder, causing her to glance down. Only then did she notice the smear of blood on her buffalo robe. His scalp was gashed and bleeding. The injury could explain why he had drifted in and out of wakefulness.

His feet cleared the rocks, the sudden shift catching her off balance. Thrown by his weight and her own momentum, Moon Hawk staggered, lost her footing and tumbled backward down the rocky slope toward the creek.

Instinctively she wrapped her arms around the stranger, protecting him as they rolled, slid and came to rest beneath a clump of overhanging willows. His body sprawled on top of hers, one leg resting between her thighs, the weight of it straining the knots of the chastity string.

She looked up to find him staring down at her, his golden eyes a handbreadth from her own. The awkward silence between them was broken only by the scolding of a chickadee and the rushing sound of the creek. Moon Hawk felt the pressure of his leg against her body, felt the strength that, even in his weakened condition, might be greater than her own. Fear nibbled at the edge of her awareness as she realized how vulnerable she was.

"Who are you?" Her voice emerged as a raw whisper. "Why have you come to this place?"

For the space of a long breath he was silent. Emotions chased each other across his face—frustration, pain and fear—the startled fear of a child who has just discovered he has lost the way home. It was a fear Moon Hawk remembered well.

"Who are you?" she asked, more gently this time.

His mouth worked. "I...don't know," he rasped, trembling as he forced each word from his throat. "Lord help me, *I don't know.*"

His eyelids closed. His head tumbled onto her shoulder and he lay still.

Chapter Three

He drifted in a swirling well of pain. During his more lucid moments, he was aware of motion and sound, the bone-jarring drag of the travois and the press of the rawhide lashings that held him to its frame. He heard the crunch of winter moccasins on snow and the deep, regular breathing of the woman who pulled the travois behind her, straining with every step. Beneath him and around him lay the leathery softness of her buffalo robe.

He realized dimly that he was a heavy burden and that he should offer to get up and walk beside her, but much as he willed it, he could not move his limbs. The cold lay like poison in the marrow of his bones, numbing his well-honed reflexes with a lethargy that made even breathing an effort. Opening his eyes brought only the blinding glare of sun and snow.

Thinking seemed beyond the grasp of his chilled brain. Every perception was blurred by pain that felt like a nail being pounded into his head. *Who was he?* The question mocked him. He was nothing and no one. A dying bird. A guttering candle. The memory was gone.

Only the woman seemed solid and real. Her face floated in the black void. In memory, she was striking—the straight nose and high cheekbones, the ripe, sensual mouth, the haunting violet eyes that seemed oddly familiar. He clung to every detail of that face—the threadlike scar that zigzagged from her upper temple to her left eyebrow, the tiny brown mole at the corner of her mouth. Her hair had been hidden by the beaver-skin cap she wore against the biting cold. Would she be dark or fair? Either way, he reasoned, she would be beautiful.

She was not a young girl—twenty-three or twenty-four, he calculated, maybe even older. And although his eye had not measured her height, he sensed that she was tall, and that she was unusually strong for a woman—strong enough to load his inert body onto the travois and drag it through the heavy snow.

Who are you? She had asked him the question in English, then in Cheyenne. Strangely, he had recognized and understood both languages. What was happening here? She was not an Indian. Neither was he. Nothing about her or about himself was making any sense.

The sun slowly vanished beyond the rim of the canyon, leaving a sullen gray sky overhead. It began to snow again, hard, dry flakes that stung like blowing sand. The constant drag of the travois through the deep drifts had chilled his body to numbness. His back and buttocks ached with cold, and his legs had lost all feeling. He wanted to call out to the woman, to insist that she stop and let him rest, but he could not rouse the strength to speak.

A willow lashed his face with its frozen branches as they passed beneath it. In the time they had been moving, the woman had scarcely uttered a word. Wherever she was taking him, he could only hope the place would be warm. Not that it mattered, since he'd likely be dead by then. Right now the idea of dying didn't seem so bad, except that if he died, he would never know who he was or what he was doing in this godforsaken place. And he would never unravel the mystery of the amethyst-eyed goddess who had rescued him.

Could she be some trapper's wife or daughter whose family had a cabin tucked away in these mountains? Or was she only a beautiful and mysterious part of his nightmare, a dream creature who would vanish along with the snow and cold when he awakened?

As the twilight deepened around him, the urge to sleep became a siren's song in his head. He was so cold that he began to feel deliciously warm and drowsy. He drifted in and out of sweet, peaceful dreams in which there was no pain, no cold, no danger. He fought those dreams with all his strength, knowing that to sink into them would be to die.

To keep himself awake, he cursed in the depths of

his throat, muttering every foulmouthed obscenity he could dredge from his sluggish brain. When he ran out of curses he began singing under his breath— nursery rhymes and church hymns, coupled with raunchy barroom ballads that would make a whore blush.

Where had he learned them, the songs and curses and patterns of speech that were stored inside his head like books in a library?

How could he remember so many things and not remember his own name or how he'd come to be here?

He could feel himself sinking again into the cozy feather bed of death. Desperately he struggled against the pull of it, chanting, muttering, and finally fixing his thoughts on the woman who dragged him down the rocky canyon on the tooth-jarring frame of the travois.

He could not turn his head far enough to look at her, but the strong, sensual cadence of her breathing drifted back to him through the snowy darkness. He could gauge the slender height of her by the angle of the travois and the length of her stride. She would be almost as tall as a medium-sized man, the body beneath the long buckskin shirt as sleek and powerful as a mountain cat's.

Some lingering impression told him he liked his women petite and voluptuous, wrapped in satin and drenched in perfume. Never mind—the thought of those long golden legs moving beneath the leather fringe was having the desired warming effect on his body. Shifting beneath the rawhide lashings, he let his fantasies wander upward. His fingertips burned as he imagined stroking the satin skin of her inner thighs, slowly, silkily, taking his time, until the moisture trickled down her legs like honey from a plundered hive. He imagined the taste of that wild honey, thick and sweet on his tongue, imagined her sudden gasp of pleasure as he burrowed like a honeybee into the fragrant folds of a rose....

He was feeling warm now, and pleasantly aroused. But his own fantasy had turned on him. The call of darkness had become too seductive to resist, luring him deeper into the erotic dream. Her face swirled in his vision, eyes closed, mouth wet and swollen, opening to release a low moan of welcome as he slid into the sweetness of cold-drugged sleep.

"Wake up!" Moon Hawk crouched beside the travois, her gloved hands gripping the man's broad shoulders. His eyes were closed, his breathing so faint it would scarcely have stirred a feather.

The storm had cleared, leaving behind a crystalline cold that cut to the bone. She felt it penetrate her damp buckskins, glazing her skin with ice as she knelt in the snow. While she was moving, the strain of pulling the travois, burdened by the heavy rifle and bullet pouch she'd found, had kept her more than warm. But now that she'd paused to check on the stranger, her teeth had already begun to chatter.

Stripping off one glove, she thrust her arm beneath the folds of the buffalo robe that covered him. The large, masculine hands she found, clasped on his chest as if he'd been laid out for burial, were like chunks of ice.

She had spent her strength to get him to the winter camp before he froze to death. The icy air had seared her lungs as she plunged through the snow, sweating with effort, afraid to stop and rest. Now the long trek was nearly over. The glade that sheltered the lodges of the Tse Tse Stus lay around the next bend of the rushing creek. But she feared she had reached it too late.

"Wake up!" She rubbed his hands vigorously, slapping them in an effort to get the blood flowing. After a few moments the chilled flesh seemed to warm a little, but the stranger had not stirred, and she feared that the only warmth she felt might be her own.

Growing more desperate, Moon Hawk pummeled his chest, shaking and pinching his arms and legs. Nothing.

It's not too late to abandon him, the warning voice shrilled again in her head. *If he dies in the camp, people will see it as a bad sign. There may be talk of moving away from here. You know that a move would be hard on the old ones in this weather. Leave him here for the foxes and ravens, before he can bring harm to those you care for. Any evil he does will be on your own head.*

This time the argument was so strong, so persuasive, that Moon Hawk's hands halted in midmotion. The tiny band of old ones, widows and children who'd been too weak to make the long trek to the Indian Territories five winters ago were her responsibility. It was she who provided game for them, she who kept vigil to protect them from the outside world.

For years they had avoided the eyes of the bluecoats. Even after a new reservation to the north, on the Tongue River, had been set aside for the Tse Tse Stus, Moon Hawk's people had voiced their resolve to stay free and live in the old way. Since they were not strong enough to fight or swift enough to run, their only defense lay in remaining as carefully hidden as a covey of mountain quail.

She, of all people, should know better than to bring a stranger, especially a white man, into their midst.

But as she hesitated, another memory, faded by time, brushed her heart like the touch of a bird's wing. She saw an aging man with a wrinkled face and fierce, dark eyes reach down to a terrified little girl and lift her into his arms. Crow Feather must have realized that the presence of a white child would be a danger to his band. Surely, then as now, the voice of wisdom had whispered that he should leave her to die on the prairie. But Crow Feather had followed the instincts of his own heart.

Faced with an even graver choice, Moon Hawk knew she must do the same.

She shook the man's shoulders harder than before. When he did not respond she raised one hand and slapped him so hard across the face that the blow almost dislocated her elbow. "Wake…up!" she muttered in English. "Do you want to die? No? Then *wake up!*"

She struck him again, a desperate, stinging blow that snapped his head sharply to one side. In the long breath of silence that followed, she heard him groan.

Her legs went watery with relief.

Staggering to her feet, she pulled on her glove, picked up the ends of the travois and flung her weight forward. The bitter wind clawed through her buckskin shirt, tightening her rib muscles so that she gasped with every step. No matter, the camp was close. Her nostrils caught the fragrance of burning pitch pine and the lingering aroma of venison stew on the dark wind. On most nights like this, her heart would be flooded with the happy sense of homecoming. But tonight was different. What would her people say when they learned that she had brought a white stranger—an enemy—into the camp?

Straining forward, she rounded the last bend in the trail. There, nestled below the high cliffs of the canyon and sheltered by a thicket of aspen, lay the nineteen lodges that made up her village. This was her family. Her world.

The nine-year-old boy who stood watch on the

creek bank flashed her a friendly grin as she approached. His eyes flickered briefly toward the travois where the stranger lay, wrapped from head to toe in the buffalo robe, trussed like a deer carcass. "Good hunting?" the boy asked.

"Good hunting." Moon Hawk returned his greeting and hurried on without giving him a chance to look more closely. Tomorrow would be soon enough for the people to know there was a *ve hoe* among them.

The lodges lay in darkness. The night was half-gone, and most of the people had long since bedded down. Here and there, a curl of silvery smoke rose through the top of a tall buffalo-skin teepee, but there were no open fires. An outdoor blaze wasted fuel and could too easily alert an enemy, of which there were many. Likewise, there were no dogs, whose barking could give away the camp's presence. The small, precious band of ponies lay up a side draw, its entrance guarded by the camp itself.

Moon Hawk's lodge stood at the far edge of the camp. By the time she reached it, her nerves and muscles were strained raw. What if she'd committed a foolish act, bringing the injured white man into the secret camp? What if his presence put her people in harm's way?

There could be only one answer to that question. If the stranger's presence proved a threat, it would be her duty to take his life.

Glancing around to make sure no curious eyes

were watching, she lifted the skin flap that covered the entrance to her lodge and dragged the travois inside. She had never kept secrets from her adopted band. But she had no wish to answer questions now. They would discover the white man soon enough.

If he survived the night.

The embers in the fire pit filled the lodge with a soft, glowing warmth. Old She-Bear, whose dwelling was nearby, had kindled the small blaze and placed a pot of stewed venison where the coals would keep it simmering. Its rich aroma surrounded Moon Hawk like a welcoming embrace.

The stranger stirred on the travois, his body straining against the rawhide thongs. Tugging aside the buffalo robe, she stared down at his face. His eyelids lay closed, the thick golden lashes frozen once more to his cheeks. His beautifully sculpted lips were blue with cold, his tawny hair and beard beaded with ice. There would be no rest for her tonight. And no peace, Moon Hawk sensed. She had brought home a load of trouble.

She took precious time to place a pot of water on the coals to heat. Then, thrusting aside her own weariness, she stripped off her damp gloves and bent to untie the thongs. The buffalo robe she'd spread beneath him was frozen to the travois, stiff with snow and ice. His body was every bit as cold, the fabric of his breeches frozen to his legs. If she did not get him out of his clothes and moving, even the warmth of the lodge would not be enough to save him.

"Wake up!" She leaned over him, rubbing his face, stinging his cheeks with sharp little slaps. He rewarded her with a groan and the twitch of an eyelid. His eyes opened to narrow slits, then slowly widened their view. For the space of a breath the lost, bewildered expression she'd seen earlier flickered across his face. Then his mouth worked, the lips flexing, hardening into a grimace.

"Holy hell," he muttered thickly. "Do you have to be so rough, woman?"

The sound of his voice, so raw and so close, sent a shock wave through her body. She stifled a gasp, forcing herself to meet his gaze. His eyes were bloodshot with cold and exhaustion, but bits of reflected fire sparked like flecks of lightning in their golden depths.

Moon Hawk suddenly felt as if her tongue had frozen to the roof of her mouth. Though in a weakened state, the stranger appeared so large and powerful, so dangerously masculine that she found herself trembling. It was as if she had dragged a wounded, half-dead he-cougar into her lodge and it had suddenly raised its beautiful head and snarled at her.

"You need to move." She spoke in English, the words thick and awkward in her throat. "You need to help me get you warm."

The corners of his mouth twitched. "I think I could manage that." His voice rasped in his throat, like the sound of breaking ice. "What did you have in mind, lady?"

Moon Hawk felt the rush of heat as his words sank home. Instinctively her hand flashed to the haft of her hunting knife. "Not what you think," she snapped, her face blazing. "I could kill you right here. Touch me, and you'll bleed!"

He exhaled slowly, his eyes drifting closed like a weary child's. Leaving him on the travois, Moon Hawk knelt at his feet, hefted one cold-stiffened leg and twisted off the boot. The thick stocking beneath smelled of wet wool. It steamed in the dry warmth of the lodge as she peeled it down his long, narrow foot, working it over the heel. The flesh of this foot was icy but not frozen.

The other foot, however, the one that had lost the boot in the snow, looked even worse than before. Worried, she cradled the foot between her palms, massaging it with her fingers, then blowing on it with her warm breath to coax the sluggish circulation to life.

"Where...are we?" He had opened his eyes again. His gaze was wary, his voice leaden.

"We are in my home," she answered with forced calm, her heart pounding, "and you are my prisoner."

"And do you give all your prisoners such delicious foot rubs?" His golden eyes flickered dangerously in the firelight.

"Only if they're in danger of losing their toes." Her fingers kneaded the long, elegant arch of his foot. His gaze scorched her flesh, stirring rivulets of heat in the depths of her body. Moon Hawk shot him a glare, forcing herself to meet his eyes. To glance away like a shy maiden would be a sign of submission, something she could ill afford.

"Who are you?" His rough voice raked her senses like the brush of an eagle's talon across her skin.

"I will ask the questions," she said in the language of her own people, testing him. "I could have left you in the snow to die, but I chose to save your life. Now I want to know who you are and why you have come here."

He hesitated. Then his mouth curled in a bitter smile. "Then, dear lady, I fear I must disappoint you," he retorted in English. "I've no more memory of who I am than a newborn baby!" He winced, his features twisting in pain. "I…"

The words trailed off, ending in a moan as his eyes closed. His head lolled to one side, revealing the gash in his scalp, which was now oozing blood.

Snatching a scrap of tanned doeskin from a nearby basket, Moon Hawk leaned across his chest to dab at the ugly, finger-length cut. Fragments of rock, dirt and hair had been ground into the wound by the blow to his head. The gash would need to be cleaned and treated with a poultice of—

Her thoughts vanished as his iron fingers closed around her wrist.

One lightning move was enough for him to twist her arm behind her back. Her free hand groped for her knife, but before she could reach it, the sudden, wrenching pressure on her elbow joint brought a gasp to her lips.

"No tricks, or I'll break this beautiful arm of yours," he growled in her ear. "I've got some questions, and I want some fast answers. Give them to me, and you won't get hurt."

Moon Hawk struggled to breathe, to think. She lay across his chest, her face inches from his own. His cat-colored eyes glared into hers. His body was hard and muscular through the heavy coat.

"Don't be crazy!" she hissed. "You're surrounded. All I have to do is scream, and—"

He twisted her arm tighter. She ground her teeth, determined not to show pain. How could she have been so foolish as to save this man? She should have left him to die in the snow!

"Surrounded?" His words grated in her ear. "Who the hell's surrounding me? I see just one woman, and while she appears to have me surrounded in a very pleasant way—"

"Stop it!" Moon Hawk's face flamed with heat as she realized how intimately they were entangled— her body sprawled across his, breast to breast, hip to hip. His eyes blazed into hers, their molten depths holding her captive as mercilessly as the grip of his hand on her wrist. "Let...me...go!" she muttered, squirming against him.

"And why should I do that?" He grimaced, his straight, white teeth flashing in the firelight. "If your aim is to thaw me out, you're doing a damned fine job of it!"

Heat seared Moon Hawk's face as she realized that her struggles had raised a ridge as hard as a hickory knot beneath his breeches. She willed herself to ignore the dampness that seeped between her legs, soaking into the rawhide webbing of the chastity string. Now, of all times, she needed to think clearly, to be strong like the warrior she was.

The man had made it clear that he wanted information. But how much could she give him without putting her people in danger of discovery? The warning voice in her head had been right. She should have left him to freeze to death in the canyon. That would have made everything simpler.

Could she kill him if she had to? Could she drag him back into the night, away from the camp, bind his hands and feet and leave him there? Or, if duty required it, could she take her hunting knife and drive the blade into his heart?

Still gripping her wrist, he reached up with his free hand, caught a ragged corner of her beaver-skin cap and pulled it off her head. The long, pale braids hidden beneath fell loose and tumbled over his chest.

Moon Hawk heard the jerk of his breath in his throat. His gaze flickered upward, taking in the lodge poles that rose above his head. When his eyes returned to meet hers, they were glazed by pain and confusion.

"Who are you?" he rasped, his grip tightening on her arm. "A white woman in a place like this—Lord in heaven, *who are you?*"

Chapter Four

He stared up into her beautiful, troubled face—a face that was, somehow, disturbingly familiar. Her hair was the rich pale gold of ripe wheat, falling in thick braids that coiled with a life of their own where they lay across his chest.

He was a prisoner, she had told him. A prisoner in an Indian lodge, held captive by a golden-haired goddess in buckskins. Hellfire, he was dreaming! He had to be dreaming! Nothing this crazy could be real!

She stirred, one of her braids brushing his throat. In his dream-haze, he found himself wanting to take those braids in his hands, to unravel them until her hair fell around him like a curtain of shimmering silk. He wanted to lose himself in that hair, to roll in it, wallow in it.

He was acutely conscious of the swelling in his groin where her hips pressed his. Crazy, how he could be bruised and broken, his limbs half-frozen, his head muddled by pain, and *that* part of him was still in perfect working order. Nothing else was, that was for damned sure. He had never felt closer to dying in his entire life.

At least, not that he remembered.

"Let me go." Her voice was a throaty whisper, her English oddly accented, with little nuances that belonged to no language he could place.

"Let me go!" she repeated, straining against his grip. "I'll tell you as much as you need to know."

"You'll tell me everything I *want* to know." He increased the pressure on her elbow joint, just enough to foreshadow the pain he could cause her. He didn't like the idea of hurting a woman, but she had said he was a prisoner. That changed the rules between them. "Everything," he snarled. "When I've heard enough, I'll let you know."

He felt the tension in her body, but she did not whimper, did not even wince. He could break her arm, he sensed, and this proud woman would still refuse to show pain.

"Where are we?" he demanded.

"In my…home," she muttered through clenched teeth.

"And your home is a teepee? Hellfire, you're no Indian!"

"I am…what I choose to be," she said with quiet dignity. "And this is where I choose to live."

He exhaled through his teeth, feeling dizzy and light-headed. Damn it, he couldn't lose his grip. Not now. "All right, then," he growled, "where the devil is this teepee? What's outside?"

"More than a hundred warriors of the people you call Cheyenne. One word from me, and they will rush in here and cut out your heart."

"Cheyenne…?" He battled the darkness that clawed at his mind, threatening to pull him back into the pit. "What band? Who's their leader?"

"I am."

He sank back onto the frozen buffalo robe, his vision swimming. Too weak to hold her, his hand lost its grip on her wrist and fell limply to his side.

She peeled her body off his and sat back on her heels, scowling at him. He gazed up at her through a fog of pain, feeling the loss of her, missing, in spite of everything, the sweet, fierce pressure of her breasts and hips against his chilled body.

"I could still let you die," she said in a tight, cold voice. "I could drag you back into the storm and let you freeze. Is that what you want?"

He swore under his breath. The woman was right. He was in no position to be giving the orders here. Not, at least, until he was stronger. His best hope for now was to put her at ease, get her to talk.

"Lady," he muttered, his head lolling like an infant's, "I'm in your hands."

"I'm *not* a lady." Her strong, tanned fingers worked at unloosing the buttons of his coat. "My name is Moon Hawk, and if you don't behave, you won't live through the night! Now, tell me who you are and what you are doing here.''

Her face swam above him, haloed by golden firelight. Maybe this was heaven, he thought, and she was an angry angel, sent to punish him for his sins. It had to be heaven. If he were in hell, she wouldn't be so beautiful.

Masking waves of pain and confusion, he forced his mouth into a teasing grin. "Sorry, Miss Moon Hawk,'' he drawled. "My memory seems to have gone south. Maybe if you can tell me how I came to be here...''

"You fell down the side of a canyon. I found you in some rocks, covered with snow. Your horse was close by.'' Her violet eyes flickered. "It was dead. I put you on the travois and brought you here.''

"Horse?'' He strained to sit up, then fell weakly back on the travois. A horse would have a saddle, with saddlebags. Inside those saddlebags, there could be personal belongings, even letters, that might unlock this logjam in his memory.

"Did you take anything off the horse? Papers?''

"Papers?'' She scowled at him as if he were a backward child. "I took only what was useful—the rifle and some bullets. Nothing else looked important.''

He groped for the words that would tell her what he needed, but the pain was tightening its grip again, blocking his efforts to speak. A chill swept through his body. His teeth began to chatter.

Her shadow moved like smoke up the walls of the teepee as she rose. "We need to get you warm," she said. "Your clothes are wet. They have to come off. It will be easier if you help me."

Her words penetrated the icy fog. Clenching his teeth, he braced his hands at his sides and struggled to shove himself to a sitting position. For the space of a breath he strained upward, as if trying to drag his body onto the edge of a precipice. Then, with a groan, he lost his grip and spiraled slowly downward, into the pit once more. Her face floated above him, fading in the black mist until there was nothing but darkness and cold. Then even that was gone.

For a moment Moon Hawk thought he had died. His eyes were closed, his body so deathly still that it was hard to believe the man had nearly overpowered her.

Still her inner voice murmured that he was dangerous, that if he perished it would be for the best. But the dread in her pounding heart told her how much she wanted him to live. Her hand fumbled at his throat, fingertips groping along the side of his neck for the jugular vein. She closed her eyes, holding her breath as her trembling fingers pressed deeper.

It was there, a pulse as faint and unsteady as the flutter of a dying insect. Moving swiftly Moon Hawk dragged the half-frozen coat from his chest and arms, leaving it to lie loose beneath him. The soft woolen shirt beneath was damp. She jerked it open in front and slipped it off his shoulders to expose more of his body to the warmth of the fire.

Under the shirt, next to his skin, he wore a one-piece suit of thick gray winter underwear. Moon Hawk's heart contracted for an instant. The last white man she'd seen in his underwear had been her own father. "Long johns," he'd called the snug-fitting garments, and for much of her childhood she'd believed them to be named after him.

As she rubbed warmth into the stranger's chest and arms, the memory tightened a little knot of pain in her throat. She seldom thought of those old days. They were so far behind her now that they rarely visited her except in dreams. Only now, with the tall, fair white man lying helpless before her, did the images come flying back like soft white flakes in a blizzard—the twinkle of sky-colored eyes in rosy faces; gentle voices, hands holding her, arms lifting her; nursery rhymes, dolls, tea parties with her tiny set of cups and saucers; curling up in her mother's blue merino shawl, filling her senses with the fragrance of lavender…

Moon Hawk willed them from her mind.

The long johns were dry on top. But the stranger's breeches were frozen to his legs. They would have to be peeled off—cut off if need be. But even more urgent was the dirty, oozing wound on his head. Hastily she gathered the things she needed—strips of salvaged, sun-bleached trade cloth for cleaning and wrapping the wound; a sharp awl made of elk bone for probing, and a wad of dried, shredded sumac bark for a poultice. Dropping the bark into the hot water to steep, she dampened a scrap of cloth and knelt behind him, cradling his head between her knees.

In the firelight, his hair was the rich, tawny color of tanned buckskin. It clung to his scalp in thick, wet curls, stained with crimson where the ugly gash, as long as her thumb, lay along the side of his head, slanting upward from his temple. The weight of his head pressed into the furrow between her thighs. His eyes were closed, his breathing shallow and ragged.

Moon Hawk bent close, straining to see in the flickering, amber light while she cleaned the bits of dirt and rock from the wound. He flinched reflexively as she touched the raw flesh, but his eyes did not open and his face remained as pale as death.

Fishing the hot poultice from the water, she held it in her fingertips to let it cool. Her eyes studied his chiseled features—the straight brows that were a shade darker than his hair, hooded eyes that lay pooled in deep shadow; the sharply chiseled nose, the clean bow shape of his mouth, the prominent, deeply cleft chin.

Why had he come here, to these lonely mountains, at the beginning of winter? There was no gold in these canyons. Mink and otter lived along the creeks, but she'd seen no traps on his horse, and none of the tools that might be used in clearing land or building a cabin. He'd been traveling light, traveling fast, most likely. Why?

A dark chill crept upward, along her spine as the thought struck her. A lone man would enter this labyrinth of canyons and hollows for just one reason. To hide.

His body jerked, his breath sucking inward as she pressed the steaming poultice onto the wound and wrapped it tightly with a strip of cloth. Why would he be running? What had he done, and who was after him?

She had seen outlaws from a distance—ragged, filthy men like the ones who had murdered her parents. They traveled in bands, like packs of mangy, starving wolves. By contrast, this lone stranger was clean and well dressed, his neatly groomed hands callused, as if from honest work.

But appearances meant nothing, Moon Hawk reminded herself harshly. He had already shown her that he could be rough, even violent. The warning voice in her head had been right. She had brought a dangerous man among her people.

It was not too late. She could drag him back beyond the camp and leave him to the cold that would have taken his life if she hadn't interfered. One more threat to her helpless little band would be gone.

But would it? What if he had not come here alone? What if there were others—cohorts following him or enemies hunting him? If this man died, her people would have no knowledge of them and no way to prepare. That, in itself, was reason enough to keep him alive.

Resolute, she lowered his head to the travois and shifted her position to his side. Once his frozen breeches were off, she could move him onto the warm bed and cover him with buffalo robes.

The man had lost his memory, she reminded herself as she fumbled with the ice-encrusted belt buckle. But then, she had known head blows to cause this condition. Usually it cleared up within a few days, as the shock wore off and the injury began to heal. She would warm him, feed him, give him time to rest and hope that nature would do its work.

The buckle was stubborn, the belt leather frozen stiff. Moon Hawk tugged it, twisted it and finally, in a burst of impatience, drew her knife from its sheath. To destroy any useful thing in this place of scarcity bordered on a crime. But she had already delayed too long. Pulling upward on the belt, she began working the blade beneath the tough leather.

"What the blazes are you doing?"

Startled, she glanced up. His eyes were open. They glinted with fury as he struggled to rise. Had he really been unconscious, or had he just been biding his time, waiting to see what she would do?

"Lie still!" she hissed. "I'm not going to hurt you! I'm just trying to get you out of your clothes."

He swore under his breath, straining upward. Then a wave of dizziness rippled across his ashen face. He sank back onto the travois, his eyes glazing. "You don't need a knife to get my pants off, sweetheart,'' he drawled, the words slurring off his tongue. "All you have to do is smile and crook your pretty little—''

"That's enough!'' she snapped. "I am not your sweetheart. I am not even interested in you as a…'' Moon Hawk felt the hot color rise in her face. "As a man!''

His eyes regarded her through drowsy golden slits. "How much do you know about men, Moon Hawk?'' his teasing voice challenged her. "How much do you know about what goes on between men and women?''

Her cheeks blazed like bonfires. Had his condition so numbed his mind he talked like a man drunk with whiskey? Or was he simply baiting her, fully aware of what he was saying and how his words would affect her?

Driven by a sudden, nameless fury, she jerked the knife upward. Its sharp blade sliced through the thick leather of his belt in a single motion. "I know enough,'' she said coldly. "I was married.''

His eyebrows lifted. "Was?''

"He died.'' Sheathing the knife, Moon Hawk fumbled briefly with the icy buttons of his trousers. Then she remembered the earlier response of his body. Her fingers froze. Her flush deepened as she jerked her hands away. "You do it,'' she muttered.

A smile tugged at the corners of his mouth as he

obeyed, working the buttons awkwardly with his bloodied, frost-nipped hands.

"How?" he asked.

"What?" The question had startled her.

"How did your husband die?"

"Bravely." Her answer was partly true. Crooked Nose had been a courageous warrior, but he had died miserably, of measles, a few moons after their marriage.

"He was Cheyenne?"

"Yes."

"And you are a white woman."

"Not in my heart." She averted her eyes from the widening gap in his breeches.

"The Cheyenne captured you?"

"No," she said quietly, "they saved me."

"And did you love your husband, Moon Hawk?"

The question probed her, irritated her. She had no wish to tell him that she had been Crooked Nose's number two wife, or that she had shared the lodge with his entire first family. Darkness had provided the only privacy, and she could count the times they had mated on the fingers of one hand. As for love—who had time for such foolishness when there were hides to scrape, moccasins to sew, meat to smoke and water to carry? Most nights, she had fallen exhausted into her buffalo robes, wanting only to sleep.

"Moon Hawk?" His low voice was like a physical touch, causing her to flinch.

She lifted her chin, her gaze defiant. "It's not your

place to question me," she said. "Who and what I am doesn't matter."

His fingers labored with the last of the buttons, but his hooded gaze lingered on her face. "It matters a great deal," he said. "A beautiful white woman, living with Indians. Can you blame me for wanting to know more about you, especially since you seem to be holding me prisoner?"

"We're wasting time," she said, her face uncomfortably warm.

"Are you aware, Moon Hawk, that your cheeks are the color of a prairie sunset?"

He had unfastened the last button, and though his body was still covered by the long johns, she felt a rising surge of something akin to panic. She fought the impulse to avert her gaze. To turn away would show him that he had the power to disturb her.

"The bed is over there." She jerked her head toward the layered pine boughs and willows, covered with buffalo robes, that lay on the far side of the fire. "Can you get those pants off by yourself?"

She saw his mouth twitch and braced herself for another teasing retort, but this time it did not come. A steely glint of determination flickered in his eyes, and she realized he had taken her words as a challenge.

Raising his hips slightly, he gripped the severed belt and shoved downward with his hands. But the trousers, though beginning to thaw, were still rigid with ice.

Watching him struggle, Moon Hawk realized he was in far worse condition than he'd led her to believe. Pain—more than his banter could hide—rippled across his pale features. Sweat glittered on his forehead as he tried vainly to loosen the half-frozen fabric and work it downward.

Moon Hawk edged forward to help him, but his eyes narrowed as she reached out with her hand. He shook his head, warning her away. "I can do this," he muttered through clenched teeth. "Just give me a…minute."

He had turned to one side and was trying to stand now. She watched him, taking his measure as he staggered to his feet. His tightly pressed lips were edged with white. His eyes were glazed. They sank deeper into their sockets as he pulled himself to his full height. Only now did she realize how tall he was. Even in his pitifully weak condition, his presence filled the small lodge with an aura so powerful, so masculine, that Moon Hawk felt her knees go liquid beneath her.

His firelit shadow loomed and flickered like a dancing giant's on the buffalo hide walls. A sensation akin to fear curled in her stomach as he loomed above her. She could feel her heart pounding against the wall of her rib cage, the sound of it echoing in her ears. *Danger…danger…*

But he was already reeling, eyes squeezed shut

against the pain. She saw him sway toward the fire and she leaped to brace him, cradling him in her arms as he went down.

He grew worse as the night wore on. Moon Hawk had dragged him to her bed and stripped away his frozen garments, willing herself to ignore the lean, muscular beauty of his warrior's body, its slumbering manhood as exquisitely sculpted as the inner surface of a shell. Tearing her gaze away, she had covered him with buffalo robes, then piled more wood on the fire. He was cold. So very cold.

He slept fitfully, shivering despite the warmth of the lodge. It was as if, when she'd first brought him inside, his body had been preserved in a state of frozen shock. Only now that the heat had begun to penetrate his chilled muscles, bones and organs did the full damage of cold and injury begin to manifest itself.

His skin was feverish, his breathing as rough and labored as the death gasps of a buffalo bull. Now and then he moaned or muttered incoherently under his breath, but even when his eyes were open there was no flicker of recognition in their golden depths.

Moon Hawk hovered beside him, tucking the buffalo robes around his body when, in his delirium, he struggled to kick them loose. Despite his fevered state, he was so strong that it was a constant fight to keep him covered. But if the fever was to be broken, it was essential to keep him warm, to make him sweat.

When he was calm enough to allow it, she would lift his head and try to force a few drops of willow bark tea into his mouth. More often than not, he would only choke and cough it back up, soaking the tawny stubble on his chin.

He lay with one arm and shoulder exposed, where he had flung back a corner of the buffalo robe. His skin was hot to the touch and, though she had changed the poultice twice, an ugly, oozing welt had formed around the head wound.

Her exhausted mind groped for other remedies— teas, washes, dressings and poultices—that She-Bear had shown her over the many seasons their little band had been together. The old woman had taken Moon Hawk under her tutelage when the young girl had shown an early talent as a healer. But providing for her people had taken its toll on Moon Hawk's skills. There was so much to remember, so many vital things she had forgotten.

She should have awakened She-Bear as soon as she reached the camp, Moon Hawk chastised herself. She had told herself she did not want to disturb the old woman. But other things, as well, had made her hesitate. In her younger days, She-Bear had been married to a warrior of the Southern Tse Tse Stus. She and her family had been camped at Sand Creek with Black Kettle's band, under a flag of peace, when a troop of bluecoats had ridden down upon them, shooting and hacking down everyone in sight. She-Bear's husband and three daughters had died in the melee. She-Bear herself had been horribly wounded and left for dead. To this day, the old woman's hatred of the *ve hoe* went deeper than the marrow of her bones.

As if thought could summon spirit, Moon Hawk felt a sudden blast of winter air. She glanced around just as the door flap lifted and a hunched, ragged figure hobbled into the lodge.

Firelight cast She-Bear's form into grotesquely dancing shadows as the old woman tottered across the floor, dragging a leg that had been rendered useless by the bullet that had shattered her hip. She stopped at Moon Hawk's side. The dead silence in the lodge was broken only by the muffled cry of the wind as she gazed down at the helpless white man.

"What have you done?" The question was a raven's croak, dark and sharp.

Moon Hawk willed herself to speak with the tongue of reason. "I found him in the canyon. If I hadn't brought him here, he would have died."

"You should have left him alone. Nothing but evil can come from his being here."

The old woman's words echoed the ones Moon Hawk had heard in her mind. For the space of a heartbeat she was stunned. Then, recovering her wits, she replied as she had replied to the warning in her head. "Crow Feather could have left me to die, too. Instead he brought me to the Tse Tse Stus and raised me as his own."

"Crow Feather brought home a child. You have

brought home a man, full-grown and dangerous. Has he spoken?''

''Some. Enough to tell me that he has no memory.''

''All the more reason not to trust him.'' She-Bear's arthritic hand brushed the bulge beneath the stained wrappings that encircled the stranger's head. Only then did Moon Hawk notice the familiar battered elk-skin medicine bag, hanging by its braided leather strap from one misshapen shoulder.

What strange, secret sense had awakened the old woman in the night and brought her here, with her lifesaving collection of roots and herbs? Had she known all along that she would find a wounded, helpless enemy? Moon Hawk knew better than to ask such questions.

''You tell me nothing that I have not told myself,'' Moon Hawk said. ''But if this man dies, his secrets will die with him. We'll have no way of knowing if he came alone, or if there are others.''

She-Bear's tangled gray hair dripped melting snow as she shook her head. ''If there are others, you would be wise to drag his body back to where they can find it. Then they will have no reason to go on looking for him. They will turn around and go back the way they came.''

Icy drops splattered on the stranger's face as the old woman bent over him. His eyelids fluttered open, and he gazed up at the two women with sleepy, golden eyes. His lips moved as if he were struggling to speak. Then, as if the effort had exhausted his strength, he slipped back into the twilight of oblivion.

She-Bear's eyes shifted in their wrinkled pits. Their sharp black pupils gazed knowingly at Moon Hawk. "He is young and strong, and very handsome for a *ve hoe*. You have been without a man for many winters, my daughter."

"I no longer have such thoughts!" Moon Hawk protested, hot with denial.

"Every woman has such thoughts. That is why I will ask Maheo to grant you wisdom." Her gnarled fingers plucked a stray shred of the poultice that clung to the wrapping. "Sumac bark is good," she muttered, "but pitch pine is better. And wintergreen for the fever." Her shoulders sagged wearily, causing the medicine bag to slip quietly to the floor of the lodge. "It is not yet dawn. This old one is tired and needs to sleep. Do not awaken me."

Without another word, She-Bear turned away and hobbled out of the lodge, her crippled leg dragging a trail of wet snow across the hide-covered floor. Moon Hawk stood gazing after her, knowing the old woman had just given her a priceless gift of trust.

A gift and a burden.

The stranger groaned, his parched lips moving as if trying to form words. Moon Hawk dropped to her knees and opened the medicine bag. Her anxious hands rummaged for the treasures that would save his life.

Chapter Five

He awoke to the trickle of melting snow and the cool brightness of sunlight through his closed eyelids. For the first few moments he lay still, his senses quivering as he took stock of his surroundings—the coarse buffalo wool against his naked skin, the crackle of pine coals and the savory aroma of venison stew with wild onion. Muffled by distance, the babble of a creek and the shouts of romping children drifted lightly to his ears.

Where was he? *Who* was he?

Memories of cold, pain and darkness swirled in his head, and with them the vision of intense violet eyes in an angel's face, framed by a nimbus of golden hair.

An angel in buckskin, with the haunting name of Moon Hawk.

Like falling flakes of snow, the impressions drifted into place, to make, at last, the vaguest kind of sense. He remembered pain and bone-chilling cold; bumping on a travois through icy diamond drifts; then the amber glow of firelight, the blessed warmth—and words. Words from the angel, transformed into a blazing valkyrie who announced that he was her prisoner.

What had he said to her? He recalled talking with the woman, but the words had vanished. He could not remember anything he'd told her. Hellfire, he couldn't even remember his own name!

Slowly and cautiously, he forced his eyes to open. For an instant the glare almost blinded him. He jerked his head to one side, triggering an explosion of dull pain above his temple. As his vision cleared, he could make out the sloping lodge poles that formed the inner framework of an Indian teepee. The entrance flap had been pushed aside. Sunlight streamed through the opening to cast a triangular patch of light on the floor. The cool breeze raised gooseflesh on his bare shoulders.

Where were his clothes? His eyes scanned the shadows above his head. On the far side of the lodge, he could make out a blurred object hanging from a pole. A stray beam of sunlight gleamed on a shirt button of polished horn. Dangling below it was a shape he recognized as one leg of his woolen trousers.

He strained to sit up and discovered that he was as weak as a kitten. His head ached and his hollow stomach growled with hunger. But no matter. He had to get dressed and get out of this place. There was something he needed to do, something important.

Maybe if he got moving, he would remember what it was.

Feeling dizzy, he finally pushed himself to a sitting position. His body stank of sweat, and his mouth tasted as if he'd eaten buzzard droppings. But never mind, the door of the lodge was open and there was no one in sight. If he could get his hands on a horse and a gun, he would soon be far away from here. But where would he go? And who would he look for? Where his memory had been there was nothing but a frightening void. Who *was* he?

He had just swung his bare legs to the floor when he heard a suppressed giggle from behind a pile of wood. Peering into the shadows beyond the pooled sunlight, he caught the glimmer of four mischievous black eyes. He jerked the buffalo robe over his lap just as two little Indian girls, about five or six years old, ran from their hiding place and, shrieking with laughter, raced out of the lodge. One of them bumped against a corner of the entrance flap, causing it to fall into place as she skittered out of the way.

A bemused smile tugged his mouth as he rose in the darkness and twisted the buffalo robe around his waist. Kids were the same wherever you found them. He could only hope those two didn't alert the whole camp that he was up and around.

His knees threatened to buckle beneath him as he took the first wobbling step. Things were beginning to come back to him now, including the woman's remark that more than a hundred armed Cheyenne braves were waiting outside. Whether that was true remained to be seen. Meanwhile speed and stealth were his only resources, and he would have to make the most of them.

Peering into the dark shadows, he edged toward the place where his clothes hung. The eyes of anyone coming into the lodge from outside would take a few seconds to adjust to the darkness. If the worst happened, that small beat of time would be his only advantage.

There was no sign of his underwear, so he stepped hastily into his breeches, buttoned them at the waist and pulled on the shirt. To survive his escape, he would need something on his feet and some kind of protection from the cold. It made sense that he would have been wearing a coat and boots when he was brought here, but he saw no sign of them now. He'd bet good money they were walking around on some high-and-mighty Cheyenne brave.

But that in itself was a puzzle. Five years ago, the Northern Cheyenne had surrendered to the U.S. army and submitted to being marched all the way to Oklahoma, where many of them had sickened and died. In the autumn of '78, the remnants of the tribe, led by their two chiefs, Dull Knife and Little Wolf, had fled the reservation and fought their way back north, determined to reach their old homeland. Halted at the Dakota border, they'd been sent back to Fort Robinson, Nebraska, where they'd broken out again in the dead of winter. This time yet more of them had been killed. The survivors now lived on a reservation in Montana's Tongue River country, where missionaries and government agents were doing their best to turn them into second-class whites.

How could he remember all that and not remember his own name?

His eyes scanned the shadows of the lodge, searching vainly for his boots. Nothing he saw came from the so-called civilized world. There were no boxes or barrels, no metal utensils, books or woven blankets. It was as if he had stepped back twenty years in time. He had no idea where he was, but it sure as hell wasn't on the reservation.

A slight rustle from outside the lodge shattered his musings. He melted into the shadows as the entrance flap parted, shooting a brief shaft of sunlight into the darkness.

His breath stopped as a willowy figure stepped into the lodge. For the space of a breath he took in the sight of her—the pale gold hair hanging loose over her shoulders, the long fringe on her buckskin tunic that fluttered with her slightest motion, the ferocity of her gaze as she peered into the darkness with sun-dazzled eyes.

It was his angel. She had not been a dream after all. But this was no time for admiration. He had questions, and only she had the answers. He would get them now.

As she glided past his hiding place, he summoned his strength and moved like lightning. One arm hooked her waist. The other clasped her mouth and jaw, jerking her head back into the hollow of his throat. She gasped and went rigid, straining against his grip. Beneath the soft buckskin, her body was hard and strong. Had she fought him, he would likely have been no match for her in his weakened condition. But she stood still, her breathing rapid, her heart pounding against the flesh of his arm. Cautiously he slid his hand away from her mouth.

"What do you want?" she whispered, her hoarse, taut voice sending a shiver through his senses.

"I want you to tell me where I am and how to get out of here," he growled in her ear.

"I can't do that. Let me go and I'll tell you why."

His arms tightened around her in an unspoken threat. "I won't hurt you unless I have to. But you're going to have to do better than that, Miss Moon Hawk. There are things I need to know, and they can't wait."

"I can answer some of your questions." Her body twisted against him. "But you're too weak to leave here. You've been sick for four days. You need to rest, to eat—"

"I'll be the judge of what I need," he snapped, interrupting her. "Get me the rest of my clothes and any horse that's fit to carry me. Then I'll be gone, and your worries will be over."

She shook her head, her fine hair catching the stubble on his chin. He could feel the determined set of her jaw against his wrist.

"What's to stop me, lady? That army of a hundred Cheyenne braves you said was waiting outside?"

She sagged slightly in his arms, saying nothing.

"I just met two of your so-called warriors," he said roughly. "They had big brown eyes and pigtails, and when they saw I was awake, they giggled and ran outside. If you've got a dozen men out there, let alone a hundred, bring them on! I'd pay a heap of silver dollars to see them!"

She stiffened against him in stubborn silence. He could feel the lightness in his head trickling down to his knees, and he knew he would not be able to hold on to her much longer.

"What else have you lied to me about, Moon Hawk?" he muttered, drowning in the sweet, smoky fragrance of her hair. "You? This place?"

"Let me go," she whispered. "Yes, I lied. I lied to protect you. There are secrets here. The less you know, the better."

"That's not good enough." He spun her around to face him, gripping her shoulders. "Nothing I've seen or heard in this place makes any sense. I don't know where I am or how I got here. For all I know, I've lost my mind, and none of this is real."

"You're right." Her gaze dropped to his chest. "None of this is real. As long as you believe that, you'll be safe."

His clasp tightened on her shoulders, as much to

steady his own balance as to hold her in place. From outside the lodge came the laughter of children and the raucous, piping call of a chickadee. The smell of meat stew, bubbling over some nearby fire, made his empty stomach clench.

"That's not true," he said irritably. "You're real. This place is real. And whatever it is you're trying to hide from me, it's already too late." He braced his legs apart to keep them from buckling. "You said my horse was killed. What about the saddle and the things in the saddlebags? Did anybody go back for them while I was sick?"

Her eyes widened slightly as she shook her head. "I tried. I went back up the canyon with the travois to get your saddle and the deer I'd shot. But there was a family of bears on the dead horse, a mother and two big cubs. The cubs had ripped the saddle apart and scattered things all up and down the creek. I didn't dare go near them."

He cursed under his breath. At least she hadn't apologized—that would have annoyed him even more. After all, this mess wasn't her fault. It was nobody's fault. It was just his dumb, rotten luck.

His right hand moved to cup her jaw, lifting her face and forcing her eyes to meet his. The irises were deep indigo, the pupils wide and black, like the dark centers of pansies. Something about her face struck a familiar chord. Had he seen her before? Even known her? He struggled to place her features—and failed.

"There are a lot of things I don't remember," he said, "but I do know that I didn't come here to hurt you or your people. Do you believe me?"

She hesitated, then gave a slight but emphatic shake of her head. "You don't understand. I'm responsible for the safety of everyone here."

"You saved my life. I owe you a debt. I pay my debts." Impatience surged in him. This argument was getting him nowhere.

"How do I know that?" she retorted. "You don't even know who you—"

Her words ended in a gasp as he seized her wrist, spun her around and pushed her ahead of him, out through the entrance of the lodge.

The flash of sunlight on snow shot a blinding pain into his eyes. Wet cold seeped upward through the soles of his bare feet, reminding him that he'd failed to find his boots. Dizzied by the light and by his own sudden motion, he began to sway. He struggled to remain upright, to stay alert to whatever might happen next. But he could not stop the onrush of darkness that swept over his senses, lingered for the space of a breath, then passed as swiftly as it had come.

It dawned on him, as his vision cleared, that he was no longer holding Moon Hawk. She was standing beside him, her left arm clasped around his back, her shoulder pressed against his side to steady him.

"Are you all right?" She glanced up at him, her features tense.

"I'm fine," he lied, squinting hard against the brightness.

A shudder passed through her body. "Go ahead and look, then," she said. "Look at my people."

By now his eyes were growing accustomed to the light. From where he stood, he could see eighteen or twenty hide-covered teepees standing among the ghost-white aspens. Their entrance flaps were flung open to the sunshine of the early winter thaw. Just outside the nearest dwelling, an ancient crone with a scarred face and twisted spine sat grinding dried herbs in a wooden bowl. A short distance beyond, a younger woman with long black braids and a pretty but careworn face was stretching a fresh deerskin on a willow frame. Behind her, at the entrance of her lodge, a very old man with milk-blind eyes sat cross-legged on a buffalo robe, staring at the sun while his hands braided strips of rawhide into a long rope.

Among the teepees there were more Cheyenne women, some of them young, others bent with age. All of them were working—some preparing food, others scraping hides or sewing moccasins. No one appeared to be idle.

A handful of brown-skinned children raced among the trees, playing a game of tag. The two little girls who'd fled Moon Hawk's lodge were there, as well as two more girls and three boys. All of them appeared to be about the same age. But strangely, there were no younger children in sight. There were no toddlers. No babies. And except for the blind old rope maker, there appeared to be no men in the camp.

He felt the women's furtive gazes on him. But none of them stared. Clearly they had known about his presence and were not surprised to see him.

"A hundred Cheyenne braves ready to rush in and cut out my heart. Wasn't that what you told me, Moon Hawk?" He glared down at her golden head.

Her breath eased out in a ragged sigh, as if she were putting down one burden and taking up another. "Go back inside," she said. "I'll bring you some food. Then we can talk."

The darkness of the lodge was a welcome retreat after the blinding glare of the sun. He sank cross-legged onto the rumpled buffalo robe where he had slept for so long. Four days, she had said. Who had cared for him during that time? Who had stripped off his wet clothes, seen to his needs, kept him warm and alive?

There could be only one answer to that question.

She reappeared in the entrance of the lodge, cloaked in a golden aura of sunlight. Her hands cradled a gourd bowl filled to the brim with savory venison stew. The mouthwatering aromas of meat and wild herbs swam in his senses as she placed it on the floor in front of him. He fought the urge to snatch up the bowl and bolt down the stew like a starving dog. That, his instincts told him, would not speak well for his manners or for his self-discipline. Both, he suspected, were about to be tested.

"Nea'ese," he said, thanking her formally in Cheyenne. "Will you share this meal with me?"

She shook her head. Her eyes were downcast, making her look demure, almost shy. He picked up a small piece of meat with his fingertips and placed it in his mouth, forcing himself to chew slowly. Where had his knowledge of Cheyenne manners come from? If only he could remember.

"Tell me about your people," he said.

Slowly she lifted her gaze. Light slanted across her face. The depths of her expressive eyes glowed like amethyst. When she spoke, it was in Cheyenne.

"Many seasons ago, the bluecoats came to take our people south, to the Indian Territories in the place called Oklahoma."

"Yes, I know. And I know what happened to them."

Her mouth twitched. "You do not know everything. Some of those in our band were not strong. The old ones, the mothers with babies, and those about to give birth, the smallest of the children—we knew they would never survive such a journey. They would die on the trail."

"And you?" He studied her, anticipating what she was about to say.

"I was strong enough. But I knew that if the bluecoats saw me, I would be sent away and my people would be punished for having me with them. By then my husband had died, and I had chosen the path of

a warrior. I went to our chief, Little Wolf, and together we made a plan.''

He stared at her, forgetting to eat. Questions
sprang to his lips, but he forced them back, not wanting to interrupt the flow of her words.

''The men who wrote the treaty had promised Little Wolf that the people could return home after a
year if they did not like their new land.'' Her eyes
smoldered with quiet anger over the broken promise.
''Our plan was that I would take those who could
not travel and hide them in the mountains. I promised
Little Wolf that I would provide them with food and
keep them safe until he returned…''

Her voice trailed off, and for the space of a long
breath, she seemed lost in herself, overcome by the
sadness of what had followed.

He touched her sleeve. ''Little Wolf came back a
long time ago,'' he said.

''I know.'' She glanced away, sunlight catching a
moist glimmer in her eyes. ''People sneak away from
the reservation on the Tongue River to visit us. They
tell us what is happening there.''

''Then you know that Little Wolf is no longer
chief.''

''Yes, the news reached us.'' She swallowed, then
her eyes widened sharply. ''But you—how can you
know such a thing if you have no memory?''

''I'm…not sure.'' Strange, how the fact had risen
from the murky pit of his mind. He remembered the
whole, tragic story—how Little Wolf, in a rage, had

murdered a brave who was pressing too much attention on his daughter. In the wake of the unforgivable act, the aging chief had given away all his possessions and moved to a lonely part of the reservation, exiled for life.

He willed himself to begin eating again. Moon Hawk watched him with eyes that reflected his own questions.

Could the reservation on the Tongue River hold the key to his locked memory? Had he been there recently, perhaps spoken with people who would recognize him? The fact that he understood some of the language told him there had to be some past connection to the Cheyenne.

"Why haven't your people gone to the reservation?" he asked her. "Many of them must have family there. And they'd be safe. They'd be fed, clothed, educated—"

"Anyone who wants to go to the reservation is free to leave!" Her eyes flashed. "I have made that clear to my people. None of them have chosen to go! We know what the reservation is like. We've heard the stories—"

"Whose stories?" His gaze drilled into her. "Yours? Are you urging these people to stay here because, if they were to join the rest of the tribe, you'd be left alone?"

She had gone rigid. Her face looked as if he had just struck her. "That's not fair," she said in a choked voice. "You don't know anything about us! You don't know anything about *me!*"

"I know what I see," he said softly. "I see a brave, beautiful, lonely woman. A white woman."

"Then your eyes betray you." She spoke calmly but her voice was strained and unsteady. "I am Cheyenne. And those of us who live free are the last keepers of the old ways."

"The old ways are gone, Moon Hawk. Gone, like the buffalo."

A curious sadness stole over her lovely face. "Not for us," she said. "The people on the reservation look to our little band for hope. As long as we are here, the old ways, the sacred ways, will survive. Crow Feather, the old blind man you saw, he is the keeper of all our stories and of bow making. And She-Bear, the crippled woman, is the keeper of healing. People such as these are our treasures, and it is my responsibility to keep them safe."

He shook his head and, for want of a fitting response, bent to finishing his meal. Maybe this was a dream after all. A lost and helpless little band of Cheyenne, guarded by a golden-haired Amazon, who'd become the self-appointed keeper of their traditions. How could anything so far-fetched be real?

A quirk of memory told him that it was not unheard-of for Indian women to become hunters and warriors. But for a white captive to do so, earning the trust of Little Wolf himself—that was beyond belief.

But never mind. This place and its people were none of his concern. All he really wanted to do was put it behind him, like some bizarre dream, and go back to the person he had been before he'd awakened in a snowbank with this wild, beautiful creature bending over him.

He locked her gaze with his, weighing his words as he spoke. "Your people can have their secrets and their old ways. All I want is to leave. Give me the rest of my clothes, and a horse if you can spare one, and I'll be on my way at first light tomorrow. You can keep the rifle and bullets for your pains—or don't your rules allow that?"

"Anything that would help me feed my people would be welcomed," she said. "But the gift makes no difference. I can't let you leave here."

He stared at her, thunderstruck. When she'd said that he was a prisoner, he'd assumed she was only bluffing. But even he could not doubt the gravity in her eyes or the resolute set of her jaw.

"What the devil—"

"We can't risk having you betray us to the bluecoats," she said quietly. "Until we know your heart, you must stay here, with us."

He muttered a low curse. "How long will that take?"

"That's up to you. When you prove that we can trust you, you'll be free to go."

He scowled, mulling over her words in his mind. Could they really stop him from leaving? Not by force, he swiftly concluded. But there were other ways to keep him here. If he was to make it safely back to civilization, he would need his coat and boots. He would need supplies, directions and, if possible, a horse. Withhold those vital things, and he might as well be locked behind bars.

"And if I fail to win your trust?" The question emerged almost flippantly. "Do you plan to keep me here forever, Moon Hawk?"

Moon Hawk had glanced away for a moment, her gaze drawn outside by a small figure that danced toward them like a windblown leaf across the clearing. Startled by his question, she turned back to look directly at him, her lips parted, her eyes darkening with an expression that made the hair rise on the back of his neck.

A leaden chill crept through his body as the answer came to him. It was the last answer he wanted.

Chapter Six

The force of his gaze struck Moon Hawk like an icy blast of wind. There was no need for words. The stranger had guessed the answer to his own question. At the first sign of betrayal he would lose his life. As the protector of her people, it would be her duty to take it.

Silence hung between them, growing heavier with each breath. She was groping for an excuse to get up and leave when a small, bounding figure appeared in the entrance to the lodge.

"Bright Wing!" Moon Hawk reached out to the little girl with the desperation of someone about to drown. Catching the small brown hand in her own, she drew the child close. "What are you doing here?" she chided. "Why aren't you playing with the others?"

"I wanted to see the *ve hoe*." Bright Wing gazed coyly at the stranger for a moment. Then, overcome by shyness, she giggled and buried her face against Moon Hawk's sleeve.

"But you've already seen him." Moon Hawk could not hold back a smile. "Weren't you the one who came running to tell me he was awake?"

"I didn't get to talk to him." Bright Wing peered at the stranger from the safe refuge of Moon Hawk's arms. He was looking back at the little girl now, his golden eyes warming with amusement. At least the man appeared to like children. Maybe he had a few children of his own, and a wife as well, waiting for him back in that other world beyond the reach of his memory.

But such things, she reminded herself, could not be allowed to matter.

"Talk to me, Bright Wing," he said in his slightly broken Cheyenne. "Let me hear what you have to say."

She giggled again, curious but still shy. "What is your name, *ve hoe?*" she finally managed to ask.

"He can't remember his name," Moon Hawk explained. "He hurt his head, and it made him forget."

"Everybody needs a name," Bright Wing said solemnly. "If he has lost his old name, we must give him a new one."

The stranger's smile was gentle. "I would be honored to have you choose a name for me, Bright Wing. What would you like to call me?"

The little girl scowled thoughtfully. Then her black

eyes began to sparkle. "You came to us out of the snow on a cold night. I will call you Etonéto."

"Etonéto." The name meant "it is cold." He tested the sound of it, then nodded with mock gravity. "It is a good name. Thank you, little sister."

Bright Wing wriggled like a puppy who had just been praised. Moon Hawk felt another smile tugging at her lips, but it swiftly faded. Bright Wing was trusting and vulnerable. Like the other children here, she had been raised without a father. She would naturally be drawn to any man who gave her notice and treated her kindly. In the case of this white stranger, such an attachment would only wound her tender young heart.

Flashing the stranger—now Etonéto—a glance of warning, she rose to her feet and took a firm grip on Bright Wing's hand. "Let's go and see what the other children are doing," she said.

Without looking back, she strode away from the lodge. She could feel Bright Wing's resistance as the little girl pulled back to wave at her newfound friend, but she did not slow her step.

Moon Hawk's thoughts churned as she walked. While the white man lay ill, she had shared her lodge with him, spending her nights in a separate bed on the opposite side of the fire. No one had questioned this—after all, she had taken up the life of a hunter and warrior, and her chastity string was firmly knotted. But now that he was awake Moon Hawk felt a growing sense of danger.

The chastity string was more of a symbol than a real physical barrier. Moon Hawk knew of many Cheyenne brides who'd worn their chastity strings for the first few nights of marriage, or even longer. This allowed the new husband and wife to become comfortable together before their union was consummated. No self-respecting Cheyenne male, however strong or needful, would violate the barrier of a woman's chastity string. But a white man? That was a very different matter.

Moon Hawk remembered the intimate way he had spoken to her when she'd first brought him into her lodge—teasing her and asking what she knew about love. She remembered the way his drowsy cat-colored eyes had grazed her features—and how, at the slightest brush of his hand, the heat had risen from simmering depths of her body to flood her face with fire. Even now, she could feel the warmth invading her cheeks, causing her cheeks to burn in the wintry air.

Moon Hawk knew she could no longer share her lodge with the white man. The reason, however, puzzled and disturbed her. Was she afraid of what he might do? Or was there something else she feared more—something inside herself?

But she had no time to waste on such a useless question. Since there was no other lodge where Eto-néto could properly stay, she would take her things and move in with She-Bear. The old woman snored like a buffalo, but there were more important things at stake than a good night's sleep. She-Bear's fireside would provide her with safety, warmth and wisdom until the disturbing stranger was gone.

Moon Hawk was still lost in thought when a desperate cry shattered her world.

The cry came from Broken Elk, a youth of fourteen who had stayed behind with the little band because of a shriveled leg. He burst into sight through the alder thicket at the far side of the clearing, his thin young face as pale as wood ash.

"Moon Hawk!" He lurched toward her on his hickory crutch, stumbling in his haste. "It's Otter Woman! I found her down the canyon by the creek! She's—" He collapsed, sobbing and exhausted, in the melting snow.

Moon Hawk felt Bright Wing's small hand go rigid in her own. Otter Woman was the little girl's mother.

Sick with dread, she dropped to a crouch, gripped the child's shoulders and gazed into her fear-filled eyes. "Can you be a brave girl?"

Bright Wing nodded, her lips pressed tightly together.

"Stay here with the others," Moon Hawk said. "I'll take Broken Elk and go and see what's happened."

"I'll keep her with me." A woman stepped forward and took Bright Wing's hand. Moon Hawk's throat ached as she watched them walk away. Life in the depths of these mountains was fraught with peril. There were wild animals, steep ledges and sudden storms that could trap anyone who failed to find shelter. Still, the little band had fared well over the years. There had been only a handful of accidents, and, except among the old ones, very few deaths.

But the horror she had glimpsed in the youth's eyes told Moon Hawk that something extraordinary and terrible had happened to Otter Woman. Bracing herself for what they would find, she sprinted toward the spot where Broken Elk had collapsed on the ground. Out of the corner of her eye, she glimpsed the man called Etonéto standing in the open entrance of the lodge. He looked of a mind to follow her, but his bare, tender feet would keep him in his place, she reminded herself. There was no time to worry about him now.

She reached down to help Broken Elk stand. "Can you go back with me to find her?"

Nodding, he gripped his crutch, caught her hand and scrambled to his feet. Crane Flying, Otter Woman's stout, iron-haired aunt, joined them with her medicine bag, a buffalo robe and an empty travois.

Moon Hawk willed herself not to look back as they hurried out of the camp, slowed only a little by Broken Elk's hobbling pace. She could feel the apprehension in the eyes that watched them go. Bright Wing's eyes would be filled with pain and fear, like a wounded bird's. Etonéto's golden gaze would be anxious, seething with frustration because he could not follow them. She-Bear's would be bitter and knowing. The others, if she allowed herself to look at them, would only reflect her own dread.

They left the clearing and trudged grimly along the creek bed. As was their custom, they kept a strict silence outside the camp. A word spoken aloud could startle game or, worse, alert an unseen enemy.

Below the ledges, where the warm fingers of sunlight had not reached, the willows drooped under the weight of glittering snow. Clumps of bright scarlet bunchberries gleamed through the whiteness. A jay, scolding raucously, darted among the bare aspens. It landed on a thin branch, its slight weight releasing a shower of snow dust on their heads.

The beauty of the day mocked the churning blackness of Moon Hawk's spirit. She had been so hopeful about the coming winter. The spot her people had chosen for their camp was secluded from view and sheltered from harsh winds. Water and forage were plentiful, and the maze of canyons teemed with game. A sense of peace and security had lingered over them all—until the night she had brought the injured white man into their midst.

Had Etonéto brought bad luck with him? Or was his presence just one more sign that the outside world was closing in on her little band?

Broken Elk's breathing rasped as he came up even with her and touched her arm. Wordlessly the youth pointed toward a broad, brushy side canyon where the women sometimes went to set their rabbit snares.

Moon Hawk felt a cold weight in the pit of her stomach as she turned off the main trail and headed into the scrub. Her hand moved instinctively to the long hunting knife at her belt. Even the air smelled of danger—acrid and overripe, like rotting fruit. The faint odor triggered a gut-clenching fear, so deeply buried that it had no name.

They found the prints of Otter Woman's moccasins in the snow—closely spaced at first, then wider, forming a zigzag pattern where she had broken into a run. Farther up the canyon they found other tracks—several sets of boot prints, closing in behind her. Otter Woman had deliberately fled up the side canyon, Moon Hawk realized. Like a killdeer protecting its nest, she had led her pursuers away from the camp, where they might have harmed the people she loved.

That, at least, would be something they could tell her little daughter.

They found Otter Woman sprawled beneath the branches of a stunted pine tree. The sight of the lifeless body, legs bloodied and spread wide, head lolling grotesquely toward one shoulder, was so like the image burned into Moon Hawk's childhood memory that her knees threatened to give way beneath her.

To keep her courage before the others, she drew from her own deep well of pain. Anger, hot and choking, boiled up in her as she stared at the blood-stained snow, and at the imprints of hands, knees and boots that surrounded Otter Woman's body.

The white men, whoever they were, had made no

effort to cover their tracks. They seemed to know they had nothing to fear from the weak little band.

A sickening fear mingled with Moon Hawk's rage. Were there more of them? Had they seen the camp? Would they be back?

Crane Flying had spread the buffalo robe on the travois. The three of them crouched in the snow to work their arms beneath Otter Woman's battered body and shift it gently onto the robe. Tears trickled down Broken Elk's homely young face as they wrapped her like an infant, covering every part of her and lashing her to the willow frame. Everyone in the camp had loved this pretty and cheerful young mother whose husband had died in the last battle against the bluecoats. Her death would be deeply mourned.

"Take her back," Moon Hawk said, speaking softly to the others. "I need to learn all I can from these tracks before the snow melts."

Crane Flying stared at her, eyes widening in her walnut face.

"Go on," Moon Hawk whispered before the woman could find the words to argue. "I'll be all right. If they were still here, we would know it by now."

Crane Flying bent and picked up the ends of the loaded travois. Sunlight glinted on a fleck of moisture in her eye, but she showed no other sign of emotion. She had endured too much sadness and buried too many loved ones to give way to open grief. Moon

Hawk understood all too well the depth of her loss. The little band had long since become one family.

Two ravens spread their wings and flapped from the top of a twisted spruce as the grim little procession moved off through the trees. In earlier times, Otter Woman's remains would have been laid out with honor and ceremony and placed on a high platform beneath the open sky. Now there would be no choice except to give her a swift and secret burial.

Moon Hawk crouched in the snow to study the tracks the marauders had left. Her eyes picked out four sets of prints, each one different from the others. One man had worn military boots, like the bluecoats, but the uneven wear on the soles told her they were too large for his feet and had probably been made for someone else. Two of the men had worn riding boots, one with a missing heel. The fourth man's feet had been clad in patched, tattered moccasins. Bandits, she swiftly concluded. The same breed of men as those who'd murdered her parents.

In the trampled snow, she could read the story of what they had done to Otter Woman—two of them holding her down while the third man took her and the fourth waited his turn. When all of them had finished, they had strangled her. The rope they'd used had left its mark against the snow.

Moon Hawk could feel the choking tightness in her own throat as she widened her field of search. Where one bandit had stood, the ground was spattered with foul, brown tobacco juice. Another had relieved himself against a pine tree. A little farther off she could see the amber-brown shards of a broken whiskey bottle, and, beyond that, the grove of aspens where they had tied their horses. A scan of higher ground showed sets of hoofprints leading toward the steep trail that zigzagged up the canyon wall. The intruders were gone. For now.

Filthy, loathsome white men. They had pushed her people to the brink of hopelessness, but that was not enough for creatures like these. Even here, where the little band wanted nothing except to live in peace, the *ve hoe* had come to torment them.

Dizzy with rage, Moon Hawk struck out toward the aspen grove. She would memorize every hoof and boot print, she vowed, every trace these monsters had left behind. And if ever the chance came to strike—

"Moon Hawk!"

She went rigid at the sound of her name. One hand flew reflexively to her knife, drawing it from its sheath as she spun around, half-crouched and ready to defend herself.

Etonéto stood beside the tree where Otter Woman had died. He was coatless, but she saw that he had managed to find his boots where she'd hidden them in the lodge, beneath a stash of beaver skins. His face wore the same frustrated, searching expression she had seen earlier that morning.

He was unarmed, and there was nothing threatening in his manner. But when she looked at him,

Moon Hawk's fury-glazed eyes saw only a *ve hoe*. A white man.

Blinded by grief and rage, she flew at him.

He reacted like an experienced fighter, widening his stance and crouching slightly to take the force of her attack. As she flung herself against him, his flashing right hand caught her wrist, twisting it so that she grunted with pain and almost dropped the knife. Had he been in prime condition, that single move would have forced her to the ground, but she was able to wrench herself away and slash upward. As he pushed her away, the blade grazed his cheek, leaving a thread of crimson in its wake.

"Stop it!" The outer edge of his hand chopped her wrist, and the knife spun into the snow. "For God's sake, stop it, Moon Hawk! I'm not the one who did this!"

"They were your...kind!" Unarmed, she continued to flail at him. Her fists pummeled his chest, thudding against his rib cage as he gripped her shoulders to hold her at bay.

"They were your kind, too, blast it, but that doesn't make you responsible for what happened!"

"Doesn't it?" His words had taken the fight out of her. She sagged against the grip of his hands, feeling drained and exhausted. Why did she allow this man's questions to challenge what she stood for? Why did his presence have to be a constant, gnawing reminder that her skin was white?

She forced herself to meet his hard golden eyes.

"I'm responsible for the safety of everyone in the camp," she said, conscious that she was breathing hard. "In saving your life, I put us all in danger. I should have left you where I found you, or dragged you back up the canyon. If those men had found your body, they might have turned back, and Otter Woman might still be alive!"

His gaze narrowed sharply. Moon Hawk could feel the pressure of his fingers, digging into her upper arms. "You're saying they came here looking for me?"

"Why else would they have come? Judging from their tracks, they're not soldiers or lawmen. But they could be after you for their own reasons." She took a step closer, challenging him with her gaze. "They could even be your friends."

He shook his head, his mouth tight and grim. "I may not remember who I am. But if I've got friends who'd do a thing like that—" he glanced toward the trampled, bloodstained snow "—I wouldn't say my life is worth much if I'd run with the likes of them."

Moon Hawk felt the weight of his hands on her shoulders. She felt the tension in his fingers, and she knew he was waiting for her to say that she believed him. But she could not bring herself to say what he wanted to hear. She had risked too much already by trusting this man.

His hands released her shoulders and dropped to his side. A cloud had passed over the sun, deepening the shadows beneath his eyes. He looked weary now.

As weary as she was. "All right, then, we know where we stand," he said. "Give me a horse and let me go. If your suspicions are true, the bastards will follow me and leave your people alone."

Moon Hawk tore her gaze away from his. She could not think clearly while looking into those tawny eyes. And she had to think clearly now for the sake of her weak little band.

What if she did as he suggested? He would be gone then. There would be no more questions, no more challenges to drag her into this quagmire of self-doubt. She would be sure of herself, sure of her purpose once more, as she had been before he came.

But her own feelings were the least of Moon Hawk's concerns now. Her first responsibility was for the welfare and safety of her people. If she allowed this white man to leave, there was still a danger that he might betray them to the bluecoats. And even after he was gone, there was no guarantee that the bandits would not return. These monsters, who preyed upon the weak and helpless, had stumbled on a ready supply of victims. She had no choice except to assume they would be back.

If he could be won to their side, this white man might prove a valuable ally. If not, he might at least serve them as a hostage.

She glanced up at him again. He was watching her guardedly, a thin trail of blood trickling from the knife cut on his cheek.

"What if you *are* one of those men?" she challenged him. "You could join them and—"

"You know better than that," he interrupted gruffly. "I met the old woman and the boy on their way back to camp. They told me what happened. I could never be one of those bastards."

"Did you know the woman they killed was Bright Wing's mother?"

The stricken look that flashed across his face gave her more reassurance than any words he could have spoken. But it wasn't enough, she reminded herself. This *ve hoe* was still the enemy.

"They'll be back," he said, confirming her own fears. "If they've seen your camp, they know there'll be easy pickings here—food, shelter, and unprotected women."

"Then help us fight them," she challenged him. "With you and that rifle, we might be able to hold them off."

He gazed at her for a long, still moment. In the silence, Moon Hawk could hear the scolding of a jay and the feathery rush of wind through the tops of the pine trees. The air smelled of snow.

"Hold them off?" Etonéto shook his head. "For how long, Moon Hawk? And what about the ones who come after them? I found your camp—or likely would have even if you hadn't brought me here. These men found it, too. Sooner or later there will be others. Whatever safety you've had in these mountains is gone."

She stared up at him, her mind refusing to accept what her ears were hearing. ''Then we'll move,'' she said. ''We'll go north—as far as we have to. There has to be someplace—some piece of land that nobody else wants, where we can live in peace!''

Again he shook his head. ''This country is filling up with land-hungry people who have no love for Indians. Get in their way, and, sooner or later, you'll be asking for a bloodbath. There's only one place where your band can be safe.''

''No!'' Moon Hawk reeled under the impact of his words. ''We won't go to the reservation! We'll die first!''

''Even the children?''

His question slammed into her like a doubled-up fist. She had spent anguish-filled nights wondering about the little ones and what would become of them—how they would make their way in the world, whom they would marry and whether they would keep to the old ways. So many questions, and none with easy answers.

''You said you'd had visitors from the reservation, so it can't be that far,'' he said. ''Show me the way, and I'll escort you there myself. If we go soon enough, we can get your people there before the winter settles in.''

A snowflake brushed Moon Hawk's cheek, melting against the warmth of her skin. The drop of moisture it left behind could have been mistaken for a tear. But it was not. Moon Hawk had not cried since that terrible day when she had discovered her butchered parents beside their wagon on the prairie.

She could almost feel Etonéto reading her thoughts. If her people went onto the reservation, she would not be allowed to stay with them. She would be sent back to a world she barely remembered and had even grown to hate. Worse, she would lose the only family she knew.

Earlier, he had suggested that she was keeping them here for her own selfish reasons. He was wrong, she told herself. Her people were free to go back to the reservation anytime they wished. All of them, even the children, had chosen to remain free.

But he was right about one thing. The threat to their tiny world was growing every day. Now a pack of beasts in human form had discovered their hiding place. How could she protect her vulnerable little band? The urgency of that one concern pushed all others aside.

The camp consisted of twenty-four women, nine children, one crippled youth, and Crow Feather, who was blind and had seen more than seventy winters. There were no able-bodied warriors among them and no guns, except for Etonéto's rifle, which Moon Hawk had not yet learned to shoot. They were helpless, at the mercy of these bandits or anyone else who came along.

They would be safer on the reservation—Etonéto was right about that, too. But even if her people were willing to go, it was too dangerous to flee now. They would be even more vulnerable on the trail than here in camp.

Etonéto was waiting for her to speak. She could feel his eyes on her, questioning and impatient. Her gaze crept stealthily upward until she could study him through the veil of her eyelashes. How tall he was, and how strong—a man of action who would know how to defend himself and others.

Slowly her mind edged toward the truth. Only with Etonéto fighting at her side did she have any chance of keeping her little band safe. But he had no ties to these people or to this place. All he wanted was to be on his way. And the reality was, she had no power to stop him. He had already found his boots. Soon he would discover how to get the other things he needed, including a horse. Then he would be gone.

There had to be a way to keep him here, to bind him to her and to her people. Force was not the answer, and there was no time for persuasion. Only one other idea came to mind.

Moon Hawk closed her eyes and took a long, slow breath to calm herself. Her heart was like a fluttering bird in her chest, and her flesh had become so warm that she scarcely felt the bite of the wind.

Looking up, she saw him through a blur of snow-flakes. His golden eyes blazed down at her, hot through the icy grayness of the storm.

Swiftly, before she could lose her courage, Moon Hawk caught the back of his neck, pulled herself upward and pressed her trembling lips to his.

Chapter Seven

He felt his pulse slam as her soft, full mouth captured his. For an instant he went rigid with surprise. Then his instincts kicked in. Her kiss was innocent, almost childlike in its awkwardness, but he was not about to let such a gift go to waste.

His arms slid around her. Beneath the supple buckskin she was all sinewy, flowing curves. The feel of her through the thin leather ignited a forest fire in his loins. He clasped her tightly, molding her to his rising hardness. Her taut body quivered against him but she did not pull away.

Oh, she knew exactly what she was doing, this golden-haired vixen. Her people were in danger, and she needed his help. This wild, clumsy seduction of hers was nothing more than bait, an enticement aimed at persuading him to stay and help her protect the camp.

Hellfire, didn't the woman understand that all she needed to do was ask? He might not remember who he was or where he'd come from, but his instincts told him he was not a man who'd go off and leave helpless women, children and old ones to be tormented by a band of filthy, murdering bastards.

But never mind. If the beautiful Moon Hawk wanted to sacrifice herself on the altar of passion, who was he to argue against it?

Her sweet lips were primly closed. It was plain to see she didn't know a lot about kissing. But he was a good teacher, he sensed, and didn't mind giving a few free lessons.

Gently but insistently his tongue brushed the edge of her full lower lip, teasing away her resistance. She gasped, then sighed as he sucked the lip softly into his mouth, letting his tongue flick light caresses along its silky inner lining. Her mouth and body melted against him. Her free arm twined around his neck.

The wind whispered around them as he held her close, his senses drinking in the feel and smell and taste of her. Even without a memory, he knew that few things in his life had ever felt as good as holding her like this, rocking her against him, feeling the sweet, aching pressure of her against his hard arousal and knowing that, for now at least, things could go no further. This was a moment of quiet magic, removed from the dark realities that churned around them. He knew, as she did, that this time was as brief and fragile as the song of a bird or a baby's laugh.

She had begun to tremble. He could feel the emotions welling up in her, crashing like waves against a bursting dam—grief, fear, loneliness and anger. And he could feel her resisting them, fighting them back. As the leader and protector of this little band she could show no weakness. In this time of loss and terror, it was her duty to set the example for them all.

How many years had she been living under this burden, putting aside her own needs and feelings, sacrificing a life of her own for the sake of this wretched little band of Indians she called her people?

Abruptly she tore herself out of his arms. Her eyes were feverish with denied need, her mouth wet and swollen. ''Bright Wing!'' she exclaimed as if she'd only just now remembered the little girl. ''She'll be crying! She'll need me! I have to go to her!''

Without meeting his gaze, she wheeled away and launched herself into a sprint for the camp. He stood where she had left him and watched her disappear through the bone-white aspens. Only when he could no longer see her did he bend and pick up the knife she had dropped. Then he followed her trail at a more thoughtful pace, the cut from her blade still stinging his cheek.

They buried Otter Woman later that day, at the base of a rockslide that had crumbled off the edge of the canyon in some long-ago time. Fifteen women trudged up the slope beneath a dark, roiling sky, two of them carrying the body between them on a travois.

The wind that chilled their tear-dampened faces carried the threat of an oncoming storm.

Moon Hawk herself rolled away the skull-sized boulders that covered the roots of an ancient pine tree, exposing a natural hollow beneath the trunk. Here they laid the shrouded body of their friend and sister, easing her into the cradle of the earth like a sleeping child. Then Moon Hawk replaced each rock as she had found it, so that no one would know the slide had been disturbed.

In less dangerous times, Otter Woman's body would have rested for a day in her lodge while her friends and family mourned her and paid their respects. Then she would have been laid out in her finest clothes, on a platform erected in the high branches of a tree. But that was not possible now. The hawks and ravens flocking around an exposed body could give away the presence of the band.

Likewise, because of the danger of discovery, the women had long since abandoned the custom of mourning aloud. Instead they simply turned around and trudged down the canyon, silent as ghosts through the veil of snow that had drifted in around them.

Moon Hawk had left Etonéto behind to help Broken Elk guard the camp. She felt the dread growing in her as they neared the clearing. Would she return to discover that he'd taken the opportunity to find the horses in their hidden corral, steal the strongest one and ride away? Or had her kiss—and the unspoken promise of more—been enough to keep him here?

The memory of that kiss haunted her now as she strode down the trail, bringing up the rear with her bow at ready. She was grateful that no one looked back at her to see the crimson stain that had crept upward into her cheeks. What had she been thinking, throwing herself at him like a reckless fool? In spite of her brief marriage, she knew almost nothing about men, especially white men. As for kissing…Moon Hawk held her face up to the snow to cool its furious heat. Etonéto had probably found her awkwardness laughable if not downright pathetic.

But he had given no sign of it, she reminded herself. His gentle lesson in kissing had nearly undone her. The memory of his teasing tongue triggered a hot, moist surge in the depths of her body. Her response to him had been as powerful as a rushing river, sweeping her perilously close to the brink of surrender. It had taken all her strength to tear herself out of his arms and flee to the safety of the camp.

She could not let herself give in to him—that much she knew. It was the *promise*, not the fulfillment of that promise, that had the most power to hold him. If she gave him what he wanted, he would tire of her and go. But if she could keep the bait dangling just out of reach…

Moon Hawk winced as she stubbed her foot on a tree root hidden beneath the snow. The pain jabbed up her leg, a sharp reminder of her own awkwardness.

What was she thinking? She had no skill with men. When it came to their desires, she scarcely knew where to start, let alone where to stop. Playing with fire would be less dangerous than the plan she had in mind.

But what other recourse did she have when the lives of her people were at stake?

By the time they neared the camp, Moon Hawk's nerves were quivering like bowstrings. Would she find him waiting, his golden eyes challenging her to make the next move? Or would she find no trace of him except his boot prints in the snow?

As they came out of the bare aspens into the clearing, her searching eyes found him. He was sitting cross-legged in the open entrance of Crow Feather's lodge, talking earnestly with the blind old warrior. Curled in his lap, her small face pressed against his soft woolen shirt, was Bright Wing.

Relief lightened Moon Hawk's dragging spirits as she hurried into the camp. She fully expected him to turn his head and look at her, but he seemed engrossed in conversation with the old man and scarcely paid her any heed.

Bright Wing, however, raised her tearstained face. At the sight of Moon Hawk, she scrambled off Etonéto's lap and raced across the clearing toward her. Dropping to a crouch, Moon Hawk put down her bow and caught the small body in her arms.

Bright Wing's breath came in little hiccuping sobs as she pressed her face against Moon Hawk's throat, but there were no tears. The little girl had wept herself dry.

Aching for her, Moon Hawk clasped the small shoulders and eased her gently away so that she could look into her stricken eyes. "Listen to me, Bright Wing," she said softly. "Your mother was a fine, brave woman. She would want you to be brave, too. Can you do that? Can you make her proud of you?"

"I will…try." Bright Wing's small voice was hoarse from sobbing, her face streaked with the salty crust of tears.

"I wasn't much older than you when I lost my own mother and father," Moon Hawk said softly. "I was all alone when Crow Feather found me and brought me home to the Tse Tse Stus. They became my people, my family. We are all your family, Bright Wing. We will take care of you."

"But who will be my mother?" The plaintive question tore at Moon Hawk's heart. She knew what the little girl wanted to hear. But how could she take on the burden of a child when she had so many other responsibilities?

A tall shadow had fallen across the snowy ground. She glanced up to find Etonéto standing beside her. Snowflakes swirled around him, blurring the expression on his face. Bright Wing tore loose and flung herself against him, her arms clasping his knees.

Only when she had a firm grip on him did she look back at Moon Hawk.

"*You* can be my mother," she declared, "and Etonéto can be my father!"

Moon Hawk felt the hot flash of color in her cheeks. Etonéto's left eyebrow twitched in silent acknowledgment. "It's not that simple, little one," he said gently. "Before we could become your parents, Moon Hawk would have to take me as her husband. I don't believe we're quite ready to do that."

"All of us in the camp will be your mothers," Moon Hawk added, desperate to change the subject, "but Crane Flying is your closest relative now. She has told me that she will take you into her lodge."

Bright Wing sighed, and Moon Hawk could almost read her thoughts. Crane Flying was a good woman, but she was dour and humorless and getting along in years. She would not have much patience with the demands of a lively child.

"I want to live with you," Bright Wing persisted. "You could teach me to shoot a bow and be a hunter."

Moon Hawk patted her small, wiry shoulder. "I will ask Crow Feather to make a bow just your size," she said. "As soon as it's finished, I will give you your first lesson. Would you like that?"

Bright Wing's tear-laced eyes danced like the snowflakes that flew around her on the rising wind. She would mourn her mother for the rest of her life. But the people in the camp would do their best to care for her and see that she was happy. They were a family, all of them.

"Run now, and find Crane Flying," she told the little girl. "Hurry, the storm is getting worse!"

Obediently, Bright Wing turned away and raced off through the blowing snow. She could not go back to her own home. Otter Woman's lodge and everything in it would need to be purified before it could be used again. She-Bear usually performed this ritual right after the burial. But now, with a fresh storm blowing down upon them, the ceremony would have to wait.

The tall pine trees swayed like meadow grass as the full force of the storm howled down the canyon. A barrage of snowflakes blasted Moon Hawk's face. She leaned into the wind, struggling to stay on her feet. Through the blinding swirl of snow, she glimpsed Broken Elk coming from the direction of the box canyon that sheltered the horses. He waved at her, signaling that the animals were secure. Then he disappeared into the lodge he shared with Crow Feather.

By now almost everyone had taken shelter. Eto-néto caught Moon Hawk's hand as they staggered across the clearing. She held on, grateful for the grip of his strong fingers as they fought for every step.

At last they reached her lodge on the far edge of the camp. Clasping each other for balance, they tumbled through the opening, letting the entrance flap drop behind them.

For a long moment they lay still, both of them breathing hard. Outside, wind gusts yowled, tearing at the heavy buffalo skins that covered the log framework. Inside, the lodge was dark, the storm muffled.

Moon Hawk lay on her side, half covered by his body. She could feel her heart, pounding with such force that the sound of it echoed in her head. She was acutely aware of his nearness—the feel of his lean, hard frame, the smoky scent of his skin and hair and the throaty rasp of his breathing against her ear.

She stirred against him, rolling onto her back in a halfhearted effort to free herself. The friction created by their entangled legs sent a lightning shaft of heat forking upward through her body. She bit back a moan.

Edging forward, he raised himself above her, his weight on his arms. He looked down at her, his expression lost in shadow.

Moon Hawk quivered as he bent close and kissed her lightly on the mouth. His lips barely brushed hers, but their tingling warmth radiated through her senses leaving her exquisitely hungry. Her lips parted, eager for more, but he drew back, still leaning above her.

"There's no need for you to be afraid of me, Moon Hawk. I won't hurt you." His voice was a raw whisper in the darkness. "And I won't do anything you don't want me to. Do you believe that?"

She gazed up at him, throbbing with need. Her body seethed beneath her clothes as she struggled for self control. She had set out to win his protection for her people. To give in to her burning needs would be to throw away the only bargain she had to offer him.

When she spoke, each word had to be forced from her reluctant mouth. "I…think we need to build up the fire…and get something to eat."

He laughed roughly as he disentangled his legs and moved off her. Moon Hawk sat up, feeling slightly dizzy. Her hair clung to her face in damp tendrils, cold against her hot skin. She smoothed it back with frenzied fingers, aware of his eyes on her. Her teeth had begun to chatter, as much from nervousness as from cold.

"We do need that fire, don't we?" His amused voice carried a sensual edge. "This shouldn't take long."

She watched his shadowy form as he rummaged for the wood that was piled against the base of the sloping wall. The fire had only a trace of red left in its coals. Etonéto stripped the bark from a dry stick of wood, shredded it with skillful fingers and placed it on the coals. Stirred by his breath, yellow tongues of flame flickered in the darkness as the bark fragments caught fire. Swiftly he added some sticks to the blaze, then a heavier section of dry aspen trunk. Soon the fire was crackling cheerfully, filling the lodge with light and warmth.

She-Bear had left a pot of her warm stew beside the coals. The fragrance of meat, roots and wild herbs curled into the air as Moon Hawk ladled the savory mixture into gourd bowls. They settled themselves on opposite sides of the fire to eat.

Food and warmth had helped to ease the tension between them. All the same, Moon Hawk watched him warily, her gaze dropping whenever he glanced up from his meal. He ate unhurriedly, with a confident air that implied all things would come to him if he waited—including her. Moon Hawk's pride warred with the needs of her heart. How she would relish proving him wrong!

And how she ached to prove him right.

The sound of the blizzard, still howling outside, added to the feeling of cozy isolation inside the lodge. But the sense of safety was only an illusion, Moon Hawk reminded herself. Somewhere beyond the camp, the man-beasts who had raped and killed Otter Woman were waiting for the storm to end.

"They'll stay holed up in this weather." Etonéto's words echoed her own thoughts. "But once the storm clears they'll be on the move again. If they need supplies, chances are they'll come back here."

"And it won't be to trade." Moon Hawk grasped at a thread of hope, then forced herself to let it go. Why should the bandits bother to negotiate when they could just as easily take what they wanted?

"How many do you think there are?"

"I counted four sets of tracks. But there could be others," she said.

"Horses?"

She nodded. "I saw the hoof marks where they'd tied them. We could use those horses, if we could get our hands on them."

He frowned thoughtfully, his long fingers balancing the empty bowl. "How well can your women fight?"

"Any one of them would die to protect the camp. But they have no weapons except their skinning knives." Moon Hawk stared into the flames, then added the only note of hope. "Broken Elk is a fine shot with a bow, almost as good as I am. And with the help of your rifle…"

Her voice trailed off as she realized what she'd been about to say. Etonéto had never told her he would help her people. She could not assume he would be there when the time came to fight off the bandits.

He exhaled sharply, and she guessed what he must be thinking. The bandits would likely be well armed, or at least rapacious enough to make the most of the weapons they had. In an all-out attack, even with the aid of one good rife, the little band of Cheyenne stood no chance of winning. Why should he risk almost certain death to aid a ragtag band of Indians he scarcely knew?

Etonéto leaned closer to the fire, reflected flame dancing in his eyes. "Crow Feather was telling me a story today," he said. "When he was a boy, his village was threatened by a band of Pawnee raiders. The men were off on a buffalo hunt, leaving no one there but women, children and old people..." He glanced up at her, the barest hint of a smile on his face. "Come over here to my side of the fire, and I'll tell you the rest."

Moon Hawk frowned. She had known Crow Feather for most of her life, but this was one story she had never heard. Had the old man made it up for the entertainment of a visitor, or had he been saving it for such a time as this?

She hesitated, watching him guardedly through the flames as he put down his bowl and settled back against a bundle of beaver pelts, his boots toward the fire. Only now did she realize how weary she was. This day of shock and tragedy had taken its toll on the entire band. But she was the one who bore the burden of responsibility for what had happened. Perhaps if she had been more vigilant, and less distracted by her own emotional turmoil, Otter Woman would be alive and safe.

Guilt and exhaustion lay on her like crushing weights. There were so many people who needed her, so many people she had come to love and care for, so many who would not survive without her strength. But right now, with the storm raging outside, all she wanted to do was to rest in the warm darkness, cradled by a pair of strong, supporting arms.

"Come here, Moon Hawk." His voice was like

the growling purr of a big, contented cat. "It's going to be a long night. We may as well stop playing games and make ourselves comfortable."

She moved, then hesitated, remembering the sensations that had raced through her body when she'd flung herself into his arms that morning. Could she control them now? Could she keep her head when all she really wanted was to abandon herself up to that same delicious madness?

"I promised I wouldn't harm you," he murmured as if he were calming a skittish horse. "I keep my promises, Moon Hawk. If all you want to do is talk, then that's what we'll do—just talk."

She edged around the fire toward him and eased into the place he had made for her. His arm dropped around her shoulders, pulling her gently against him. She nestled into his warmth, savoring the solid strength of his body and the clean male aroma of his skin. The scent of him, a white man's scent, stirred memories buried so deep inside her she was scarcely aware of them—the safety and comfort of strong arms holding her, the sweet, masculine fragrance surrounding her like a child's much-loved blanket.

He had buried memories, too, Moon Hawk reminded herself. She sensed their presence every time she looked into his restless golden eyes. When those memories came back to him, Etonéto would be lost to her. He would be a stranger, with a stranger's life. She had to be prepared for that.

"Tell me Crow Feather's story." Moon Hawk

forced herself to break the silence. "I thought I knew all his tales, but I don't remember that one."

"Hmm…where was I?" His mouth brushed her damp hairline as he spoke. Lost in the feathery contact of his lips, she roused herself to answer him.

"You were telling me that the men were gone from Crow Feather's village, and the Pawnee were coming to raid."

She felt him nod, the tawny stubble on his chin scratching her temple. "That's right. And while the Pawnee were still far off, the wisest woman in the village thought of a plan. They would cook up a delicious stew, but instead of wild onion they would chop up the stems and bulbs of the death lily…"

Moon Hawk listened as he related Crow Feather's story, taking pleasure in the rough, husky timbre of his voice. For the moment, the story itself mattered less than the telling of it, the sensual cadence of his speech and the stir of his breath against her hair. But then, suddenly, what he was saying began to penetrate her awareness, and she knew that Crow Feather had told the story for a reason. She pulled away and sat up, wide-eyed and quivering.

"We could do that here! Etonéto, it could work!"

His cat-colored eyes narrowed cautiously. "It wouldn't be simple. There would be plenty of risks involved—"

"But what else can we do to protect ourselves against those awful men? If it works, we could end up with their guns, their horses—"

"And if it doesn't work, we could all end up dead, or worse. I'm not saying it's a bad idea, Moon Hawk. Just that we'll need to plan and carry out every step. And we'll need backup plans we can fall to if something goes wrong."

"Yes, and—" Her lips parted in sudden silence as his words sank home. *We,* he had said. *We.*

Etonéto was not leaving. He was going to stay and help her people.

Impulsively Moon Hawk leaned forward and pressed her lips to his. Her kiss was every bit as clumsy and overeager as the first one had been. She told herself that she was only trying to show gratitude, but when he caught her and pulled her close, she knew that this was what she had wanted all along, what she had wanted all through this harsh and draining day. His arms were a refuge, his sensual, searching kisses a medicine to soothe her battered spirit.

Her senses exploded as his tongue penetrated her mouth, the tip touching hers in a caress that sent shooting stars rocketing through her body. With a long sigh she gave herself up to the sweetness of it. Her lips opened to welcome the intimate invasion. Hungry for the feel of him, her frenzied hands roamed over his shoulders, his back, his chest.

Her breath stopped, then quickened as his hand slid upward beneath her long buckskin shirt. The feel of his callused palm on the bare skin of her back sent shivers of pleasure through her body. When his thumb lightly brushed the outer curve of her breast she could not hold back a moan. Her couplings with Crooked Nose had been brief and furtive, something to be endured out of wifely duty. No one had ever touched her like this, aroused her like this, loved her like this.

Her loins contracted sharply as his hand cupped her breast. Dizzy with need, she strained upward toward the exquisite pressure of his stroking fingers. Her nipples felt swollen, sensitive almost to the point of pain, but all she wanted was more—his hands, his mouth, his lean, golden body.

Her thighs were slick with moisture, her body aching to contain him, to feel his hot, passionate thrust deep inside her. She had been without a man's strength for so many lonely nights. She had been so alone, so cold.

With a little whimper, she shifted against him, the motion pulling the chastity string tight against her legs. The sudden, sharp pressure sent a jolt of awareness through her body.

What was she thinking? She was not alone. She had a whole extended family to feed and protect. Her only reason for being here with this strangely compelling white man was to entice him into fighting for her people. Her own needs could not be allowed to matter. Keep him wanting—that was the strategy she'd planned earlier, and it still made sense. He had said he would stay. But there was no promise that he

would not change his mind, especially if she made
the mistake of surrendering too soon.

Nudging her chin upward, he kissed her again.
Moon Hawk's head swam as his lips took her higher
and deeper. His hand stroked her breast in a sensu-
ous, circling motion that caused the liquid heaviness
in the depths of her body to seethe and shimmer. She
fought to awaken the voice that had shrilled caution
in her mind on the night she'd found him half-dead
in the snow. Where was that voice now, when she
needed it? The voice of warning—the voice of She-
Bear? She had to find it again.

"She-Bear!" She almost shouted the name as she
pulled away from him. "I must go to her! I have to
talk with her about our plan! We're going to need
her help—"

"She can wait." His voice was husky with desire
as he caught her hand and drew her gently back toward him. "Nobody's going anywhere in this storm.
Not She-Bear, not the bandits and not us."

"But I have to go to her!" Moon Hawk twisted
out of his reach and scrambled to her feet. If she did
not leave now, she would be hopelessly lost.

Face flaming, she plunged toward the entrance of
the lodge, fumbled for the entrance flap and shoved
it aside. She would spend the night safely and sen-
sibly—in She-Bear's lodge. In the morning, when
her mind was clear and her purpose strong, she
would deal with Etonéto. Bracing herself, she
stepped outside.

The howling blast of wind, snow and sleet struck her like a solid wall. Moon Hawk staggered and fell to her knees as the full force of the storm swept over her. The night was black, and so thick with flying snow that she could not even see the other lodges in the camp. The wind tore at her with icy claws, so cold and sharp that it seemed to be ripping the skin off her face. She could hear nothing except the roar of the wind, see nothing except blinding sheets of snow. She tried to move forward, then to turn back, but she could scarcely breathe, let alone crawl. The wind seemed to be sucking the very air from her lungs.

Suddenly there were strong hands, groping for her in the storm. Moon Hawk gasped with relief as they found her, clasped her by the waist and dragged her back the way she had come.

She tumbled into the firelit warmth of her own lodge, to lie wet and shivering on the floor. Etonéto crouched above her, his eyes narrowed with concern.

He had spoken the truth. While the storm raged outside, no one would be going anywhere.

Chapter Eight

"You crazy fool!" He glowered down at her, forcing the words from a throat that was still choked with fear. "I've seen storms like this! I've seen what they can do to people who get lost a dozen paces from their own doorways!"

And he had, he was sure, even though he couldn't remember when or where. He only knew that when Moon Hawk had flung herself away from him and gone dashing out into the blizzard, his heart had gone cold in his chest, and all he'd been able to think of was that he had to bring her back or die trying.

Now she lay sprawled on the buffalo skins that covered the floor of the lodge, gazing up at him with wide, uneasy eyes. Was she afraid of him? Hellfire, she hadn't acted frightened when she'd kissed him. And when he'd taken her in his arms for another lesson in loving, she'd melted and sizzled like tallow on a red-hot stove. What kind of game did the woman think she was playing?

His first impulse was to seize her in his arms and take up where they'd left off. But she was trembling like a child, as if still reeling from the terror of the storm outside. And he was reeling too, stunned by the utter panic that had swept through him when she'd disappeared into the swirl of wind and blinding snow.

What if he had lost her?

Then again, what had given him the idea that she was his to lose?

Her pale braids lay like soggy ropes, pooling water on the buffalo hide that covered the floor. Her eyelashes were beaded with melting snow. Her chattering teeth made her lower lip quiver. She looked as pathetic as a wet puppy. Under the circumstances, there was only one thing he could do.

With a ragged sigh, he reached for a buffalo robe and tucked it around her shivering body. He felt her go tense, but she did not protest as he worked his arms beneath her knees and shoulders and lifted her against his chest. Her sinewy frame was a solid weight in his arms as he carried her close to the fire and settled her gently against the pile of beaver pelts.

Slowly he eased himself down beside her. When she didn't move away, he encircled her shoulders with one arm and pulled her against his side. Moon Hawk paused to remove the leather thong that held her large, sheathed hunting knife. Then she nestled against him like a cat seeking warmth.

"Better?" he murmured against her hair, and felt

her nod. The warmth of the fire began to settle around them, easing the tension.

"Those men are out there, too," she said. "Maybe the storm will take care of them for us."

"Maybe. But there's plenty of shelter in these canyons—caves, overhangs, deadfalls. Unless they're real greenhorns, they'll have found a safe place to hole up and wait for the weather to clear."

"Maybe they were just passing through." She was grasping at straws now. "Maybe they were on the run and just happened across Otter Woman. They could be far away by now."

"We can't count on that," he said. "We have to prepare as if they're coming back, and we may not have much time."

"Do you really think Crow Feather's idea will work?"

He desperately wanted to tell her yes. But in truth, the scheme that had arisen from the old man's story was fraught with risk. They could not be certain how many bandits there were or how well armed they would be. It worried him as well that so much depended on She-Bear's skill with herbs. At this point, he didn't even know whether the old woman would have what was needed, let alone know how to use it. The number of things that could go wrong with their plan was enough to make him feel dizzy.

But worry was useless now, with the storm raging outside and shadows dancing on the walls of the lodge. Moon Hawk's damp head rested in the hollow of his shoulder. Her body nestled trustingly against his side, and he sensed that this night would be remembered as one of the sweetest times of his life. He knew almost nothing about her, and even less about himself. But something told him that, when the time came, if he died protecting her, his life would be well spent.

But tomorrow could wait. What he wanted tonight was to learn more about the woman at his side—this amazing creature who was so strong and yet so vulnerable. He wanted to understand her, to know her to the depths of her untamed spirit. And he wanted to understand why he felt such a mysterious connection to her, as if they had met in a time beyond memory.

She stirred beside him, and he sensed that if he did not speak now, the chance would be lost.

"Tell me about your life with the Cheyenne, Moon Hawk," he said, his lips skimming her hair. "I want to know everything you can tell me—how you came to be here, why you chose to live as a man—the whole story."

"Why?" she murmured drowsily. "Why should it matter to you?"

"Because *you* matter," he whispered, nuzzling her eyebrow. "Because I have a strong, courageous, beautiful woman in my arms, and I want to know all about her." He lowered his head to brush a tingling kiss along the crest of her ear. "And because if I don't have a good story to occupy my mind, I'll be tempted to forget my manners and make love to you this very minute."

And so, because she felt so warm and safe with him, Moon Hawk pushed aside her natural reticence and allowed the words to flow. She told him how her parents had died, and how Crow Feather, who was now old and blind, had found her on the prairie and brought her home for his widowed daughter to raise.

"Once I'd gotten beyond grieving for my parents, growing up with the Cheyenne was wonderful," she said. "I'd always wanted brothers and sisters, and I soon discovered that the whole band was my family. They treated me as one of their own. I never wanted for playmates, or for some grown-up to give me affection and discipline and teach me what I needed to know."

Moon Hawk closed her eyes, basking in the memory of those days, when the prairies teemed with game, and it was possible to leap onto a horse and ride for days without seeing a *ve hoe* trail or outpost. Now all that had changed. The world of the Tse Tse Stus was growing smaller every day.

"You told me you'd been married."

"Yes." She willed herself not to flinch at the unspoken questions behind that statement. "I was… sixteen. My foster mother had died, and my grandfather, Crow Feather, was beginning to lose his sight. He could no longer hunt meat for us."

Moon Hawk remembered that time well. She had

been of marriageable age and was well trained in the wifely duties of foraging, cooking, skinning, tanning hides and sewing them into garments. But conflicts with the *ve hoe* were on the rise, and the young men of the tribe knew that having a white-skinned wife could be a magnet for trouble. None of them had tried to court her.

"A warrior named Crooked Nose—a kind man and a good hunter—offered to take me as his second wife. His first wife was big with her fourth baby and needed help in the lodge. For three good horses and the promise that he would provide for my grandfather, I went with Crooked Nose and became his wife."

"And did Crooked Nose keep his promise?"

Moon Hawk sensed an underlying edge in Etonéto's soft-spoken question. "While he lived, he kept it well, and my grandfather never went hungry. But Crooked Nose did not live long. A traveler brought the red spot sickness to our winter camp. By the time it had passed, my husband and his two older children were dead."

Moon Hawk swallowed her emotion as the memory swept over her. So many sick. So many dead. She herself had survived measles as a young child and so was safe from the ravages of the disease. But Crooked Nose had been a good man, and she had grown to love his stripling son and his pretty daughter, who'd been only a few years younger than Moon Hawk herself.

"With Crooked Nose gone, there was no one to feed the family," she said, taking up the story. "That was when I became a hunter. My grandfather taught me to shoot a bow. At first I was clumsy and brought home only a little meat. But as my skill grew, I began to take pride in what I could do. I needed no man's help to provide for Crooked Nose's family and for my grandfather. After a time I began to provide for others as well."

She paused for a moment, her eyes gazing into the flames. Etonéto had begun to toy with one of her long braids. His deft fingers had untied the rawhide thong that held the end. Now, little by little, he began to unravel the damp plaits, letting her hair fall loose in shimmering waves that were the color of moonlight.

"Was that when you started dressing as a brave?" he asked.

"It was easier to ride and shoot in men's clothes," she replied, her senses tingling as he stroked her hair. "At first I only wore them to hunt, but over time, I gave up women's clothes altogether."

No, not altogether, Moon Hawk reminded herself. She still wore the chastity string, though it had been shortened from the usual style so that it would not bind her legs when she straddled a horse. She had long since ceased to question why she wore it. Despite being amid her little band of women, children and old ones, the chastity string had become a symbol of her hard-won freedom—a reminder that no man was her master.

Etonéto had finished one braid and started on the other. Nestled beside him Moon Hawk felt warm, safe and contented. But now his gentle, patient fingers were stirring the embers of the flame that had roared through her body earlier. The ache in her loins had reawakened to become a low, pulsing throb.

"Don't you get lonely, Moon Hawk?" His lips grazed her temple as he spoke.

"There is no time to be lonely here."

"But you're a beautiful woman—and too young to put yourself away like an old maid's trousseau. Don't you ever wish for a man's arms to hold you on long, cold nights...like this one?" His thumb stroked her cheek as he spoke, the simple touch igniting flames that raced through her body in a wild conflagration.

"Such a wish would be foolish." Her voice came out breathy and trembling. "There are no men—no suitable men—here. And I have learned not to need..."

His thumb slid down her cheek and along the edge of her jaw. Lifting her face he kissed her, slowly, sensuously, his mouth exploring and caressing hers with such exquisite restraint that she whimpered aloud. Her hand caught the back of his neck, fingers raking his damp, wavy hair as her body turned to liquid flame in his arms.

This was far too dangerous, the warning voice

shrilled. She was safer outside in the blizzard than in the arms of this strong, gentle stranger who made her heart dance every time their eyes met. But she was already beyond listening to caution. She knew almost nothing about this man, but her sense of connection to him went deeper than flesh, deeper than trust. It was as if she had been his from the moment she'd found him beside the creek, half-frozen and covered with snow.

Was this how love felt? Moon Hawk had no way of knowing. She had respected Crooked Nose and been grateful for his help, but the sweet, hot yearnings that raged in her now, with Etonéto, had never been a part of her brief marriage. She felt as if her own spirit animal—the falcon—had been freed from its tether to soar into the sky for the first time.

Who had he been before he came here? Moon Hawk pondered the question as she lay in his arms and realized it no longer mattered. She knew him here. She knew him now, and whoever he was, he had become a vital part of her world.

Perhaps he would never recover his memory. Perhaps he would remain Etonéto forever, here at her side with no ties to that other life he had known. She could easily wish that for herself. But for him…?

The question swirled and faded from her mind as his hand stole beneath her buckskin shirt to recapture her waiting breast. She gasped, reeling with pleasure as he caressed her swollen nipple. Her body arched upward, begging for more. Her fingers tore at the buttons that fastened the front of his shirt, wanting to touch his skin as he was touching hers. For the space of a breath he paused to help her, his touch swift, his eyes burning into hers like hot coals.

"Moon Hawk, if you want me to stop—"

"No," she whispered, her carefully laid plans scattering like storm-blown snowflakes. "No, don't... don't stop."

He had loosened her hair from the long, tight braids. It spread around them, falling over his knees. His fingers smoothed it into a pale gold fan. "You're so beautiful," he murmured, kissing her eyes, her cheeks, her throat. "So beautiful..."

Her hands found his bare skin beneath the unbuttoned shirt. His flesh was as smooth and hard as river stone, all muscle and sinew, his chest dusted down the center with a soft, crisp triangle of hair. Moon Hawk's trembling fingers traced the tawny trail of it where it narrowed downward to disappear beneath the waistband of his trousers. There she paused, her heart racing.

"Wait, you little wanton." The words emerged as a throaty chuckle. "There's time. That storm outside isn't going anywhere." Lifting her hand, he pressed a kiss into its palm. Then he sat up and moved to kneel above her,

She lay back against the beaver skins as he took his time undressing her—peeling off her leather leggings and moccasins, warming her chilled feet between his hands. Moon Hawk had never been touched with such playful tenderness. The warning voice whispered that he must be a very experienced lover. But then, what did she know of such things? She only knew that his hands and lips were sweet fire on her skin, and all she wanted was more of him. All of him.

Bunching the fringed hem of her buckskin shirt, he worked it over her head and tossed it aside. Moon Hawk lay bathed in firelight, wearing nothing but her doeskin breech cloth and, beneath that, the knotted chastity string. He swore softly as he gazed down at her, and she sensed the struggle in him. This was a man who did not know who he was or what lay lost and waiting beyond the reach of his memory. Their loving could leave a trail of pain and regret when that memory returned.

But tonight he needed her, and she wanted him more than she had ever wanted anything in her life. She wanted to forget the grief and terror of the day. She wanted to put aside her lonely burdens and, for just this night, lose herself in loving and being loved.

Bending close, he brushed a trail of kisses down her belly, his lips skimming the hollow of her navel and nudging aside the leather strap that held the soft doeskin breechcloth around her hips. His hand stroked the sensitive inner surface of her thigh. She moaned, her legs parting at his touch, opening the way for more. The chastity string bit into her skin.

He saw it as his hands tugged away the breech-cloth. Moon Hawk had expected him to be startled, or at least puzzled, but he seemed to know what he had just found and what it meant.

"Moon Hawk, are you sure—"

"Take it off," she whispered, feverish with need. "I've worn it long enough."

He fumbled with the first of the intricate knots, but the thin leather strips had been tied together for so long that each joining had melded into a solid lump. When he began to mutter, Moon Hawk groped for, and found, the hunting knife that she had tossed on the floor. Without a word he took it from her and slid it from its sheath. For the space of a breath their eyes met. His were molten with need, their gaze intense and searing, and she realized that even if she'd wanted to, she could not stop him now—not any more than she could stop herself.

She closed her eyes as the knife severed each strand of the chastity string. For the first instant she felt a flash of dread, as if the blade were cutting into her own flesh. Then a sweet sense of release swept over her. She was a woman, with a woman's body, and she felt as if she had been born for this man— to be found by him, to be loved by him.

His fingers touched the wet, pulsing quick of her, triggering waves of sensation that shimmered through her senses like silver fish through dark water. She arched upward against the exquisite pressure, her hands reaching, pulling him down to her. This time he did not stop her when she found the waistband of his trousers. Her fingers flew at the buttons, breaking two of them in their haste. She had undressed his beautiful body once before, but that first time his maleness had been cold and slumbering. Now he jutted toward her, swollen and hot and hard.

Time seemed to stop as he kissed her, tongue thrusting in a feverish dance that spoke of what was to come, fingers opening her, gently stroking her until she almost screamed with need.

"Yes," she whispered, unable to think of anything but having him. "Yes...now!"

He entered her in a long, smooth thrust that set off shimmering bursts of fire. Moon Hawk arched to meet him, wondering how anything could be so perfect as the feel and fit of him inside her body. A little sob worked its way out of her throat.

He paused, kissing her cheeks, her eyes. "It's all right," he murmured thickly. "I won't hurt you."

"You're not...hurting me," she whispered. "It's just that I've never...never felt..." Words failing her, she pushed upward with her hips, drawing him into her. His breath stopped for an instant. Then his arms went around her, holding her close as it began—the pulsing, thrusting rhythm that carried her higher and higher until she felt as if she were soaring in the sky. She cried out as the bursting came, her legs holding him deep as he shuddered, gasped and lay still in her arms.

He lay with his head propped on one elbow, watching the play of dying firelight on Moon Hawk's sleeping face. They had made love again and again, until both of them were deliciously spent. She had tumbled over the edge of exhaustion and into slumber. But he had lain awake for the rest of the night, cradling her in his arms, listening as the soft rush of her breathing mingled with the sounds of the storm outside.

Now the fire had burned down to flickering embers, and the first rays of dawn glimmered through the entrance flap of the lodge. He watched the soft flow of light and shadow across her features, thinking how beautiful she was and how completely she had given herself to him. Right now there was nothing he wanted more than to wake up beside her every morning for the rest of his life.

But how could a man think of the future when he knew nothing about his past? Through the blackest hours of the night, he had struggled to remember even the smallest detail of his life. But the effort had been like staring into a thick fog. No names came to his mind, and no faces except one—a woman's face framed by a halo of pale gold hair. A woman who looked strangely like Moon Hawk and yet, he sensed, was not.

Who was he? Did he have a sweetheart? A wife? Children? Was someone waiting in a place he no longer remembered, heart aching, eyes scanning the horizon for the sight of him?

Lord, why couldn't he remember?

He had just spent a night in heaven, with a woman

who was as passionate and courageous as she was beautiful. Only now, stretched out beside her in the cold dawn, did the ugly truth of what he'd done sink home. Moon Hawk had opened herself to him— heart, soul and body. But he'd had no right to take what she offered so freely—not until he knew what lay in the darkness of his forgotten past.

Who had he betrayed last night? Who had he hurt? The questions haunted him as he sat up, cursing under his breath. If he could be certain he was free, he would kiss her awake this very minute and lay his life at her feet, but such an act was unthinkable for a man who was a stranger to himself.

Moon Hawk smiled in her sleep. The sight of her, so happy, so innocent and so beautiful, tore at his heart and filled him with self-loathing. He could not risk hurting her any more than he already had. For the rest of his time here, he would ask to move in with Crow Feather and Broken Elk. That would give Moon Hawk the safety she needed.

Taking care not to wake her, he eased to his feet and slipped into his clothes. He had brooded long enough. It was time he put himself to use, and he could start by going outside to see how much damage the storm had done.

His coat was still missing, so he flung a buffalo robe around his shoulders before slipping outside and closing the flap behind him. Above the towering walls of the canyon, he could see the pewter gleam of an early-morning sky, still dotted with fading stars. The storm had passed, leaving an eerie silence in its wake. In the camp, the canyon wind had sculpted the snow into deep, white drifts. No one else had come outside, but he could see fresh smoke curling above one of the lodges—the one where the old woman, She-Bear, lived.

For a moment he weighed the wisdom of disturbing her. She-Bear was a vital part of the plan he and Moon Hawk had discussed. If she could not do as needed, they would have to find another way to defend the camp, and there might not be much time to prepare.

He turned toward the old woman's teepee, then hesitated. As leader of the little band, it was Moon Hawk's place to speak with her people. The last thing he wanted was to undermine her authority. And yesterday, old She-Bear had bristled with distrust every time she looked at him. He could only guess what was behind those looks, but clearly she had no love for white men.

Moon Hawk would be awake soon, he reminded himself. It would be best that she deal with She-Bear. Meanwhile, he would be wise to check around for any sign of trouble.

He prowled the boundaries of the camp, gazing up and down the canyon as the sky paled into dawn. The wind had blown down limbs and toppled trees in the night, but except in the camp itself, the snowfall was not as heavy as he'd expected. It took a few moments of puzzling and staring up at the high, bare ledges before he realized what must have happened.

The blizzard had spent itself sometime in the night. After that, it appeared that the canyon had become a funnel for a freakish wind—a wind that had scoured much of the snow from the higher ground and blown it with galelike force into the camp.

A cold sweat broke out under his clothes as the implications of what he was seeing sank home. The camp itself was bogged down in snow. But much of the surrounding country had been swept bare. Unless the bandits had holed up in the bottom of the canyon, they would be able to move much more freely than either he or Moon Hawk had anticipated. Mounted, they could strike and run while their helpless victims were still snowbound.

His anxious eyes scanned the rocky slopes as he struggled to guess what the brutes might do. Maybe Moon Hawk had been right. Maybe they had done their deviltry and moved on. But he wouldn't bet money on it. Not in this country where supplies, horses and women were as scarce as gold. Even if the outlaws were on the run, they would be tempted by the easy pickings.

With a ragged exhalation he turned back toward the camp. He had hoped to let Moon Hawk sleep, but he could not wait any longer to alert her to the danger. Without the snow to contain them, the bandits could strike anytime they chose.

He had just crossed the creek when a sound echoed down the canyon, chilling his blood and shattering the morning's uneasy peace.

It was the scream of a frightened horse.

Chapter Nine

Wheeling, he plunged toward the sound. It had come from the direction of the sheltered side canyon where, Moon Hawk had told him, the band kept its precious horses. Maybe a prowling cougar had leaped onto one of them. If he could get there fast enough, he might be able to scare the cat off. Most cougars were shy creatures and tended to flee from humans. All the same, he wished he'd taken the time to find out where Moon Hawk had hidden his rifle.

As if the thought had summoned her, she appeared from behind him and shoved the rifle into his hands. She had flung on her long shirt and moccasins, but her legs were bare, her eyes were swollen with sleep, and her hair was an uncombed tangle in the early morning light. Her bow and her quiver of arrows were slung from one shoulder.

She raced past him without a word, heedless of the cold as she ploughed through the drifting snow. Their harsh breaths left white clouds on the winter air as he followed close behind, letting her choose the path through the thick pines that screened the mouth of the side canyon.

As the trail wound upward, they could hear the horses, snorting and whinnying. Whatever had spooked them, it couldn't be far away. He paused long enough to chamber a shell and cock the rifle, then hurry after her, up along a wind-scoured rockslide to the top of a low rise. From there they could see down into the sheltered, grassy hollow where a half-dozen ponies—poor, scrawny-looking creatures—were clustered in the lee of a pine grove, shifting and snorting nervously. Etonéto could see no sign of cougar or bear or anything else that might have scared them. But the hair on the back of his neck was bristling, a sign that something was wrong.

The hollow was a well-chosen hiding place, sheltered from the weather and surrounded by towering cliffs. A makeshift fence of brush and fallen tree trunks had been laid across the narrow entrance to keep the horses from wandering out, but the barricade was scarcely necessary. The animals were securely hobbled and had no better place to go.

On the far side of the hollow, a spring trickled from a crack in a high, jutting ledge. Where the water splashed downward, the rocks were coated with a sheen of ice that glinted like quicksilver in the faint morning light.

Etonéto's eyes were tracing its path down the cliff-side when he heard Moon Hawk gasp. Her hand reached out to clutch his arm.

"What is it?" He followed the direction of her gaze but could see nothing amiss.

"There," she whispered, pointing. "At the bottom of that ledge, where the water comes down."

At first he could see nothing. Then, as his eyes strained into the faint light, a dark form took shape at the foot of the rocks. It emerged in his vision as the dark body of a man, lying low.

"Take cover and stay back!" Rifle at ready, he flattened himself against the rocks and began edging his way down the slope into the hollow. Ignoring his urgent whisper, Moon Hawk paused to slip her bow off her shoulder and nock an arrow. Then she followed his path, flowing like a shadow behind him.

Had the intruder spotted them? Etonéto peered through the brush fence, expecting at any second to hear the whine of a bullet, but the only sounds in the hollow were the gurgle of the spring, the milling of the horses and the croak of a passing raven. The smaller birds had fled or fallen into silence. Even the wind was still.

"He hasn't moved," Moon Hawk whispered, and it was true. They were close enough now to make out the faded red plaid of the man's coat where he lay screened by low brush. From the moment they'd first spotted him, he had not so much as stirred.

"Stay back while I take a look," Etonéto hissed. "I mean it. Stay put."

This time Moon Hawk did as she was told. As he moved beyond the fence, a swift backward glance told him she had raised and drawn the bow. Even now, with danger all around them, he could not help admiring her fierce courage.

But neither the bow nor his own rifle would be needed here. As he circled the prone figure, coming in from behind, Etonéto saw the bloody gash at the back of the greasy, unkempt head and he knew that this intruder would never move again.

He took a moment to scan the ledges for signs of the man's cohorts. Seeing no danger, he slid the man's pistol from its holster. Then he beckoned to Moon Hawk.

She came into the open, moving cautiously, eyes alert, bow drawn. Her lips parted when she saw that the man was dead, but only when she had walked around him and inspected the soles of the ill-fitting military boots did she lower the bow and allow the string to slacken.

"He's one of them." Her voice was leaden. "I recognize those boots from the tracks around Otter Woman's body."

"From the look of things, I'd say he was trying to come down these rocks and slipped on the ice."

"But what was he doing here? And where are the others?" Her eyes searched the cliffs around them. "Maybe they were all trying to come down this way and ambush the camp from the pine thicket. Or maybe they wanted to run off the ponies, maybe use them to draw us away from the camp.''

Etonéto scanned the snow. The only hoofprints he saw were from unshod horses, and the only human tracks were their own. ''There's no sign the others made it down,'' he said. ''They may have given up after this one slipped and fell.''

''Or the rest of the bandits were coming a different way.'' She stared down at the broken body in the snow, as if trying to glean some satisfaction from an enemy's death. When she looked up at him again, her eyes blazed with urgency.

''We have to get back and warn the camp. It may be too late for our plan.''

''How many ways are there for them to get down here?'' He laid a hand on her arm, turning her away from the battered corpse. He kept the contact as they toiled upward out of the hollow toward the rise.

She took her time answering his question. ''There's a long, easy trail, the way you would have been coming when your horse fell. But that trail is on the far side of the canyon. It doesn't make sense that they'd cross over and come back down.''

''What's on this side—besides the way our friend back there came down?''

''Another trail, shorter and steeper. That's the way they probably left yesterday, and that's the way they'd most likely try to…come back.'' Her breath caught as an icy gust of wind struck her face, sweeping her tangled hair behind her. Her eyes were blood-shot, her lips blue with cold.

A lovely young woman like Moon Hawk should not have to bear such a harsh life, Etonéto thought as they moved up the slope. She belonged someplace warm and safe, where she could eat civilized food, sleep in a downy feather bed and wear pretty clothes in soft colors that enhanced her beauty. She belonged where she could be cherished, pampered and loved—loved by him, every day and every night for the rest of their lives.

But what was he thinking? He had spent the past night making love to Moon Hawk. He knew every curve and hollow of her exquisite golden body, the feel of her, the scent of her, the taste of her. He knew every nuance of her breathing and the exact timbre of the sweet little cries that rose from her throat when he brought her to her peak.

In one night, she had become so much a part of him that he could not stand the thought of life with-out her. But until his memory returned he was not free to offer her tomorrow, let alone a lifetime, es-pecially when there was no way to know if either of them would live through the next few hours. To-morrow could not be allowed to exist for them. They had only the memory of last night. And now.

That the bandits would strike was becoming more and more of a certainty. As defenders of the helpless little band, the two of them would be at the forefront of the coming danger. If he died—or if, God forbid, she did—he did not want anything left unsaid between them.

In the wind-sheltered lee of a high boulder, he caught her shoulder and pulled her around to face him. He knew they needed to get back to the camp. But he also knew that if he did not speak to her now, he would regret it to the end of his days.

"We have to hurry." She strained against his grip, her eyes anxious.

"I know. And we will. But I have to say this now, before our time runs out. Will you listen to me, Moon Hawk?"

She gazed up at him uncertainly, waiting.

"I don't know what's going to happen down there in the camp," he said. "Right now I don't even know my own name. But I know that I can't let you go without telling you that I love you."

Her eyes widened, the pupils as large and dark as the centers of purple pansies. Her lips, still swollen from last night's kissing, parted and quivered, but she did not speak. He could feel the urgency in her, the need to get back to the people who depended on her, and he knew he could not take much time.

"Whatever the day brings," he said, gripping her shoulder with his free hand, "whatever happens tomorrow and after that, never forget what I'm telling you now. I love you, Moon Hawk. And if fate is kind enough to let us be together, I want to spend the rest of my life taking care of you and making you happy!"

Her hand reached up and gently brushed the stubble on his cheek. "Until you came, I had never known a man's love," she whispered. "And I had never known the feel of love here—" Her fingertips touched her breast. "To know is enough, Etonéto. To ask for more would be greedy. It would anger the spirits. But you have given me so much happiness—"

Her voice broke as he caught her close and held her for a long moment, tight and hard, as if trying to press her into his body. She trembled like a bird in his arms. "We have to get back to the camp," she said. "If something happens—"

"I know." He released her, feeling as if he were tearing flesh from flesh. If the attack came when she was not there, she would never forgive herself—or him.

They took a shortcut across the rockslide, leaping from boulder to boulder until they reached the trees at the bottom. There they paused to catch their breaths. From the direction of the camp, fresh smoke curled skyward, a sign that people were up and stirring.

"Do you know how to use this?" Etonéto held out the Colt revolver he had taken off the dead bandit. A quick check had revealed five bullets in the cylinder.

She shook her head. "I'm better with the bow."

"Take it anyway." He checked the safety, then thrust it into her belt. "I'll show you how to use it when we get back to camp. Save it for close range, where you won't have to worry about your aim.''

A chill passed through his body as he imagined the circumstances under which she might have to use the pistol. To a pack of woman-hungry outlaws, Moon Hawk would be a prize. If they could corner her alive, they would be on her like a pack of rabid wolves.

A bright flicker caught his eye, causing him to glance up. Now he saw it again, the glint of morning light on something metallic, high in the rocks above the ledges. His heart lurched as he realized what it was.

''There,'' he whispered, but Moon Hawk had already seen it. For an instant she froze in horror. Then she wheeled and broke into a run, headed for the camp.

Etonéto stayed put long enough to analyze what he had seen. It appeared that the bandits' plan was to spread out along the ledges and shoot down into the camp from above. Then, when most of the people were dead, wounded or fleeing for their lives, they could move in and take what they wanted.

Moon Hawk's running figure flashed through the trees. He plunged after her, all his instincts screaming. There would be no time to prepare and no chance to set the trap they had planned in the night.

The enemy was close, and the time had come for him, for Moon Hawk, and for her little band of Cheyenne to fight for their lives.

* * *

Moon Hawk was sprinting into the camp when the first shot rang out. She heard the whine of the bullet and saw Crow Feather collapse in the entrance of his lodge.

No! Moon Hawk dived for the old man, catching him in her arms, cradling his body as he had cradled hers on that long-ago day when he'd found her on the prairie. But she was already too late to save him. The crimson hole in his buckskin shirt told her the bullet had gone straight through his heart.

The traditional wail of mourning sprang to her lips, but she gulped it back. Grieving for the dead would have to wait. Her first duty was to save the living.

Broken Elk came stumbling out of the bushes. He was still arranging his clothes when a second bullet sang past his head and struck a tree behind him.

"Get down!" Moon Hawk flew at him, knocking him to the ground as a third shot splattered the snow beside them. How many bandits were up there in the rocks? She had counted four sets of tracks. With one of the men dead, that left three. But there could easily be more. Many more.

Keeping low, she dragged Broken Elk behind a rock, where they would be less exposed. Women were darting among the lodges, catching up stray children, making easy targets as they ran for the shelter of the trees. But the shooters clearly wanted to pick off the men first—one blind elder, one gangly, crippled youth, and Etonéto. They would save the women for different sport.

The sharp crack of a rifle rang out from somewhere behind her. A scream echoed off the cliffs as one of the bandits tumbled from his hiding place and pitched onto the sharp rocks below. A wild volley of rifle shots rang out from the ledges, all of them aimed at Etonéto's hiding place behind the massive stump of a fallen pine tree. How many? Moon Hawk counted shots from five different vantage points. Her heart sank as she realized how many others there might be. Even now, while the fire from the ledges kept her people pinned down, more *ve hoe* outlaws could be working their way along the trail toward the camp.

How many shots did Etonéto have left in his rifle? Not enough, Moon Hawk realized. When she'd rescued him from the snow, she had hidden the leather bullet pouch beneath the floor of her lodge and forgotten about it. Now all their lives depended on her getting it to him.

Broken Elk had caught sight of Crow Feather's body sprawled at the entrance of their lodge. The young man had begun to weep, his thin shoulders heaving as he struggled to hold back the sound of racking sobs. Moon Hawk shifted her weight onto one elbow and seized his arm.

"Be still!" she whispered. "Find your courage, little brother. Our grandfather would want you to be a brave warrior. Make him proud of you."

He turned his tear-splotched face toward her. "How can I be a warrior? I can't even walk without a crutch, and I'm…afraid." It was a disgraceful admission, wrenching in its honesty. Moon Hawk's heart ached for the boy.

"We're all afraid," she said more gently. "But the women and children need a man to protect them. Get your bow and arrows, then lead them to the horse pasture. When they're all safely inside, stay and guard the entrance. Etonéto and I will try to hold them off here, but if we fail…"

She let the words trail off and saw his resolve harden. When Etonéto's next shot rang out, drawing a hail of gunfire, the boy took advantage of the distraction to seize his crutch and lunge for his weapons, which lay just inside the lodge, near the old man's body. Keeping low, he seized them and lurched off in the direction the women had taken, determined to do a warrior's duty. He would be all right, she thought. If he lived.

Moon Hawk watched long enough to make sure Broken Elk was out of rifle range. Then she made a zigzag dash for her own lodge. A bullet whined past her head as she dived for the entrance. She had gambled that the bandits would not shoot at a woman, but either she'd been dead wrong or, dressed as she was, they'd mistaken her for a male.

Frantically she rummaged for the leather bullet pouch. Finding it, she crawled back to the entrance, lifted the flap and flung the pouch toward the spot where Etonéto lay, protected by the uprooted tree. Her arm was strong and sure. He caught it deftly and flashed her a grim smile, then bent to reloading the rifle—none too soon. A hail of bullets exploded from the cliffs. This time they were aiming at *her*.

Dodging and rolling through the trampled snow, Moon Hawk made it back to the rock where she and Broken Elk had taken shelter. She heard the bark of the rifle, followed by a long shriek as another man fell to his death.

At once the gunfire shifted back to Etonéto. Moon Hawk struggled to gather her own wits. The shooters were too high for her arrows to reach. She would be more useful at the foot of the trail, where she could pick off any bandits who might try to come down into the canyon.

Etonéto's next shot sent a shower of rocks tumbling over a high ledge. Taking advantage of the commotion, Moon Hawk sprang up and sprinted for the tangle of aspen and willow that grew along the creek.

From his hiding place, she heard him curse. ''Where the hell do you think you're going?'' he shouted. ''Get back here!''

Ignoring him, she plunged ahead. She could only hope his impulsive shout hadn't drawn attention to her movements. The thick scrub would help screen her, but if the shooters happened to spot her directly below them, she would be an easy target.

Crouching low, she clawed her way through the

snowy tangle of willow and chokecherry. A sharp branch gouged her cheek, drawing blood. Moon Hawk swallowed a little cry of pain. If she could make it to the trailhead without being seen or heard, she could hide behind an outcrop of boulders that jutted over its narrow base. That would give her a clear bow shot at anyone coming down into the canyon.

Behind her, the report of Etonéto's rifle echoed off the ledges. He was firing rapidly in an effort to draw the shooters' attention away from her. She was dizzy with fear for him, but she could not stop now. Taking advantage of the distraction, she cut away from the creek and plunged through the snow, into a clump of bare aspens.

Looking ahead through the ghost-white trunks, she could see the boulders that marked the trail. The firing continued behind her as she raced through the trees.

Just in time, she remembered that if she approached the boulders straight-on, her tracks would be visible to anyone coming down the trail. Gasping with effort, she cut back the way she had come, circling to approach the rocks from the rear. The distance had never seemed so far.

By the time she reached the back of the outcrop, her heart was threatening to burst through the walls of her chest. She collapsed, panting, against the rocks, her breath forming white clouds on the frigid air.

She did not hear the footsteps approaching from behind until a rough, smelly hand clamped over her mouth.

Instinctively Moon Hawk began to struggle, kicking, twisting and clawing. But more hands seized her, jerking her off balance. Her head struck a jutting rock, stunning her for a few precious seconds. When her vision cleared, she found herself securely pinned to the boulders, with two grinning, bewhiskered faces leering down at her.

"Well, now, what we got here, eh?" The dark, fleshy man held her left wrist in one hand while the other hand covered her mouth. He reeked of stale tobacco, and his voice was a nasal whine. "My gawd, Ike, it's a white woman! An' a purty one at that!"

"Glory be, is this our lucky day or what?" the smaller, thinner man chuckled. "Think we oughta save her for the others or take our turns here and now?"

"Hank told us to sneak in and bushwhack that sonofabitch with the rifle," the first man said. "He'll be madder'n a riled skunk if'n we don't do that first."

Ike's wiry fingers tightened painfully around Moon Hawk's left wrist. Forcing herself to remain calm, she lay quietly, gathering her strength for the chance to catch the men off guard.

"If you ask me, Hank's been gittin' too big for his britches lately. I say we have our fun now and let him worry about the rifle. Maybe if we git lucky, they'll shoot each other.''

''An' if we don't, Hank'll have our balls for supper. We can't have it both ways, Ike.''

The small man's eyes narrowed thoughtfully. Then he broke into a broad grin, revealing a line of yellow, rotting teeth. ''Who the hell says we can't? We'll stick it to 'er and let 'er squeal. If that don't bring the bastard out of where he's holed, nothin' will! When he comes chargin' to the rescue we'll just plug 'im between the eyes and finish what we started. How's that for a plan?''

A sickening weight stirred in Moon Hawk's stomach. She imagined Etonéto hearing her cries and racing to help her, as he surely would. In her mind's eye, she saw the bullet strike, saw him stagger and fall.

Whatever happened, whatever these filthy beasts did to her, she could not allow herself to make a sound. Not if she wanted Etonéto to live.

The big man chuckled as he removed his hand from Moon Hawk's mouth. ''Hell, you's a right smart one, Ike! You shoulda been a schoolmaster.'' His greasy fist caught the hem of her long, fringed shirt and flipped it up over her bare thighs. ''Lawse,'' he breathed, ''I ain't seen pussy that color since we went on the run. I'm hard as an anvil already. Come on, help me tie 'er hands. I'll butter the bun while you keep a lookout for her friend out there. Then we can trade off.''

"It was my idea," Ike snarled testily. "I go first. You keep watch."

The big man swore, then sighed. "All right. We can tie 'er hands to that quakie over there. That soft ground'll be easier on the ol' knees. C'mon, help me drag 'er."

Moon Hawk knew she would be helpless once her hands were tied. She lay still, listening to the pop and whine of gunfire from farther down the canyon. Her muscles ached with tension as she waited for an opening, any vulnerable moment that would allow her to move.

That opening came as the two men were shifting positions to drag her to the tree. Moon Hawk's strong legs struck first, kicking upward to club the smaller man in the face. Ike tumbled backward, cursing as he clutched his broken, bleeding nose.

She'd expected the big man's reflexes to be slow, but he had her in a headlock before she could draw her knife. Moon Hawk writhed in his grip, almost suffocated by the stench of his thick, sweaty arm against her face. Her hands flailed as she struggled to reach her knife. If she could get a grip on it, she might have a chance to fight them off and escape. But she was already losing the struggle. She could feel herself growing weak and dizzy as his grasp shut off her air supply.

Working her mouth open, she bit down with all her strength into the man's arm. He screamed in pain as her teeth sank into his flesh. Moon Hawk hung on with the tenacity of a wolverine, fighting nausea as she clamped down harder and harder. By the time he let her go, blood was oozing down his arm, and he was bawling at the top of his lungs.

Moon Hawk rolled free of him and sprang to her feet, dagger flashing in the morning sunlight. But Ike had already drawn his pistol and was pointing it at her head.

"Hold it right there, you hellcat," he snarled. "And drop that damned pigsticker. Either you promise to be nice to me an' my friend here, or I put a bullet right between them purty blue—"

"Moon Hawk!" A deep, clear voice rang across the canyon. "Where are you? Are you all right?"

Etonéto. Moon Hawk's heart plummeted. Had he heard the big man scream or had he simply become worried about her? Either way, he was headed right into a trap.

"Stop, Etonéto!" she screamed. "Go back!"

But she was already too late. As she sprang toward the man with the pistol, she saw the weapon swing toward a figure in the trees. The gunshot rang out the instant before her body struck Ike's arm.

The world seemed to end as she saw Etonéto reel backward and collapse in the snow.

Chapter Ten

"No!" The cry broke from the shattered depths of Moon Hawk's soul as she fought her way clear of Ike's thrashing body. The pistol, which she had knocked out his hand, lay in the snow a few paces away. Only one thought was driving her now—to reach Etonéto. But reason shrilled that she had to get the weapon now, before either man had the chance to use it again.

Kicking herself free, she crawled forward and groped in the deep snow for the gun. As her fingers touched the cold steel grip, the big man seized her ankles. Moon Hawk felt herself being jerked backward. The brambles beneath the snow raked her bare belly, leaving long scratches as the buckskin shirt bunched upward beneath her arms. He was crouched over her hips now. Moon Hawk could hear him breathing hard. "You git back, Ike. By gawd, I've earned the right to first poke at this pussy! I'm gonna take 'er from behind like a—"

The words ended in a gurgle as a rifle shot rang
out from the far side of the canyon. The big man
slumped to one side, clutching his throat as he died.

Gasping, Moon Hawk worked her knees beneath
her and scrambled to a crouch. Ike was on his feet
now, but he went down in the next volley, his chest
riddled by bullets.

Would she be next? Moon Hawk did not wait to
find out. Keeping low, she cut a zigzag path through
the underbrush, a path that would take her to the
clump of aspens where she had seen Etonéto fall.
Bullets ricocheted off the cliffs, striking the earth
around her as she ran. From the long trail on the
canyon's far side, she could hear shouts and the
sounds of horses.

Her lungs were almost bursting by the time she
found Etonéto. He was sprawled on his back in the
snow, his eyes closed, his face ashen. Blood was
flowing from a wound on the side of his head, stain-
ing the snow a deep, bright crimson.

With a cry, she dropped down beside him and cradled his head in her lap. There was nothing to stanch
the bleeding except her own buckskin shirt. She
pressed the wound hard beneath her breasts while her
fingers groped the side of his neck for a pulse. After
a few frantic seconds she found it—the barest flutter,
like the wing beats of a dying insect.

She packed the wound with fresh snow, which she
held in place against her belly. Her lips moved in
prayer, first to Maheo, the giver and protector of all

life, then to the white man's god, the god of her childhood, to whom she had not prayed in years. "Let him live…oh, let him live…"

Through the bare trees she could see the riders, fifteen or twenty of them, coming down the long trail into the canyon. They were not bluecoats, but they were clearly white men, warmly dressed and well mounted, their rifles drawn from their scabbards. Were they bandits, too? Moon Hawk's heart sank as she realized the answer to that question made little difference. Whoever they were, she had no strength left to fight so many. Her people would be at their mercy.

The gunfire from the ledges had ceased. The leader of the newcomers, a lean, hawkish man with graying whiskers, directed a half-dozen men up the steep trail toward the ledges to look for any remaining bandits. The rest of the group rode single file along the creek, in the direction of the camp.

"Marshal! Over here!" One of the men had spotted Moon Hawk. The leader wheeled his horse from the head of the line and trotted the animal over to the clump of aspens where she knelt with Etonéto's head cradled between her breasts. Sunlight glinted on the silver star that was pinned to the vest beneath the man's open coat.

"What the devil?" He swung off the horse, drew his pistol and strode into the trees. Bloodied, frozen and exhausted, Moon Hawk gazed up at him with the desperation of a wounded animal.

"Please…" she whispered, her teeth chattering. "He's alive but he's hurt. Please help him."

The marshal's grizzled eyebrows met in a scowl as he called for blankets, holstered the pistol and knelt in the snow to inspect Etonéto's injuries. Moon Hawk watched his every move as he tugged off his right glove, pulled a bandanna out of his pocket and sponged away the blood.

"Looks like just a scalp wound," he grunted. "Not so bad in itself, but my guess is he's got a bad concussion to go with it. Saw my share of these injuries as a medic in the army. Sometimes the men got better in a few days. Other times, they just lingered and…"

His voice trailed off as he stared down at Etonéto's face. His sharp gray eyes widened, brows bristling intently as he leaned closer.

"Good Lord," he muttered. "I know this man!"

Once again the snow was melting. Water dripped off the bare aspen branches to splatter on the muddy ground below. The creek flowed high and brown with runoff from the early blizzard. Chickadees piped and scolded from the berry thickets, happy for yet another reprieve from a long, cold winter.

Moon Hawk sat cross-legged in the open doorway of her lodge, thinking how her life had crumbled around her in the past three days. No part of who she was or what she cherished remained untouched. It was as if everything that was dear and familiar had been wrenched out of her grasp, leaving her alone and empty.

With the need for secrecy gone, Crow Feather had been buried in the traditional Cheyenne way. Dressed as a warrior, his body had been carried on a platform to a remote part of the canyon and raised high on a scaffold made of lodge poles. Tears had streamed down Broken Elk's young face as he slaughtered the horse that would carry Crow Feather's spirit across the four rivers to the place of the dead. The animal fell without a sound beneath the scaffold.

Moon Hawk had embraced the youth as he turned away. "You are the keeper of Crow Feather's stories now, little brother," she had admonished him. "Never forget the words he spoke to you."

Even now, with the bittersweetness of memory, the old man's arms seemed to enfold her like a soft blanket. His voice murmured on the warm south wind, brushing her face like a caress.

"Nestaévahósevóomatse, Nam Shim," Moon Hawk whispered, her throat burning with the sting of unshed tears. "Until we meet again, Grandfather."

Crow Feather's loss was not the only change. From where she sat, she could see across the bustling camp, where her people were packing their meager possessions for the trek to the reservation, which was to begin at first light tomorrow. They would be escorted to the agency on the Tongue River by Marshall Sam Rafferty and his posse, who had trailed the bandits all the way from South Pass to this secret canyon and had now taken on a far different mission.

So far, at least, these new *ve hoe* had treated the Tse Tse Stus with kindness and respect. They were good men who would keep her people safe, Moon Hawk tried to reassure herself. But even if they were not, she no longer had any choice in the matter.

"I was hired by the government to uphold the law," Marshall Rafferty had told her after the ceremony for Crow Feather. "These Indians of yours are breaking that law by living off the reservation. In the absence of the army, it's my job to take them there, and even if it weren't my job, I'd do it anyway, for their own safety."

Moon Hawk had been too dispirited to argue with him, but his manner had softened at the sight of her stricken face. "You're welcome to come back to South Pass City with us," he'd said. "I know some folks there who might be willing to take you in."

Moon Hawk had replied with nothing more than a slight shake of her head.

"Well, you can't stay here," he'd insisted, his exasperation growing. "And you can't expect to follow these people onto the reservation! No matter what you've told me about their being your only family, you're a white woman, not a blamed Cheyenne, and you've got a future to consider. Now, where do you want to go?"

"I...don't know," Moon Hawk had replied, forcing each word to take shape in her benumbed mind. "I need time to think."

And she was still thinking as she sat beside the bed of the man she had loved with all the passion of her lonely heart. His pulse and breathing were stronger now, and the scalp wound was already healing; but he had not opened his eyes nor given any other sign that he was aware of her. Marshal Rafferty planned to take him by horse travois to the Cheyenne agency on the Tongue River, where there was a dispensary with a doctor who could look after him until his elder brother could be summoned to take him home.

Etonéto. Moon Hawk's lips formed his name as she brushed back a lock of tawny hair from his pale forehead. But he was no longer Etonéto, she reminded herself. He had another name now, and a family who owned one of the biggest cattle ranches in the territory. He had a whole life that, if he recovered, she could not expect to share.

Whatever happens…never forget what I'm telling you now. I love you, Moon Hawk. And if fate is generous enough to let us be together, I want to spend the rest of my life taking care of you and making you happy…

The words came back to Moon Hawk as she gazed down at his unconscious face. But they were only words, spoken by a man who no longer existed except in her own memory.

"So, how is the *ve hoe* this morning? Has he

awakened from his long sleep?'' She-Bear, lugging a rolled buffalo hide beneath her arm, paused at the entrance of the lodge. She looked gaunt and frail and old.

''He is the same,'' Moon Hawk replied. ''But you should not be working so hard. Sit here in the sun with Etonéto, and I will load your things on the travois.''

The old woman shook her head. ''When other people do my work, I will be ready to die.'' She paused with a sigh and lowered the hide to the ground. ''But I will stop and sit with you a while. Who can say if such a chance will come again?''

The words, so calmly spoken, stabbed into Moon Hawk's heart. How she would miss this gruff old woman. How she would miss all of her people.

''I found your chastity string on the floor of your lodge. Did I not warn you what would happen if you rescued this man, my daughter?''

Moon Hawk willed herself to ignore the hot color that flooded her face. ''You did. And you were right. But I am not sorry for what happened. I think it was time for such a thing to happen.''

She-Bear's eyes softened for a moment, as if she were remembering her own young womanhood and the husband she had loved. Then her gaze narrowed and sharpened. ''Remember your words when the hard times come. And they will come, Moon Hawk. The kind of happiness you have known does not come without a price, one you are only beginning to pay."

Moon Hawk glanced down at Etonéto's sleeping face and knew that the old woman's words were true. She would never regret loving him, but her heart was already aching.

"What will you do if he dies?" She-Bear asked.

Moon Hawk shook her head, unable to answer.

"And what will you do if he lives?"

"I don't know," Moon Hawk whispered. "The marshal—the man with the star—tells me he belongs to a powerful family with more land than a man can walk across in three days and more cattle than stars in the sky. I have seen enough of the *ve hoe* to know that a man from such a family would not want a woman like me."

Moon Hawk jerked herself back from the brink of self-pity, knowing it would only render her useless. After all, what were the problems of one foolish woman compared to the trials awaiting her people, who were losing the very thing they cherished most—their freedom?

She imagined them living on the reservation, eating whatever the *ve hoe* chose to give them, dwelling in ugly log houses that could not be moved when it came time for the land to rest. She pictured them freezing in ragged cloth garments, forced to learn the white man's ways, attend the white man's schools and practice the white man's religion. She thought of the diseases that spread like ravaging fire when the Tse Tse Stus came in contact with the *ve hoe*. By remaining isolated, the band had been able to keep these sicknesses at bay. Now there would be no escape.

One way or another they would all be lost, unless she could find a way to save them.

Moon Hawk felt a new sense of purpose kindle and begin to burn inside her. She might be separated from her people, but she could not, *would* not, abandon them to a bleak future on the reservation.

"What will you do?" She-Bear asked her for the third time, and suddenly Moon Hawk knew the answer to that question.

"I will search out a new home for our people," she said. "A safe place where the bluecoats cannot follow them and bring them back."

The old woman stared at her, then slowly nodded. "I have heard of such places," she said. "Far to the north, I was once told, there is a line the *ve hoe* have made on the ground to mark the end of their country. The bluecoats will not cross that line for anything. It is their law. But our people have no such law. We can cross the line when we want to. All we need is a place to live."

"I will search out some land for us!" Moon Hawk vowed. "When I have found it, I will come for our people and take them there—in the spring, when the snow is gone."

The old woman's mouth widened in a toothless grin. "We will move like shadows! The bluecoats will never catch us. It will be like old times, my daughter, only better!'' Her gnarled hand reached out and squeezed Moon Hawk's wrist so hard that the small clawlike fingers dug into her flesh. ''The memory of your promise will keep our feet moving lightly on the trail to the Tongue River. Our spirits will be strong through the long winter, knowing we will be together again in our own place.''

Someone called to She-Bear from across the camp. The old woman hobbled away, dragging the rolled buffalo skin behind her. Moon Hawk might be the provider and protector, but when it came time to move the camp, She-Bear was the one in charge.

Moon Hawk gazed after the small, hunched figure, crushed, suddenly, by the growing weight of the promise she had made. What did she know about getting land and keeping it? The Tse Tse Stus and people of other tribes did not believe that land could be owned. The earth was their mother—how could they own a part of their mother? But to the *ve hoe*, the ownership and control of land was everything. They worked all their lives to get and keep it. They fought for it, died for it. And if one of them found a piece of land that was not owned by anyone else, he would be swift to claim it.

She needed to get some land that no one else could take away. And she did not even know where or how to begin.

Beside her, Etonéto stirred and moaned in his twilight sleep. Moon Hawk stroked his cool forehead, her fingers smoothing back the tangle of damp, tawny hair. Over the past few hours he had become more and more restless. Was he trying to wake up? She watched him now, her heart pounding.

"I'm here, Etonéto," she whispered, calling him by the name she knew best. "You're safe. All of us are safe. Open your eyes and see."

But he only sighed and settled back into stillness. What was he seeing in his mind? she wondered. Who would he be when—and if—he awakened?

The marshal had told her his family was rich. She thought of the land her people so desperately needed. For a fleeting moment she weighed the idea of pleading for his help, then swiftly decided against it. If he offered, she would accept gratefully. But she would not ask. It would hurt too much to have him refuse.

The wind had shifted, sending a cool breeze down the long funnel of the canyon. Etonéto shivered as it touched his skin, and Moon Hawk reached for his coat, where it lay next to his bed. As she smoothed it gently over him, her fingers skimmed a hard, flat object that appeared to be sewn into the coat's lining. Puzzled, she examined it through the thick flannel fabric. It was oval in shape, about half the size of her palm, and as thick as a small slab of bark. Only it didn't have the feel of bark. Its hard, smooth weight suggested metal, or even glass.

Bending closer, she inspected the coat. Where the object had been slipped into the lining, the seam had been hastily and clumsily restitched. Even now, she noticed that a strand of mismatched thread was hanging loose. Unable to resist, she gave it a slight tug. The seam unraveled, revealing a gleam of metal as the hidden object tumbled out into Moon Hawk's hand.

It was a miniature portrait, framed in a silver filigree that was as delicate as winter frost. The glass was scratched and clouded, the image beneath murky with age, but Moon Hawk recognized it at once. Tearless sobs worked their way up into her throat as she cradled the portrait in her palm, her eyes staring at the small, pale face—staring as if she had seen a ghost.

Ryan Tolliver opened his eyes. At first he saw only the blur of sunlight—a blinding triangle bordered by darkness. But as his vision began to clear he realized he was inside an Indian lodge, lying on a bed of pine boughs covered with soft buffalo robes. His head ached dully, and his stomach felt as hollow as the inside of a Pawnee drum. How long had he been asleep, and where the hell was he?

For the space of a long breath he closed his eyes, filling his senses with the drip of melting snow, the chatter of winter birds and, from farther away, the bustling sounds of an Indian camp. It was all right, he reassured himself. Wherever he was, he was alive and safe.

Only when he opened his eyes again and turned his head did he see the beautiful golden-haired woman kneeling beside him. She was dressed like a man in a long, fringed buckskin tunic. Her braids shone like pleated sheaves of ripe wheat where they hung down over her breasts.

She was gazing at him, her violet eyes wide and expectant. But as he looked back at her, a shadow passed across her face. Her shoulders sagged, as if she had just been dealt an invisible blow.

Their gazes locked and held for what seemed like an eternity before she spoke.

"You don't know me, do you?" Her husky whisper carried an undertone of sadness.

Ryan stared at her, and suddenly the memories came rushing back—his meeting with Horace Mannington, the old man's missing granddaughter, and the five-thousand-dollar reward that would open the wide world to him if he could bring her back to St. Louis.

With effort he found his voice. "You're...Molly Ivins, aren't you?"

A fleeting, animal wildness flashed in her eyes as she shook her head. "Molly Ivins is dead. She died on the prairie a long time ago. My name is Moon Hawk."

"But you're—"

"No," she said, interrupting him. "It's my turn to ask questions and your turn to answer. I know who you are. But why have you come here, and where did you get...this?"

Her extended fist opened like a clenched flower.

Clasped in her hand, so tightly that the silver edges of the frame had cut into her palm, was the portrait of Florence Mannington Ivins.

He struggled to a sitting position, bringing his gaze level with her own. His head throbbed, and his vision swam with odd little blotches of light, but he forced himself to speak calmly and clearly. "Your grandfather gave me that portrait of your mother when he sent me to find you and bring you home."

She drew back warily. "You're lying. I had only one grandfather. His name was Crow Feather. And I *am* home."

He studied her stubborn, sunlit face—as beautiful as the face in the portrait but with a strength Florence Ivins had never possessed. Her skin was a rich, sun-bronzed gold, her cheekbones wide and high, her blue eyes as sharp and fierce as a falcon's.

Molly Ivins was nothing like the dazed, beaten captive he had expected to find among the Cheyenne. She was every inch a warrior, as proud and untamed as a golden mustang.

Making love to such a creature would be unforgettable, he mused. But he would be a fool not to keep his distance. She was Horace Mannington's granddaughter, not some little backwoods tart, and the man who trifled with her could expect to pay dearly.

She would not follow him meekly back to St. Louis, that much was certain. By the time he turned her over to Mannington, Ryan suspected, he'd be forced to earn every cent of that five-thousand-dollar reward. But earn it he would. If he had to hogtie the woman and sling her over the rump of his horse, by heaven, that's exactly what he would do!

And if this battle of wills began to weaken his resolve, he would remind himself of the shimmering Nile, the teeming plains of Africa, the crumbling palaces of Rome, and how he yearned to see them all.

"This isn't your home, Molly," he said, feigning a patience he did not feel. "Your home is in St. Louis, in a fine, big house, with a lonesome old man whose only desire is to put things right."

"Put things right." It was more of a challenge than a question, flung at him with the disdainful flare of one elegant nostril. "I don't see that—"

"Listen to me, Molly." His voice dropped in pitch, forcing her to listen closely. "Your grandfather, Horace Mannington, is one of the richest men in the state of Missouri. His daughter—your mother—was a beauty. She had an army of wealthy suitors, and he expected her to make a profitable match. When she married your father, a poor schoolmaster—"

"My father wasn't poor! My mother always said we were rich because we had everything we needed!"

Ryan bit back a cynical smile. Lord, the woman had no notion of wealth. She had never seen how the upper classes lived—the grand houses, the food, the clothes, the lavish balls and parties. What a shock it would be to her innocent eyes. She would not adjust well to such a life, he thought. Either she would run away or she would remain a social misfit, an outsider to the end of her days. But that was not his problem. Once he left her with Mannington and collected his payment, his job would be done.

"Your grandfather didn't approve of the marriage," he said, taking up the thread of the story. "In fact, he was so angry that he disowned your mother—his only child. They never saw each other again."

"And now he wants me to go to him." Her voice was expressionless, as were her riveting violet eyes. Was she bitter or only sad? And why did her manner make him feel like a low-bellied snake? He was doing her a favor! Most women would have been delighted to hear the kind of news he had just delivered.

But Molly Ivins was not like most women.

He was grasping for something else to say to her when a movement through the open entrance of the lodge caught his eye. A lanky figure in a Stetson, looking out of place but strangely familiar, was striding toward them.

"Ryan Tolliver!" The man broke into an awkward lope that carried him across the clearing. "You mule-headed son of a gun, I should've known you were too ornery to die!"

Ryan blinked up at the leathery, grinning face. "Sam? Sam Rafferty? What the devil are you doing here?"

"Trailing the Benton Creek gang with a posse from South Pass. We got the bastards, too, and saved the territory the cost of a trial and a hanging. Good riddance to the whole lot, I say. But now we're saddled with marching these Cheyenne holdouts north to the agency before the next storm sets in. Judging from the looks of them, it'll be a slow trip." He paused. "Hungry?"

"I could eat the hind leg off a bear!" Ryan answered with a grin, but he was acutely conscious of Molly's silence beside him. U.S. Marshal Sam Rafferty was a longtime family friend, but his timing was not the best. Ryan sensed that Molly was slipping away from him, and it would not be easy to approach her again.

"We're camped up the creek a piece," the marshal said. "Got some good beans and bacon on the coals, but you'd best not be on your feet just yet. I'll have one of the boys fetch you a plate, along with some hot coffee. Then you can eat while we visit."

Ryan was aware that Molly had risen silently to her feet. She moved past him like a shadow and, murmuring something about having work to do, ducked through the entrance of the lodge and strode out into the sunlight. Ryan gazed after her, seized by a strange sense of loss. Something was happening here, he sensed, something that lay beyond the depths of his understanding.

The sound of a throat clearing reminded Ryan that Sam Rafferty was beside him, watching him with curious eyes. "I'll go see about those beans," Sam said, rising to his feet. "I won't be but a minute."

"Take your time," Ryan said, meaning it. He needed a few minutes to collect himself, to grapple with the fact that he had awakened in a strange place with only a vague idea of how he'd arrived. He remembered the sudden snowstorm. He remembered the owl that had spooked his horse and sent the animal careening down the slope of the canyon. But he remembered nothing about the Benton Creek gang and nothing about the arrival of the posse.

As he sat soaking up the sunlight, his eyes were drawn to the figure of a little girl who flitted across the clearing like a windblown leaf. A small, pretty thing who looked no more than five or six years old, she was dressed in buckskins and wrapped in a tattered piece of blanket. Her black braids flew behind her as she ran.

She came nearer, then stopped as she caught sight of him. For the space of a heartbeat, she stared. Then her small face broke into a grin. She sprinted toward him, shouting in Cheyenne.

"Etonéto! You're awake! You're—"

She stopped in her tracks, suddenly tongue-tied, as if seeing a stranger for the first time. A shyness stole over her face. For an instant she hesitated. Then she wheeled and bolted away like a startled fawn.

Chapter Eleven

Moon Hawk walked slowly along the bank of the creek. With every step, she filled her memory with images of this place, where she had been happier than she ever expected to be again in her life.

The aspen trunks were white against the dark, ledges. The swollen creek ran high and wild, flooding over its banks onto the lower parts of the path. Where Moon Hawk had to cut above the water, the rocks were sharp through the soles of her moccasins.

Finding a high flat rock above the creek, she settled herself where she could look down at the rushing water. The smell of wet leaves was sweetly pungent, like old, damp leather. The plaintive winter call of a chickadee echoed against the cliffs.

Would she ever return to this lonely canyon? No, she concluded sadly, she could never truly return. Even if she found her way back here, her people would be gone. Etonéto would be gone—as he was gone already. Etonéto had been part of this place.

But Ryan Tolliver was a stranger here. A hard edge had replaced the tenderness she had known in him. The tenderness of a man who no longer existed.

Ryan was determined to take her back to St. Louis. Would she go? Part of her wanted to stay here in this canyon, to guard it as a sanctuary for her people. But the canyon had been violated, just as Otter Woman had been violated, and it would never be safe again. She would have to find another way to keep her little family together.

Ryan had said that her grandfather was rich. But what did that mean? Among the Tse Tse Stus, a rich man was one who had many horses and a good supply of meat and buffalo robes. A rich man was one who shared his bounty with those in need. Would her grandfather be wealthy in the same way? Moon Hawk sighed. From what she remembered and had heard of white men, they counted their wealth in gold and silver coins, which they kept locked away in great iron boxes where no one could take them. While the poor among them went hungry, they gathered more gold and silver, which they spent on huge stone houses that shut out the fresh air and could not be moved when the land was tired.

A flash of movement along the path caught her eye. Moon Hawk's hand moved reflexively to the haft of her knife, then relaxed as she recognized the small, darting figure of Bright Wing.

Reaching down, she helped the little girl scramble up onto the rock beside her. Bright Wing's face blazed with puzzled hurt, as if she had just been punished for no reason.

"What is it?" Moon Hawk slipped an arm around the rigid shoulders and drew her close.

"Etonéto."

Moon Hawk's breath stopped as she waited for the little girl to go on.

"I was outside your lodge, and I saw that he was sitting up." Bright Wing choked back a sob. "I ran to him, only…" Her words trailed off. She gazed up at Moon Hawk with bewildered eyes. "It wasn't Etonéto. It looked like him, but it was somebody else. And he didn't even know me."

"That sometimes happens when people hurt their heads," Moon Hawk said, hiding her own dismay. "Etonéto's head was hurt twice, and there are many things he doesn't remember—not even you, little one."

"But he was my friend!"

"I know." Moon Hawk gathered the little girl close, thinking how much loss her young spirit would have to bear—her mother, her home, and two people she had learned to trust. What would become of this beautiful child in the years ahead?

"Everybody is getting ready to move," she said. "I don't want to move. I want to stay here."

"I know, so do I." Moon Hawk's arm tightened around her. But you must go with the others, and I…will have to find a new home."

Bright Wing pressed her face into the hollow of

Moon Hawk's shoulder, her tiny hands clinging fiercely. "Why can't I stay with you?" she demanded. "Why can't you be my mother?"

"That isn't possible now," Moon Hawk answered, aching. "I have no home, no place to keep you safe. For now, at least, you will need to stay with Crane Flying on the reservation."

"But Crane Flying says you will find a new home for us. That's what She-Bear told her."

Moon Hawk felt the weight of her own words, their power almost crushing her. Already the news had spread. What had begun as a wish had solidified into a promise. Her little band had always depended on her. Now they would be waiting for her to keep that promise.

What would happen if she failed?

"Getting the land may take a long time," she said, not wanting to set the child up for more disappointment. "First I'll need to find a piece of land where there'll be game and water and plenty of grass for the ponies. Then I'll need to make sure no one can come and take it from us. That probably means buying it with *ve hoe* money. Right now I don't have any money."

"Crane Flying says you will come for us in the spring, when the snow is gone. She says we will follow you to the new land, and that we will all live there together."

Moon Hawk felt her heart contract. "I will do everything I can to get the land by spring, but it may take longer. Will you be patient, little one? Will you stay on the reservation with Crane Flying and do as she tells you?''

Bright Wing nodded, her black eyes glowing with trust. ''When you come back for us, will you be my mother?''

The knot around Moon Hawk's heart tightened. ''All that I do from now on will be for you and for our people,'' she vowed. But one look at Bright Wing's face told her it was not enough.

She hugged Bright Wing hard, wondering if she could ever love a daughter of her own as much as she loved this sweet, trusting little girl. ''I wish I could promise you that,'' she whispered. ''But things happen, things we don't expect or want. All I can tell you is that I'll do everything I can to come back. And when I do...we'll talk about what happens next.''

It was a feeble promise at best. But Bright Wing seemed to understand. She flung her arms around Moon Hawk's neck and held on tightly. As Moon Hawk stroked the glossy braids she knew there was only one way to keep the promise she'd made—a way that would demand all the courage she possessed.

By the time the sun rose above the canyon rim the next morning, the camp was empty. In the gray time before sunrise, Moon Hawk had embraced each of her people. Broken Elk had struggled to be a man, hiding his tears behind a stoic mask. Bright Wing had clung sobbing to her neck. She-Bear had clasped Moon Hawk's face between her gnarled hands and stared into her face as if she would never see her again. In a way, she was right. As Moon Hawk stood beside Ryan Tolliver and watched the sad procession trudge up the steep trail on the north side of the canyon, Moon Hawk died. And Molly Ivins was reborn.

Riding up the long south trail behind Ryan, Molly willed herself not to look back. Clinging to the past would destroy her. She had to focus on the future—her own and that of her people. Only by returning to the world of the *ve hoe* could she get the money she needed to buy a home for her beloved little band.

Outwardly she had not changed. She still wore her long braids and her fringed buckskin. She still carried her knife, her bow and her quiver of arrows. She had even made herself a new chastity string. She had put it on last night in the solitary darkness of her lodge, after Ryan had gone off to spend the night in the camp of the white men. As she rode away from the world she had known, the light pressure of the leather knots against her thighs was familiar and comforting.

She would leave the string in place for as long as she and Ryan were alone together. She had been reckless once. She could not afford to be reckless again.

Ryan rode a stone's throw ahead of her, sitting like a man who'd lived in the saddle, his broad shoulders relaxed, his lean hips shifting easily with the motion

of the horse. For now, Moon Hawk was grateful that
the narrow trail did not permit them to ride abreast.
She would have been at a loss for conversation this
morning, with her mind such a turmoil. Was this how
it felt to be white—always torn between one thing
and another, always wanting what you couldn't
have?

Every time she looked at Ryan she wanted to feel
his arms around her. But it was Etonéto she wanted,
not this cold-eyed stranger who treated her like a
piece of baggage to be delivered to its destination.
Not once that morning had he spoken to her with
warmth or affection or good humor. He had not even
flashed her a smile.

And that was just as well, she reminded herself.
The distance between them was like a river. As long
as she was on one side and he was on the other, her
heart would be safe. But, at the same time, there were
things she had to know about this journey and what
she would find at its end. Only he could answer her
questions.

Soon they would reach the top of the canyon
where the trail leveled out. There, Molly resolved,
she would force herself to move alongside him and
bridge the awkward silence.

Ryan shifted in the saddle, feeling sore and tired
and out of sorts. The coffee he'd had that morning
lay in the pit of his stomach like a pool of thick black
tar. His head ached, his eyes burned, and the memory

of the dream that had kept him tossing and fevered all night refused to go away.

Behind him, Molly Ivins rode as silently as a shadow. That was just as well—it was too early for talk, and if she were to guess about the dream he would probably get an arrow right between the shoulder blades. All he wanted to do right now was sink into his own thoughts and be quiet.

How had this muddled condition come about? Ryan's frustration grew as he struggled to reconstruct the events of the past few days. Sam Rafferty had mentioned that the posse had found Molly cradling his wounded head in her arms and that she had been his nurse the whole time he was unconscious. But how long had he been here between the time his horse fell and the arrival of Sam's posse? What had happened during that time? What had he told her? And what had triggered that mind-searing dream? These missing pieces of his life were driving him crazy.

He had chosen to bed down with the posse rather than cause talk by spending another night in her lodge. The ground had been cold and rock hard beneath his borrowed bedroll. He had slept fitfully at best—except for one tormenting dream, in which Molly was lying naked in his arms and he was kissing her small, perfect breasts, burying his face in their sweetness. Her nipples had risen and hardened as he caressed them with his tongue, coaxing little catlike moans of pleasure from her throat. She had arched against him, hips rising, thighs parting...

He had awakened then, damp and sweating beneath the scratchy woolen blankets. For one confused moment he had reached out for her, wanting to hold her close in the darkness. Then the snort of a pack mule had jarred him back to reality. For the rest of the night he had lain wide-eyed, staring up at the stars, cursing as he battled the urge to roll out of his blankets, stride back to her lodge and make the dream a reality.

Now, his disposition soured by a restless night and the worst coffee he'd tasted in three years, Ryan wanted nothing more than to hunch into his coat and shut out the world. But his mind was spinning with questions, and he knew that he would not know peace until he had answers.

The trail had leveled out above the canyon. Now they were riding along the rim, following a route that would lead them eastward through the passes and down into the valley of the Big Horn. Sunlight glittered on patches of melting snow. A plump, furry marmot, drawn out of its den by the thaw, whistled from a rock slide and ducked out of sight at their approach.

Glancing over his shoulder, Ryan saw that Molly had nudged her horse to a trot and was gaining on him. She rode bareback like an Indian, sitting astride her spotted mustang with a natural grace that any horseman would envy. Her hair glistened like corn silk in the morning sun. The fringe on her buckskin tunic fluttered in the warm southern breeze.

She pulled up even with him. Ryan greeted her presence with a nod. There were things that needed settling between them. Now, he supposed, was as good a time as any.

"You haven't told me where we're going," she said. "How long will we be on the trail?"

Ryan squinted at the horizon. "Six days if we're lucky. Longer if the weather turns bad. We're headed for the ranch that belongs to my family. We can get some food and rest there, and my brother's wife should be able to rustle you up some clothes. From there we'll take the buckboard to Fort Caspar and catch the stage to Laramie. Have you ever ridden on a train?"

Her eyes widened and she shook her head.

"We'll be taking the train to St. Louis," he said. "I'll telegraph your grandfather and he can meet us at the station."

"My grandfather." She spoke the words as if she were tasting some strange new food. "I've never seen him, never spoken with him. What can you tell me about him?"

Ryan hesitated. He had never really liked Horace Mannington. In their dealings, he had found the man pompous and self-serving. But telling Molly that would only dishearten her. "Your grandfather's an ambitious man," he said truthfully. "He made his fortune buying land when it was cheap and reselling it to the railroad. My brother and I have done business with him in buying new parcels of land for the ranch. He's always been honest and fair.''

"And as a man?" she asked softly. "Is he kind? Is he gentle? Is he brave?

"In all honesty, I can't say as I know him that well. But I saw for myself how much he wanted you back. He was almost weeping when he told me how you were lost.''

Molly frowned. "Then why did he wait so long to look for me?"

"Most people thought you were dead. Your grandfather put up a reward, a big one, but it stood unclaimed for years. Then I heard a rumor about a white woman living among the Cheyenne. Since I already knew about you, I contacted your grandfather and offered to see if I could find you.''

"For the reward."

"Yes."

Her violet eyes darkened. An eternity seemed to pass before she spoke. "But the marshal told me your family was rich. Why would you need money?"

"My family has land and cattle. They don't have five thousand dollars to give to a wild younger brother who wants to travel the world.''

"I see." She fell into silence and would have dropped back behind him on the trail, but Ryan had questions of his own. Slowing his mount, he waited for her to draw even with him again.

"Now it's my turn for questions," he said. "I

woke up yesterday with a big empty hole in my memory, and I need to fill it.''

"What…do you remember?" Her hesitation hung heavy on the morning air.

"A snowstorm. And my horse falling off the trail—the same one we just came up. After that, there's nothing.''

She exhaled nervously. "Then you already know much of the story. I found you unconscious in the snow, not far from your dead horse, and pulled you home on a travois. You recovered and stayed with us until the bandits came.''

"And how long was that?"

"Not long. A few days." She paused. "You didn't remember who you were or why you had come to us. You needed a name so we called you Etonéto.''

Etonéto. That was what the little girl had called him before she darted away in fright. Aside from that, the name meant nothing to him.

"When the bandits came, you could have left us," she said, "but you stayed and helped us fight them. They had just shot you when the marshal came with his men.''

"And found me with my bleeding head in your lap." Ryan knew the rest of the story. But even after what she'd told him, he sensed that something was missing. Who had he been in those empty days? Who was Etonéto?''

"How is it you speak the language of my people?" she asked, changing the subject.

"You mean white people?"

His response had stung her. He saw the flash of anger in her eyes, and he was immediately sorry.

"You know what I mean," she said, "and your joke wasn't funny. I'm just wondering how a man who grew up in a wealthy family, on a big cattle ranch, came to speak Cheyenne."

Ryan made a show of leaning back to check a loose knot on the leather string that held his bedroll in place. The delay gave him a few seconds for her irritation to settle before he spoke. "I never was content to stay and work the ranch like my brother Morgan. When I was younger I lived wild, wandering the mountains the way my father once had. Sometimes I worked as a government surveyor. Other times I hunted and trapped on my own. Years ago, I spent a winter with a band of Cheyenne in the Dakotas. Later on I lived with the Arapaho and picked up some of their tongue, too. I've been told I have a gift for languages. Words just seem to sink in without much effort on my part."

Ryan did not add that he had learned much of the languages from women. Even among the Cheyenne, who placed a high value on chastity, he had found no shortage of warm beds and willing bodies. The fact of it made him neither ashamed nor proud. It was simply a part of his past.

Molly flashed him a scathing glance, and he realized she had guessed the truth and probably despised him for it. Well, that was just too damned bad, Ryan told himself. He was who he was, and this woman was his ticket to the boulevards of Paris, nothing more. What she thought of him didn't matter.

''Let's ride.'' He kneed the horse to a trot, moving out ahead of her on the trail. He was at a loss to explain the need to get away from those wide violet eyes, or the feeling that her look had touched something inside him—a memory, a dream that floated just beyond his reach.

They rode in silence for much of the day, pausing only to rest and water the horses. Molly kept to the rear, picking the smoother, easier parts of the trail to spare her unshod mustang.

There were times when she had to force her eyes away from the proud outline of Ryan Tolliver's shoulders and the leonine set of his head. This was not the man she had loved, Molly reminded herself. He had been someone else on that night when the blizzard had trapped them inside her lodge. So had she, and the less she dwelt on that memory, the better.

The trail wound downward through open meadows and stands of pine and aspen. They rode as long as the light held, but darkness caught them at last in a narrow canyon, sheltered by overhanging ledges. A trickling stream ran down the rocks, nourishing a patch of grass that would do for the horses.

While Ryan unloaded and hobbled the horses, Molly gathered wood and stacked it into a fire. When he ignited the flame with the touch of a match, it struck her how long she had been without such a simple convenience. What would she do in a world of trains and carriages and machines and doors with locks on them? A world of loud noises and dirty, crowded streets? The changes she was about to face were almost unimaginable.

The night was cold and clear, the stars like a glittering river above the canyon. Molly and Ryan huddled on opposite sides of the fire, gazing wearily into the flames. Molly had placed her buffalo skins near enough to the fire for warmth, but at a discreet distance from Ryan's own bedroll. He had done the same. They were polite strangers now, with separate plans, separate reasons for making this journey together.

"How do you buy land?" she asked him, as they chewed the jerked elk meat that served as their evening meal. "How much money does it cost, and where do you get the paper that says no one else can take it?"

Ryan's features appeared drawn and exhausted, and she realized he had pushed himself too hard, too soon. He looked as if he wanted nothing more than to fill his belly and collapse into slumber. But at her question he stopped eating and stared at her through the flames.

"What the blazes are you thinking?" His voice was an exhausted croak. "Is that why you haven't clobbered me with a rock and lit out for the back

country, Molly Ivins? Have you got some cockeyed
scheme to buy a home for your ragtag little band of
Cheyenne?''

She glared back at him, taken aback that he had
seen through her purpose so easily. Was she that
transparent? That childlike in her innocence?

''Why else would I have come with you?'' She
flung the question back at him. ''To live in a noisy
city, in the house of a rich old man I've never met?
To wear petticoats and corsets and tight shoes that
hurt my feet? My grandfather buys and sells land,
and he has money! You told me so yourself!''

He groaned. ''It's not that simple, Molly,'' he said.
''Horace Mannington isn't going to donate land to a
bunch of penniless Indians. And even if he did, you
couldn't keep the government from sending your
people back to the reservation.''

''I could...if I took them north, beyond the line
where the bluecoats could not follow.''

''To Canada?'' He swore under his breath. ''You
don't know anything about Canada, or even whether
your people would be allowed to stay there. They
could freeze, or starve, or be wiped out by bandits.
The reservation may not be heaven on earth, but at
least they'll be safe there.''

''Safe? Like sheep are safe? Like horses pulling a
wagon are safe?'' Molly felt herself trembling. ''To
be free matters more than safety, Ryan Tolliver, and
if you don't understand that I feel sorry for you!''

Her rich, passionate voice stirred Ryan as he studied her golden beauty across the fire. He had always valued freedom, but only on his own terms—the freedom to go where he wished and do what he chose, with no obligation to others, no burden of responsibility. But Molly spoke of freedom in a deeper, broader sense.

Ryan thought of his brother, Morgan, who had spent his adult life running the ranch. Morgan, who responded to the needs of every human and animal on the ranch. Morgan, who had taken on a wife with a baby daughter who wasn't even his and found a richness that he, Ryan, had never experienced. In his strong, nurturing way, Morgan was as free as any man on earth.

But this, Ryan told himself, was no time to take stock of the life he had lived. Not when his mind was heavy with fatigue and his punished body ached in every joint and muscle.

"I'm going to get some sleep," he growled. "You want to talk philosophy, we can do it in the morning."

Without another word he turned away and tumbled into his bedroll. He was too tired and confused for talk, too weary for anything except sleep.

He heard her moving away from the fire, rearranging her bed of buffalo robes. Then he heard her breathy, feminine little sighs as she settled herself for the night. From a faraway butte, the call of a solitary wolf floated on the wintry air—a sad, lonely sound that echoed in Ryan's mind as he slipped into darkness.

He did not know when the dream began. He only knew that she was in his arms again, her lithe, muscular body rippling beneath him as he stroked her, readying her for his thrust. The nest of curls that crowned her open thighs was crisp and wet against his hand, her nub so swollen and sensitive that she gasped when he pressed her with his fingertips. He kissed his way down her body, pressing his face against the slim curve of her waist, then the flat, sweet firmness of her belly, then lower, lower still. She moaned out loud as his tongue explored her velvety folds to find the exquisite little peak at their center. At the first touch she exploded against his mouth, whimpering, arching against him as he pleasured her, taking his time. Only when she was wild with need did he slide upward and enter her. She was so wet, so warm and tight...

Ryan's body shuddered into wakefulness. For a long moment he lay on his back, staring up at the sharp diamond pinpoints of the stars. The dream had seemed so real—the heat of her body, the silken texture of her skin, the tiny heart-shaped mole on her breast that he had kissed again and again.

He turned onto his side to face the dying embers of the fire. The night was moonless, but in the reddish glow he could make out a dark, huddled form sitting on the far side of the fire.

"Molly?"

"I couldn't sleep," she whispered. "I'm sorry, did I wake you?"

He raised up on one elbow, every intimate detail of the dream etched sharply in his mind. How could it have been so real? Ryan wondered.

And then he knew.

"There's something I need to ask you," he said softly. "The answer might be painful for you, but I want the truth. I *need* the truth. Do you promise to give it to me?"

He sensed her hesitation, as if she already knew what he planned to say. Slowly, almost painfully, she nodded. "All right. Ask your question."

He began awkwardly, groping for words. "I need to know about the time I was with your people, the time I don't remember."

"I've already told you—"

"No. You haven't told me this. There are things I keep remembering, and I need to know why." He took a deep breath, as if he were about to plunge off a precipice. "Molly, during that time…were you and I lovers?"

Chapter Twelve

Molly stared into the dying coals, gathering her courage. The memory of that night in his arms was seared into every part of her. But, knowing it would not be the same for Ryan, she had hoped he would not remember it at all.

"Molly?" The thread of steel in his voice left no doubt that he wanted his answer—wanted it now. Raising her head, she met his gaze through the smoky darkness.

"Yes," she said, forcing all emotion from her voice. "Yes, we were lovers."

She heard the low intake of his breath. "For how long?"

"For just one night. But we were different people then. Now it's over."

"But how did it—"

"No," she said, cutting him off. "You asked me a question and I answered it. Now go back to sleep and pretend it never happened, or that it was only a dream. It's finished, and I don't want to talk about it anymore."

He exhaled tensely. "All right," he said in a flat voice. "But I have one more question. A question I have every right to ask."

She scowled at him across the fire, her silence implying consent.

"I usually take...precautions," he said. "But in this case I don't remember anything about what happened. Is there any chance that you might be..." He trailed off, groping awkwardly for the delicate word.

"You mean, is there any chance you might be turning me over to my grandfather with your baby in my belly?" Molly's laugh carried a bitter edge. "Don't worry, Ryan Tolliver, the answer is no. Put your mind at rest and go back to sleep."

At least she had no cause to lie, Molly reflected. That very afternoon her moon time had begun, its flow light and spotty as usual. Her cycles were so irregular, the bleeding so sparse, that she'd long wondered whether she would be able to have children.

Pulling her buffalo robes around her, Molly lay down again with her back to the fire and to Ryan Tolliver. She did not want to talk about what had been the most wonderful night of her life. To talk about it would be to expose the memory and spoil it forever.

She closed her eyes, knowing the days ahead would be filled with the torment of looking at Ryan, knowing that he was aware of what had happened between them but no longer remembered or cared.

Whatever the day brings, whatever happens tomorrow and after that, never forget what I'm telling you now. I love you, Moon Hawk...

His words drifted back to her, so haunting and bittersweet that they tore at her heart. It was best not to think of those words, Molly told herself, best not to remember them at all.

The man who'd spoken them had died when an outlaw's bullet creased his scalp. Etonéto, the love of her life, was lost to her forever.

For the next five days they rode hard, stopping only to rest and water their mounts. When they slept it was only because they were too exhausted to go on. They would feed and hobble the horses, down a few mouthfuls of food, collapse into their bedrolls and fall asleep, exchanging as few words as possible. It was as if both of them wanted to get the journey over with, to end it with no entanglements and no regrets.

But Ryan could not end the dreams that made sweet torment of his nights. He would wake up in the darkness, physically aroused and aching with desire, fighting the temptation to join her where she slept, slip between her soft buffalo robes and make the dream real.

Would she welcome him? Would she draw her knife and fight him off like the wildcat she was, or would she simply turn to ice, defying his efforts to reach her? Ryan would never know, because he knew better than to try it. She was Horace Mannington's granddaughter, and whatever had happened between them was history. When they reached St. Louis, he would deliver her to the old man, claim his reward and walk away. He wanted to leave no regrets, and no ties behind.

Sometimes, as they rode, he thought about her wild scheme to buy land in Canada for her Cheyenne. A craftier woman might have tried to charm him out of his reward money. But Molly was as guileless and straightforward as a child. Ryan had to admit he liked her for that. He liked her for a lot of reasons—just one more incentive to get this trip over with. His dream of seeing the world was about to come true, and no woman was going to hold him back.

On the evening of the fifth day, they rode down the eastern slope of the Big Horns and mounted the last low ridge that overlooked the Tolliver ranch.

Looking down through the twilight, on the big rambling house with its cluster of corrals and outbuildings, Molly felt her heart creep into her throat. She had not set foot inside the house of a white family since her childhood. Suddenly the idea of being enclosed by solid walls filled her with a sense of panic. She no longer knew how to behave in a house. She had forgotten how to sit properly on a chair, how to eat at a table with a knife, fork and spoon and how to sleep in a bed that was high off the floor.

And what about the people? What would Ryan's wealthy family think of her? Would they laugh at her? Would they whisper about her behind her back?

The sky was darkening, and it had begun to snow, big, feathery flakes that settled on Molly's hair and clothes without melting. She knew they needed to get off the mountain. But at this moment, moving forward required more courage than she possessed.

Ryan touched her arm, something he had not done in the past five days. "Don't worry, you'll be fine," he said as if reading her thoughts. "Come on, now, the snow's getting worse."

"I don't need to stay in the house," she said. "I'll be fine in the barn with the horses."

He only laughed and moved ahead of her to pick out the trail through the flying snow. In the gathering darkness she could see the faint glow of the lantern that had been hung from the porch of the house. Ryan had told her that her presence would be no surprise. His family had heard about the search for Horace Mannington's missing granddaughter and had even been shown her mother's portrait. They would know her on sight.

Would her grandfather's wealth and status make it easier for them to accept her? Molly's knuckles whitened where they gripped the reins. She tried to tell herself it didn't matter whether these people liked her or not. But somehow it did. It mattered terribly.

The door of the house flew open as they rode into the yard. Two figures appeared in the pool of light that flooded the porch. One, a man, was tall and rangy like Ryan. The other, a woman, was small and delicate. Her skirts fluttered in the wind as she hurried down the steps and sprinted toward them, heedless of the swirling snow. The man followed, passing her with his long stride.

Ryan gave a joyous war whoop as he saw them. The exuberant burst of sound, coming from a man who had been so reticent on the trail, gave Molly a start. She shot him a wide-eyed glance—all she had time for before the couple reached them.

Flinging himself out of the saddle, Ryan enfolded them both in a big, laughing bear hug. The diversion gave Molly time to ease a leg over the mustang's back and slide wearily to the ground. She was standing beside the horse when the woman broke away from Ryan and spun toward her.

"You poor dear, you must be frozen!" The woman stripped off her woolen shawl and tossed it over Molly's shoulders. She was only a little taller than She-Bear, and she had the prettiness and energy of a darting hummingbird. "You're Molly, of course," she said. "You look a lot like your mother's picture. I'm Cassandra. Come on inside and get warm. Let the men put away the horses. That's what men are for!" She laughed, her bright blue eyes crinkling at the corners. Snowflakes had settled like tiny white blossoms on her flame-colored curls. "We're so glad you weren't caught somewhere in this beastly storm! Now that you're here, I'm hoping the snow will last a while, so that you and Ryan will have to stay with us.''

As she chatted, she ushered Molly across the yard toward the sprawling house. Sturdily built of rough stone and polished logs, the structure loomed above them like a mountain. Molly's heart slammed against the walls of her chest as they mounted the front steps, but Cassandra Tolliver's friendly warmth helped to ease the way.

"You'll be all right," Cassandra murmured, slipping an arm around her waist. "I can imagine how it must feel, leaving the world you've known for so many years. But you're among friends here, Molly. There's no reason for you to be afraid."

Inside, the house was bright and warm. A wide wooden stairway led upward from the entry to an unseen second floor. Off to the left was an open parlor furnished with braided rugs and big, cozy leather chairs. A fire crackled in a huge stone fireplace, flooding the room with a cheerful glow. Beyond the parlor, through a wide, sliding doorway, Molly could see a dining room with a long wooden table set with white plates and silver utensils.

Cassandra bustled past her, skirts swirling with the energy of her steps. "You must be starved!" she said. "Wait here while I tell Chang there'll be two more for supper. Then I'll show you to your room."

Molly murmured her thanks, struggling to remember even the most rudimentary manners as Cassandra swept off through the dining room into what Molly presumed to be the kitchen, judging from the mouth-watering aromas that were floating through the open doorway.

As she waited in the parlor, Molly became aware that she was not alone. A subtle prickling at the back of her neck alerted her to the fact that she was being watched.

Instinctively her hand crept to her knife. Her fingers tightened on the haft as she pivoted slowly, her gaze scanning the room. For the space of a breath she saw no one. Then she heard a giggle.

Peering at her from over the back of a big leather armchair were two identical pairs of wide black eyes.

Startled, Molly gasped and stumbled backward. At this, two very small boys erupted, laughing, from behind the chair. They were, perhaps, two years old, with smooth golden skin and twin thatches of straight black hair. Clad in nightshirts of striped flannel that hung just past their knees, they were as alike as two seeds in a pod.

But it was not just the fact of twins that struck Molly with amazement. Except for their nightshirts and their trimmed hair, they could have been Cheyenne children, dark and quick and constantly in motion. One of them started toward Molly but tripped over his nightshirt and tumbled onto the braided rug. The second boy stumbled over him, and in a flash the two of them were rolling on the bright rag surface like two romping puppies.

"Jacob! Joshua! Where are your manners?" Cassandra, flushed and laughing, waded into the fray and swept them both up in her arms. "We have a guest. Say hello to Miss Molly."

In an instant, both children became as shy as violets. One of them buried his face against Cassandra's collar. The other put his hands in front of his face and peered at Molly from between his small brown fingers.

"They're yours?" Molly asked, surprised. "But they look like…" Her voice trailed off as she realized she might have uttered some forbidden insult.

"Didn't Ryan tell you?" Cassandra responded, unabashed. "He and Morgan are half brothers. Morgan's mother was a full-blooded Shoshone. The boys look a lot like her people."

"They're beautiful," Molly said.

"We think so, too." She turned toward a silent figure in the doorway—a strong-looking young man with pale skin and narrow, slanting black eyes. He was clad in a gray high-necked tunic and, when he walked into the room, Molly saw that his black hair hung in a long, thin braid down his back. It was hard not to stare. She had never seen anyone like him.

"Take these two little monkeys and put them to bed, please, Thomas." Cassandra passed him the twins, who went to him eagerly, squirming and giggling in his arms, all but destroying his dignified mien. As he carried them out of the parlor, she turned back to Molly and took her arm.

"I'm going to put you in the room where I stayed when I first came here," she said. "It's small, but the view from the window is wonderful. Thomas and Johnny can bring you up a hot bath after supper, but meanwhile, we'll need to get you out of those wet buckskins." Her sharp eyes measured Molly's stature as she guided her toward the stairs. "Morgan's first wife was about your size. She left behind a trunk filled with clothes. They're a bit out of style, but I'm sure we can find you something presentable to wear."

"Out of style!" Molly stared at her, struck by the ludicrousness of what she'd just heard. Suddenly she burst into exhausted laughter. "Do I look like someone who would know about style? Do I look like someone who would care?"

In an instant Cassandra was laughing with her. "Oh, mercy!" she gasped. "What was I thinking? Come on, let me show you to your room before I make a complete fool of myself!"

They had climbed about halfway up the stairs, still laughing, when a blast of cold wind struck them from below. Molly looked down to see Ryan and Morgan coming in through the front door, lost in conversation as they stamped the snow off their feet. How much had Ryan told his brother? Molly wondered. Did Morgan know about her past? Did he know what had happened between her and Ryan?

Molly had no chance to ponder the questions. She and Cassandra were nearing the top of the stairs when a small pixie of a girl with red-gold hair darted out onto the landing above them, squealed with delight and flew down the stairs to fling herself into Ryan's open arms.

"Rachel!" He swung her around dizzily, making her shriek with laughter before he caught her close in a big bear hug. "How's my best girl? Did you miss me?"

"Did you bring me a present, Uncle Ryan?" She gazed up at him with devastating blue-green eyes. Cassandra's daughter looked to be no more than three years old, but she was clearly an accomplished charmer, accustomed to getting her own way.

Molly watched, mystified, as Ryan fished in his coat pocket and came up with something small and dark that glinted in his hand. "Here you are, *mademoiselle*," he announced with a flourish, "a genuine, honest-to-goodness flint arrowhead."

The little girl took the gift, examining it with obvious delight. Molly turned away from the sight of them and followed Cassandra onto the landing, a hollow ache seeping into her heart. She had just seen a side of Ryan that he had not revealed to her in the time she had known him.

Except when she had known him as Etonéto.

Supper had never smelled better. Ryan's mouth watered as he waited at the table, his senses feasting on the aroma of Chang's braised beef with onion gravy and fresh, hot biscuits. It had been a long and hungry ride from the Absaroka Mountains. Hungry in more ways than one. Maybe now that he was home, those maddening dreams of making love to Molly would end.

Morgan sat on his right, at the head of the table. Ryan had never seen his brooding half Shoshone brother look more contented. Having a wife and family had been just what Morgan needed.

Here on the ranch, surrounded by so much love and laughter, Ryan sometimes caught himself wishing for the same thing. He was not yet ready to pay with his freedom, but maybe one day, if he could find a spark of the magic that flashed between Morgan and Cassandra whenever they looked at each other...

Ryan's thoughts trailed off as Cassandra and Molly entered the dining room side by side. His mouth went dry as he stared. Molly had traded her soggy buckskins for a gown of soft rose silk that brought out the color in her cheeks. Cassandra had unbraided her hair and brushed it to a fine golden sheen. Wavy from the braids, it hung almost to her tiny waist in a rippling cascade that all but took his breath away.

A nudge from Rachel, who was seated on Ryan's left, jarred him back to reality. "She looks so beautiful!" the childish voice piped. "Are you going to marry her and have babies, Uncle Ryan?"

Ryan had not blushed in as many years as he could remember, but he was aware of the hot color creeping into his cheeks. Molly, too, had turned pink and lowered her golden lashes.

He had made love to this woman. He had clasped her naked body in his arms, entered her, filled her, made her his. Why couldn't he remember except in those accursed dreams that left him gasping in his sleep? Looking at her now, he ached to remember every detail—her softness, her sweet, blazing heat…

Morgan had risen to help Molly into her chair. Remembering his manners just in time, Ryan did the same for his sister-in-law. Across the table, Molly sat nervously, perched on the edge of her chair, staring down at her reflection in the shiny white plate as Chang and his son Thomas carried in platters of steaming food. Her eyes widened at the sight of such bounty.

They paused long enough for Cassandra to murmur a brief grace over the food. Then Morgan, playing the part of the gracious host, filled Molly's plate with generous helpings of meat, vegetables and biscuits.

"Thank you," Molly murmured, looking overwhelmed. "I haven't eaten food like this in years." She gazed at her plate but made no move to eat. It took a moment for Morgan to realize that she was waiting for someone else to pick up a utensil so that she could follow their example.

He obliged her by dishing up his own meat and

vegetables, then picking up his fork. He felt her eyes on him as she mirrored his every move. Following his lead, she took small, even bites, cutting the meat and buttering the biscuit as he did. Ryan could not help admiring her resourcefulness. Molly was no fool, he thought. She would do all right in this frightening new world. And no man would be able to resist her stunning beauty.

"This food is delicious," she said in an obvious effort to make polite conversation. "Did you make it, Cassandra?"

Cassandra laughed and tossed her untamable copper curls. "Hardly! The older man who brought in the platters is Chang, our wonderful cook. The kitchen is his kingdom, and he guards it like a tiger."

"The younger man is his son?"

Cassandra nodded. "The whole family—Chang, his wife Mei Li, their two sons, the sons' wives and their babies live on the ranch in their own house. As you can imagine, it's quite a lively place. When I take you to visit them tomorrow, Molly, I'll tell you all about them."

Ryan flashed his sister-in-law an appreciative glance. Cassandra was making every effort to put Molly at ease. Despite everyone's good intentions, however, Molly still looked as if she were ready to bolt at the first sign of danger. Her vulnerability touched Ryan. Settling in to her new life was going to take some time. But here, in the warmth of this family, was a good place to start.

"You didn't answer my question, Uncle Ryan!" Rachel piped. "Are you going to marry her?" She inclined her pert little head, with its nimbus of flame-gold curls, toward Molly. "I think she's pretty! Pretty enough even for you!"

Morgan's cheek muscle twitched, and Cassandra choked on a giggle. Molly flushed as pink as her gown and lowered her gaze to her plate. It remained for Ryan to answer.

"I'm just seeing Miss Molly back to her grandfather in St. Louis," he said. "After that, she'll be on her own."

"But you could still marry her!" Rachel insisted. "You need a good wife and some babies to settle you down. That's what my mama said—"

"That's enough, young lady." Cassandra shot her a stern glance. "Uncle Ryan has answered your question. Now finish your supper."

Ryan glanced at Molly. Her eyes were downcast and she was eating in slow, careful bites, the fork resting awkwardly in her weather-roughened fingers. His gaze lingered on her hands—hands that could shoot a bow, skin a deer, raise a teepee and caress a lover. Strong, beautiful, amazing hands, the nails short and broken, the skin reddened and chapped. They revealed more of the woman she was than the pretty rose gown or the gleam of her moonspun hair in the lamplight.

Lord, but he was going to miss her.

Chapter Thirteen

Wrapped in her buffalo robe, Molly stood alone on the front porch, watching the silent snowflakes drift out of the midnight sky. The wind was sweet and cold on her face, but the odors it carried—the pungent, loamy scent of horses and cattle, the lingering aromas of food from the kitchen, and even the soapy fragrance of her own freshly washed skin and hair—were alien to her senses. It had been too long, she thought, aching for the clean, mossy smell of the canyons. She would never become accustomed to living in the white world.

The days ahead loomed like black clouds, roiling with uncertainty. Thoughts of the train, the noisy city and the white grandfather she had never met stampeded through her mind. Beneath the borrowed flannel nightdress, her skin was clammy with fear. Even the delicious supper she had eaten that evening lay like a cold lump in the pit of her stomach.

It was not too late, she thought. Her buckskin

clothes and moccasins, along with her knife, bow and arrows were still in the upstairs bedroom. Her tough little mustang was in the corral. She could leave now, while the ranch slept. Nobody would miss her until morning, and by then she would be deep in the mountains. She knew how to survive there, even in winter. And no one, not even Ryan Tolliver, would be able to find her. She would be safe and free.

But her people would not be free, Molly reminded herself. By now they would be on the reservation, suffering all the humiliations of a defeated people. Instead of gathering their own food, they would be lining up outside the agency storehouse, standing like beggars in the snow to receive their ration of salt pork and moldy flour. Government teachers would already be rounding up the children for school, and missionaries would be rubbing their hands together at the thought of new conversions. Her people would be waiting for her, clinging to the hope that she would come back and take them to their new land. She had made them a promise, one she could not break.

"Are you all right, Molly? You should be in bed at this hour." Ryan had come out onto the porch, moving so silently that she was not aware of his presence until he spoke.

She swallowed a startled gasp. "I'm fine. Just couldn't sleep, that's all." She gazed into the lacy swirl of snow. "I'm sorry, I don't mean to be ungrateful. Your family has been so good to me. It's just that there are so many changes. Even here.''

Ryan moved up alongside her, leaning his arms on the porch railing. He was fully dressed, but his hair was rumpled and his shirt looked as if it had been hastily buttoned in the dark.

"Were you worried about me?" she asked, hoping he had been.

He nodded, gazing at the snow. "I heard you open your bedroom door and go down the stairs, and I thought you might be trying to leave."

"And you didn't want your five-thousand-dollar reward to sneak off into the mountains and disappear?" Molly could feel the edge in her own voice. "Is that why you got down here in such a hurry?"

He muttered something under his breath. "My first thought was that you could get hurt or lost or frozen in the storm. I didn't even think about the damned reward until you mentioned it."

She reached out beyond the railing, caught a snowflake and felt it melt in her hand. "I thought about leaving," she said. "Even in the storm, I wanted to go."

"Why didn't you?" He had turned away from the railing and was looking at her, his eyes hooded in shadow.

"I remembered the promise I made to my people—and the only way I have of keeping it."

He groaned. Unbidden he moved behind her and slid his hands around her waist, pulling her back so that her head rested against his shoulder. The feel of him, so close, so tender, raised a bitter lump in Molly's throat. Wisdom whispered that she should pull away. He was no longer the man who had loved her. But he still had the power to steal her heart—and to break it. She would be a fool to lower her guard.

But tonight she felt alone and afraid. She needed his warmth, his strength. Molly settled back against him with a sigh, savoring the feel of his arms sliding around her to draw her close.

"Those Cheyenne of yours are like children," he murmured against her hair. "The time comes when you have to back away and let them be responsible for themselves. You're a beautiful young woman, Molly. As Horace Mannington's granddaughter, the whole world would be open to you. You could study or travel, marry well, have a family, do whatever you like. Don't throw away your life on a foolish promise."

His words—the sort of words Etonéto would never have spoken—jarred her back to reality. "I gave my word," she said, her body stiffening against him. "That's something I take very seriously and so do my people."

"Your people are white." His voice grated with impatience. "The sooner you get that through your pretty head the happier you'll be."

"My people are the Tse Tse Stus—the Cheyenne!'' She tore herself away and wheeled to face him.

"Molly, listen—"

"No, *you* listen!" She spit the words at him. "I'll force myself to behave like a white woman if that's what I have to do. But my heart is Cheyenne! My soul is Cheyenne! And my people will always come first! Never forget that!"

She would have spun away and fled, but his hand caught her wrist, stopping her momentum with a force that whipped her back against his chest. His arm flashed to grip her waist, pinning her against the hard length of his body.

His eyes burned into hers with a heat she could feel even in the icy darkness. Was he about to kiss her, or would he curse her, fling her aside and stalk off into the night? Molly's heart hammered the walls of her chest as she realized what she wanted—what she had wanted for all those days and nights on the trail with him. She yearned to hold him in her arms, to feel the caress of those tender lips.

Whatever happens tomorrow and after that, never forget what I'm telling you now. I love you, Moon Hawk.

His words echoed in her memory as she flung caution aside and raised her face to his. His eyes darkened above her. His breath rasped in his throat as he leaned down toward her, then abruptly checked himself.

"I thought we agreed this wasn't going to happen," he muttered, his voice thick and husky.

"You're quite...right." Molly drew back from him, her legs weak beneath her. "I'll try to remember that in the future."

Choking on her own emotions, she spun away from him and fled across the porch, into the house.

The storm passed swiftly, its thick clouds rumbling across the open prairie like the ghosts of vanquished buffalo. In its wake, the land glittered stark and white against a sky of crystalline blue. The air was so cold that the steamy breath of the big draft horses coated their whiskers with ice.

Since the snow was not deep and the weather clear, Morgan had pronounced it safe to take the wagon to Fort Caspar. From there, Molly and Ryan would ride the Wells Fargo stage to Laramie, where they would board the train for St. Louis.

Molly sat on a low box behind the wagon seat, bundled in a mountain of quilts and blankets. She had protested that she was accustomed to cold, but Cassandra had insisted on wrapping her so thickly that Molly could scarcely move. For the first few miles, the hot bricks beneath her feet had kept her so warm that she was almost sweltering. Now the bricks had cooled, and she was beginning to feel grateful for the blankets.

Ryan and Morgan shared the wagon seat and took turns driving the team, an easy task since the massive bays seemed to know the road by heart. Molly watched the frozen landscape, only half listening to their talk about ranch business—the cattle, the horses, the plans for a new bunkhouse and the prospects for next summer's hay crop.

She was grateful for Morgan's quiet presence. Over the past three days the tension between Ryan and herself had become so oppressive that she had dreaded being alone in his company. At the ranch, she had spent most of her time with Cassandra, playing with the children, visiting the noisy, happy Chang household, and planning the clothes she would need for the trip back east.

Molly cared little about the gowns and petticoats and lacy underthings in the trunk and would gladly have gone back to wearing her buckskins, but she had no wish to hurt her new friend's feelings. Cassandra had been as excited as a little girl with a new doll and a wardrobe of doll clothes. Nothing would do except that Molly try on every item of clothing in the trunk that wealthy Helen Cummings Tolliver had left behind when she'd divorced Morgan and returned to her home in the East. The elegant gowns fit Molly as if they'd been made for her. But in the end Molly had chosen only two dresses and a warm, hooded cloak, all three pieces subdued, warm and serviceable, for the journey.

Beneath the cloak, she wore one of the dresses now, a plain dark blue serge with a high neck and long sleeves, decorated with black piping on the cuffs and collar. The fabric was itchy, the bodice and waist so constricting that it resisted her every move. The underclothes were even worse. The tightly laced corset cut off her breath, and the fabric of her drawers bunched uncomfortably between her thighs. She had dim memories of her own mother wearing similar garments. Even so, it amazed her that white women managed to move, work and function in such clothes. Molly yearned for the freedom of her buckskins.

They reached the Platte River bridge where the fort stood to guard the crossing. The fort itself had changed little since that long-ago day when Molly had crossed the Platte in her parents' wagon. But since the end of the Indian troubles, a sprawl of shacks, saloons and stores had sprung up outside its walls. The Oregon trail had faded in importance since the building of the Union Pacific Railroad, but there were still travelers who passed this way—travelers who needed food, rest and, in many instances, a good time.

Molly had not been in a white town since her childhood. From her seat in the back of the wagon, she stared in open dismay at the ramshackle buildings that sprawled along the road like mange on a dog. Most of them had been thrown up using whatever material was available—logs, tin, clapboard and even canvas. The largest structure appeared to be a saloon. A dozen horses were hitched to the wooden rail outside. One of them raised its tail as the wagon passed and plopped a steaming pile of manure onto the muddy snow. From behind the door, which was coated with peeling red paint, came the sound of raucous laughter and the tinny tinkle of a piano.

The sound of the piano brought a sudden, sharp stab of memory. Molly's mother had played the piano. The music her gifted fingers had coaxed out of the battered old upright in their parlor had filled their home with magic. Molly had cried when her parents sold the piano to help pay for the journey to Oregon. "We'll buy another piano," her father had promised. "And when we do, Molly, you shall learn to play it."

She pushed the memory aside as the wagon rolled on toward the gates of the fort. Now they were passing one of the few buildings that had an upper floor. A woman, her face gaudily painted, her hair hanging loose, leaned out over the sill of an upstairs window, talking with two young cowboys in the street below. She laughed without humor, flashing crooked teeth as the two youths mounted the porch and entered the front door.

Molly stared down at her gloved hands, trying not to think about what would happen next. When she glanced up again, she saw that Ryan had turned around in his seat and was watching her with narrowed eyes.

"Are you all right?" he asked in a low voice.

Molly nodded mutely.

"We won't be staying out here," he said. "The

fort commander is a friend of Morgan's. He'll put us up in the guest quarters. Nothing fancy, mind you, but the place is clean and safe. It has two bedrooms, so you'll have some privacy."

"Thank you." Molly already knew the rest of the plan. Morgan would be staying the night with them at the fort. Tomorrow at dawn, he would load the wagon with supplies and head back to the ranch, leaving Ryan and Molly to catch the overland stage. Again she was grateful for Morgan's presence. She would not have to endure a night alone with the man who loosed a freshet of pain in her every time she looked at him.

"Are you hungry?" he asked.

Molly shook her head. The lurching of the wagon over the long, rutted road had left her with a queasy stomach, and the sinking weight of her spirits only made things worse. The last thing she wanted right now was food—unless it was a bowl of She-Bear's hot venison stew, eaten beside a crackling fire in the evening shadows of her lodge.

Lanterns flickered here and there as the twilight deepened, masking the worst of the squalor in soft blue shadow. Concealed by the hood of her cloak, Molly let her gaze wander. In a doorway, a ragged man was drinking from a brown bottle, spilling whiskey into his scruffy beard and down his filthy leather shirt. Behind him, at the entrance to an alley, two rack-ribbed dogs tore at a muddy deer hide. A pretty girl with young, frightened eyes, her cheeks rouged, her bodice unfastened, sidled back and forth outside a dimly lit saloon.

At the Tolliver Ranch, Molly had seen the best of *ve hoe* life. Here she was seeing a far different side— not the worst, she was sure. But she knew that where she was going, sights like these would be common; and the kind of warmth and acceptance she had found with Ryan's family would be all too rare. As a woman who had lived with so-called savages, she would be regarded with suspicion, loathing and pity. Even as the granddaughter of a wealthy man, she could expect to find few allies and certainly no true friends.

Low in the western sky, three bright stars glimmered through the dark winter clouds. Her people were seeing those same stars, Molly reminded herself. They lived under the same sky and breathed the same air. She was in their thoughts as they were in hers, and that link to them would keep her strong. All that she did in the days ahead, she would do for them.

The Union Pacific depot teemed with passengers, most of them waiting to catch the last eastbound train of the day. Ryan cursed under his breath as he stood in the long ticket line. The stage had lost a wheel on the open prairie, delaying their arrival in Laramie by almost three hours. With the sun low in the sky and an icy wind raking the platform, Ryan's patience was wearing thin.

Glancing back over his shoulder, he could see Molly huddled in the lee of a brick wall, guarding their valises. Her hood had fallen back to reveal her pale hair, which Cassandra had twisted and pinned into a knot at the nape of her neck. Even the prim dress and hairstyle could not hide her spectacular beauty. Ryan had been hesitant to leave her alone, even for such a short time. But there was no reason to think she would wander off, he reminded himself. In a big town like Laramie, she would be lost without him, and she was smart enough to know it.

He had to admit she'd behaved well on the grueling stage ride. In fact, behaving well did not begin to describe Molly's conduct. One of the passengers on the crowded stage had been an exhausted-looking woman with a fretful, squirming two-year-old in her arms. Molly had taken the little boy on her lap and entertained him with songs and whimsical finger games. When he'd begun to flag, she had eased him into sleep with a Cheyenne lullaby, sung so softly that it was little more than a whisper in the child's small ear. Only Ryan, among the passengers, had heard and understood. While she cradled the sleeping child in her arms, he had let his eyes rest on her beautiful, tender face. In that moment he had known that he could not delay in getting her to St. Louis. Otherwise he was in grave danger of losing his heart.

He had closed his eyes and forced himself to think of Athens. He had imagined walking the ancient, cobbled streets in the footsteps of Plato and Socrates, imagined the taste of olives and raki on his tongue, the scent of patchouli and the flash of dark eyes...

The distraction had worked. Almost.

"Sir?" The ticket agent's bespectacled face stared up at Ryan through the barred window. "Where to, sir?"

Ryan tore his gaze away from Molly's huddled figure. "Two tickets to St. Louis, with sleeping berths."

"I'm sorry, sir, the sleeping cars are full. Unless you want to wait and leave tomorrow, you'll have to travel the night sitting up."

Ryan groaned. He had already weighed the wisdom of staying in Laramie and boarding the train tomorrow morning. But the prospect of spending a night in a hotel with Molly was fraught with temptation. The noisy, crowded semiprivacy of the Pullman car would be safer, if less restful, and they would reach St. Louis that much sooner. Now even that choice was gone.

"Sir?" The ticket agent's voice had taken on an impatient edge. Behind Ryan, the line pressed forward.

"Hey, mister, the train's pullin' out any minute. We ain't got all day!" a voice called out, and others muttered in agreement.

With a sigh, Ryan pushed his money through the iron grille and pocketed the tickets. He could always exchange them in the morning if he and Molly decided to stay the night. And right now, the prospect of—

"Damned hellcat!" An enraged male bellow shattered Ryan's train of thought. Heart slamming, he whirled toward the place where he had left Molly with their bags.

"She cut me! The bitch cut me!" A husky, well-dressed man was reeling backward, his hand pressed to his left cheek. Facing him, poised in a battle crouch, knife drawn and glinting, was Molly.

"I'll show you, bitch!" The big man lumbered toward her, undaunted by the weapon. Molly danced catlike on the balls of her feet, ready to spring in any direction. Even so, she was unprepared for his quickness. In a lightning lunge, he caught her wrist. She gasped with pain as the knife dropped from her hand. But the shock lasted only for an instant before she began to fight, kicking and clawing like a wildcat.

"Let her go!" Driven by a burning, protective rage, Ryan shoved his way through the gathering crowd. By the time he reached her, Molly had torn off the man's tie, scratched his cheek and left muddy boot marks up and down his once-immaculate charcoal-gray trousers.

"I said, let her go!" Ryan seized the stranger's collar and jerked hard. As the big man spun around, Ryan used the momentum of his weight to fling him to the platform. He landed with a breathy grunt, rolled onto his back and lay there, momentarily stunned. Molly scrambled for her knife. Only as she crouched over the man, gripping the weapon, did Ryan glimpse the terror in her eyes.

"It's all right, Molly," he said quietly. "He can't hurt you now."

"Hurt her!" the man sputtered, working himself onto one elbow. "Bloody hell, I only offered to buy her a drink! When I accidentally touched her hair, she came at me like a wild animal! But she'll pay—both of you will pay! You can't assault the mayor's brother in public and expect to get away with it!"

Ryan stifled a groan as the big man struggled to sit up. He didn't relish spending the next few weeks in jail, but the ordeal would be far worse for Molly.

The shrill blast of the Union Pacific train whistle shattered the air. Steam hissed from the pistons as the huge locomotive inched forward. The train was pulling out.

"Come on!" Ryan grabbed Molly's arm with one hand and snatched up both valises with the other. She sprang into motion, petticoats flying as they sprinted for the moving train.

The bleeding man's curses echoed in their ears as Ryan caught the bar, leaped onto the bottom step and swung Molly up into the passenger car beside him. The car was nearly full, but there were two seats together against the rear wall. Flung back and forth by the jerking momentum of the train, they staggered down the aisle and collapsed, giddy with relief, onto the empty wooden bench.

Ryan had let her go ahead of him, so that she was sitting next to the window as the train pulled out of the depot. She stared at the raging man on the platform until he was no longer in sight. Then she turned back toward Ryan, her eyes wide, her lips trembling.

Ryan had just finished stowing their bags beneath the seat. The sun was low and red in the sky, softening the ugliness of the empty stockyards outside the train. "Are you all right?" he asked, his voice an exhausted rasp.

"Yes."

"Blast it, Molly!" he said, knowing he dared not leave the words unsaid. "You're not with the Cheyenne anymore! This is civilized country, and you don't go around pulling knives on people, especially when they might be the mayor's brother! Do that again, and you're liable to end up in jail!"

"I'm used to taking care of myself," she said with a note of defiance, "and I didn't like the way he looked at me or the way he touched my hair—"

"Damn it, you could have called me." His voice had dropped to growl of frustration. "So help me, Molly, if that bastard had done anything to hurt you—"

Suddenly they were no longer talking. Ryan was kissing her, not gently but fiercely, desperately, with a hunger that reached upward from the depths of his soul. Molly had told him they'd been lovers. Maybe he would never remember that first time. But he understood it now, as he took her soft lips again and again, aching for what was no longer his.

Her arms slid around him as she returned his kisses, wild with need, heedless of the other passengers in the car. They held each other close as the train rumbled into darkness.

Chapter Fourteen

Ryan stared out the window as the train chugged across the bleak Nebraska flatland. Outside, the night was dark and silent. Flakes of lightly falling snow peppered the glass, only to be blown away by the forward motion of the train. Now and again, within sight of the tracks, Ryan glimpsed the bulky outline of a barn or the huddled shapes of horse and cattle.

Molly slept like a child, her head cradled in the hollow of his shoulder. The sweet, clean fragrance of her hair stole into his nostrils, filling his senses, making him wish that this night could go on for as long as he willed it. But that was not to be. A few hours from now, the sun would be up. With the daylight would come the cold realities that had to be faced.

That he loved Molly was beyond question. She had brought him to his knees, made him want to be a better man than he had ever been. If he thought it would make her happy, he would go straight to Horace Mannington and ask for her hand. But nothing about Molly's happiness—or his own—was that simple.

Molly wanted a homeland for her Cheyenne. He wanted the freedom, and the means, to travel the world. Join the two of them together, and the outcome would be two frustrated, unhappy people deprived of their dreams. He would not want that for Molly. He would not want that for himself.

But if, somehow, he could find a way to help her...

She stirred against his shoulder, whimpered and settled back into trusting sleep. Ryan brushed a trail of light kisses along her hairline, his heart swelling with tenderness. What did wilderness land cost in Canada? How much could she buy for a thousand dollars? Two thousand? Could he give up Africa for Molly's dream? Egypt?

Without Molly, there would be no reward, Ryan reminded himself. It was only fair that he share the money with her. But he would not tell her now. He would wait and surprise her after the cash was in his hands. She would have, at least, a part of her dream. And, with enough money left over to get him to Europe, he would have a part of his.

But they would not have each other. That would be asking too much of life. He could only hold her in the darkness of the train, fill his senses with her warmth, and know that it would have to last him forever.

* * *

When the train stopped in Omaha the next day, Ryan sent a wire to Horace Mannington to let the old man know their arrival time. He was also able to purchase two separate berths in a crowded sleeping car. Molly would not be spending another night in his arms.

By now Molly had withdrawn into silence. On the train, she sat with her cheek pressed to the window, gazing sadly out at the farms, towns and cities they passed. Her longing for the country she called home was a barrier between them, a wall of pain that Ryan could feel but could not penetrate.

Last night she had been lonely and frightened. In her need, she had turned to him. But now, in the bleak gray light of a winter morning, he was her betrayer. He had torn her from her mountains and her beloved Cheyenne. When the time came, he would leave her with a stranger, collect his thirty pieces of silver and walk away.

Ryan's eyes traced her profile against the frosted glass. Molly would thank him one day, he told himself. Even if she failed to buy the land she wanted, how could she not thank him? She would have ease and comfort to the end of her days. She would have beautiful gowns, parties, wealthy suitors, everything a young woman could wish for.

But no, he reminded himself, this was Molly. She would want none of those things, and even if he gave her the reward money, she would hate him to the end of her days. Maybe she already did.

And there was nothing he could do except try not to care.

As the train neared St. Louis, Molly grew more and more nervous. She had lain awake all night in the jouncing berth, staring into the darkness and listening to the nasal snores of the large, redheaded woman in the bed above her. This morning she had not bothered to look into a mirror, but she knew that if she did, she would see bloodshot eyes, pale cheeks, hair that she'd scarcely bothered to comb. Her grandfather would not think he'd gotten much of a bargain. But this morning she was too disheartened to care.

The train wheels clattered beneath her feet as she stuffed her nightdress into her valise. Ryan would be waiting for her over breakfast in the dining car. He would wolf down his bacon and eggs as if he hadn't a worry in the world. After all, why shouldn't he be happy? By the end of the day, he would have a pocket full of money, and she would be out of his life for good.

Heat flooded her face as she thought of that first night on the train when his kisses had set her on fire. She had been frightened and needy, and Ryan's arms had given her a last, brief refuge. Now even that was gone. For the first time since the death of her parents, she was truly alone.

But this was no time for self-pity, Molly lectured

herself. The Tse Tse Stus were still her people. She was still a warrior. No matter what happened, she could not let herself forget that.

Three winters ago, alone in the mountains, she had faced a charging bear, taken its life with an arrow and brought its skin home to Crow Feather. Now she was about to face a different enemy, just as strong and just as frightening. She could not, would not, give in to her fears.

Softly, in a voice that barely rose above a whisper, Molly began to chant. The song was one that Crow Feather had taught her, a song of a warrior's courage. The steady cadence of the words flowed through her, calming her terror as she sang. She felt the strength and the love of her people, and for a moment she was Moon Hawk, the brave one, who smiled in the face of fear.

She would keep the song inside her, Molly vowed. Whenever she was afraid, she would sing it in her mind. She would be a warrior in this strange place, so that the spirit of her grandfather—her true grandfather—would see her from across the four rivers and be proud.

Buckling her valise, she stepped out of the sleeping compartment. Back straight, head high, she strode down the aisle toward the dining car.

Ryan checked his pocket watch as the train pulled into St. Louis. Three-fifteen. The train was on time. If Horace Mannington had gotten the wire from

Omaha, he, or at least his driver, should be waiting on the platform.

In the wire, Ryan had requested that Mannington have two bank drafts, for twenty-five hundred dollars each, drawn up and ready. He would endorse one and give it to Molly at their parting, or maybe it would be safer to give her the cash, so that she would understand its value. But then, how could she keep it safe? It might be better to put it in the bank and give her the account book. He would just have to play the cards as they fell. But he was as nervous about the next hour as she was. Part of him just wanted it over and done with. Another, deeper part of him could not bear the thought of letting Molly go.

He glanced at her, where she sat beside him, staring through the train window at the ugliness of stockyards, slums, warehouses and factories. She had said little today, but he sensed a new stoicism in her, a thread of steel that he could not help admiring. Her glorious wheaten hair was awkwardly twisted and pinned atop her head, with one stray curl falling onto her pale cheek. She had discarded the blue serge gown she had worn for the past five days for a simple dove-gray military-style jacket and flaring skirt. On most women the costume would have been too severe, but Molly looked stunning in it.

Yes. Yes, we were lovers…

The whispered words drifted back to Ryan now, causing him to curse his lost powers of recollection. If he could choose one thing to take away from this experience, it would not be the reward money, but the memory of her miraculous body quivering in his arms, her husky little love cries filling his ears as brought her to her peak again and again…

Ryan felt the train jerk and sway as the brakeman applied pressure to the wheels. Steam hissed from the slowing pistons as the great iron horse glided into the depot and stopped alongside the platform.

Beside him, Molly's body had gone rigid. She pressed toward the window, eyes scanning the platform for a face she had never seen but somehow felt she should know. Horace Mannington was her single living blood kin. Ryan could only pray that the old man would make her feel at home.

"There." Ryan reached past her to point out a graying man with muttonchop whiskers, elegantly dressed in a bowler hat and a brown woolen great-coat with a fur collar. Mannington appeared to be alone, but from what Ryan knew of the man, his aides and bodyguards would be close by. He rarely went anywhere unaccompanied.

Passengers crowded the aisle as they filed from the car. Molly was still staring out the window when Ryan nudged her. "Time to go," he said softly.

She looked up at him. Her lips parted as if she were trying to speak, but her nerves had clearly gotten the best of her. Ryan ached for her as he gathered up their valises and offered her his arm. She looked so vulnerable that it almost broke his heart. The thought flashed through his mind that it wasn't too late. He could grab her and keep her on the train until Mannington had given up and left. Then he could buy another set of tickets, this time for a private compartment, and make love to her all the way back to Wyoming.

But even as the thoughts were passing through Ryan's mind, he and Molly were exiting the train and he was helping her down the steps and onto the platform. Horace Mannington waved a gloved hand as he saw them. Molly's fingers tightened on Ryan's arm as he strode toward them, trailed at a distance by three of his minions.

"My dear girl!" He seized her hand but made no move to embrace her. "You can't imagine how I've looked forward to this moment! You're the very image of your mother!"

Molly hung back for a moment, like a wild mustang mare trapped in a corral. Ryan could feel the strain in her as she took a deep breath, met the old man's gaze and said softly, "Hello, Grandfather."

Mannington smiled broadly, flashing two gold teeth. "We have so many years to make up for, Molly. My driver is waiting with the carriage to take us home. We can talk on the way."

Keeping a solid grip on Molly's hand, he pulled her away from Ryan. His arm dropped around her shoulders, as if he were taking possession. Molly's eyes flashed warily but she made no move to resist as he turned with her in the direction of his carriage.

Ryan could understand that the old man was happy

to see his granddaughter. But he had not expected to be ignored and dismissed. Irritated, he caught Mannington's sleeve, causing him to glance back. "Excuse me, Mr. Mannington," Ryan said. "Before you take Molly home, I believe we have some business to settle."

Mannington raised one grizzled eyebrow, as if he had just been reminded of something unpleasant. "Of course," he said with a note of impatience. "Talk to my clerk, Mr. Carroll, over there. He'll take care of you."

As he ushered Molly toward the carriage, she turned and, straining backward, flashed Ryan a desperate farewell glance. Ryan fought the urge to charge after them, sweep her into his arms and carry her back to the train. He had known all along this moment was coming, but he had never guessed that Molly would be hustled away without so much as a chance to say goodbye, or that the sight of her leaving would tear him apart.

"Mr. Tolliver!" Ryan turned at the sound of his name. Phineas Carroll, Mannington's chief clerk, was standing on the platform, flanked by two hulks who, though dressed in suits, had the look of seasoned brawlers.

Apprehension crawled like a spider up the back of Ryan's neck as he approached the three men. He had never liked Carroll, a prissy little toad whose air of self-importance far outweighed his station. And what were the two thugs doing with him? Were they anticipating some kind of trouble?

Without so much as a polite greeting, Carroll slid an envelope from his vest and presented it to Ryan. "Mr. Mannington instructed me to give you this for your trouble," he said, turning away almost before he had finished speaking.

"Wait." At Ryan's sharply spoken command, all three men froze. His eyes held their gazes as his fingers tore off the end of the envelope and drew out the paper it contained. Only when he had unfolded it did he glance down.

His fingers held a single draft, written on Horace Mannington's bank account, for the sum of two hundred dollars.

The rage that boiled up in Ryan was slow to build, but as the seconds ticked past, it seethed to a white heat that spilled over as ice. When he finally spoke, his voice was flat and cold.

"Your boss promised me five thousand dollars, Carroll. This doesn't even amount to a down payment."

The little man cleared his throat nervously. "Uh, yes, I hear you, Mr. Tolliver. Do you have anything in writing to support your claim? Any witnesses?"

"I have Horace Mannington's *word,* damn it. I thought that was enough." Ryan's fist crumpled the envelope and the draft it had contained. "My family has been doing business with his company for more than twenty years! We've never had any reason to believe he would cheat us!''

''Nor do you have any reason now.'' Carroll's milk-blue eyes were as bland as a child's. ''Mr. Mannington insisted on paying your expenses for the trip from Wyoming. As for anything else he may have promised you...'' His gaze narrowed behind his gold-rimmed spectacles. ''Unfortunately, it's quite impossible to give you what you're asking, Mr. Tolliver. Mannington and Company is temporarily short of funds.''

Ryan blinked in stunned disbelief. ''You mean Mannington is broke?''

Phineas Carroll winced visibly. ''Please, Mr. Tolliver, that's such a crude word. Mr. Mannington is hardly a beggar, and I am still in his employ. But, land speculation, as you know, is a risky business. Some of our investments of late have been, shall we say, disappointing? In any case, much as Mr. Mannington appreciates the return of his granddaughter, our present circumstances don't allow—''

The clerk's words ended in a gurgle as Ryan seized him by his lapels and yanked him off his feet. ''Circumstances or not,'' he growled, ''you can tell your boss—''

The two thugs moved. By the time Ryan realized his mistake, it was too late. One man caught his arms and twisted them painfully behind his back. The other went to work with huge sledgehammer fists.

Ryan awoke two hours later, bruised, bloodied and slumped into a second-class seat on the westbound Union Pacific.

"You say she lived with the Indians?" The tall, hatchet-faced housekeeper circled Molly, her lips pursed in disapproval. "Well, that much I can believe! She certainly smells like one of the filthy creatures! And those dreadful clothes are going straight to the rag pile. No lady has worn that style in ten years!" She glanced at her employer. "She's going to be a challenge, Mr. Mannington."

Horace Mannington shrugged wearily. "Do whatever you have to. There's a lot riding on this girl, and we haven't much time."

The housekeeper sniffed. "Well, the first thing she's getting is a good bath. Meanwhile I'll have some ready-made clothes delivered. They'll have to do until we can get a dressmaker in to take her—"

"I understand you, and I can speak for myself," Molly interrupted. "You don't have to talk about me as if I were a stray dog you'd just brought home."

Her grandfather sighed. "We know that, Molly, my dear. It's just that there are so many things to be done. All of them for your own good."

Molly's gaze crawled upward to the high ceiling of the sitting room, which was painted sky-blue and decorated with painted flowers and plaster angels. Just to get to this room she had walked through such a maze of chambers and hallways that she feared she might not be able to find her way out again. The house was like a gigantic, windowed cave, the furnishings so fine and delicate that she was almost afraid to touch them for fear they would soil or shatter.

"Please can't we begin with making me over tomorrow?" she pleaded, softening her tone. "I've come such a long way, and I'm so tired." She glanced at her grandfather. "And we've had so little time to talk."

Horace Mannington turned away to select a cigar from a gold box on a marble side table. Molly had hoped her grandfather would be wise and patient like Crow Feather. She should have known better. "We'll talk at dinner," he said. "That will be soon enough. Meanwhile, you be a good girl and do as Mrs. Hoffman tells you."

Molly bit her lip to keep her silence. If she'd been rash enough to speak, she would have told her grandfather and this bossy old woman that she, Moon Hawk, had been a leader among her people and would not tolerate being treated like a backward child.

But that would serve no purpose. She was here for one reason only—to help her people. She could not afford to make enemies, especially in this house.

Mrs. Hoffman glided to the parlor door as if she had wheels under her skirt instead of feet. Turning, she motioned for Molly to follow her. "Come along, girl. Your grandfather has charged me with transforming you into a lady overnight. A bit like making a silk purse out of a sow's ear, I'd say, but I shall do my duty. I trust you'll be wise enough to coöperate. That will make things less unpleasant for both of us.''

Obediently Molly trailed the woman down the hall and up the back stairs to the second floor. She had sensed that the reunion with her grandfather might be difficult. But not in her worst moments of fear had she expected to be treated with such cold contempt as she had found in this house.

She thought of Ryan, but the memory was tainted with bitterness now. She had hoped he would stay in St. Louis for a few days to help her settle in. But Ryan had not even taken the time to wish her luck and say goodbye. He had collected his reward and passed out of her life, as if nothing had ever mattered to him except the money. She was alone in this noisy, bewildering city. Alone in this huge, empty cavern of a house.

She was left with no connection except to her people. From this night forward, all that she did would be for them.

Scrubbed raw and clad in a clean flannel nightdress and robe, Molly sat at one end of the long dining table, picking at her plate of roast lamb, boiled peas, mashed potatoes and stale, buttered bread. The vast dining room was dark except for the single lamp on the table. The tired-looking black woman who'd brought in the plates had vanished without a word.

Molly had expected to be ravenous, but it was hard to feel like eating when her grandfather sat across from her, watching every bite that went into her mouth. At least she'd had the chance to practice her table manners at the ranch and on the train. Otherwise she might have disgraced herself.

"I'm assuming those savages ruined you." His statement came without warning, striking her like a slap across the face. She stared at her grandfather, too stunned to answer.

"It's something I need to know," he said. "If you're not a virgin, we'll need to come up with a reason for it."

"I don't consider myself…ruined." She forced the words out of her tight throat. "I was married for a short time. My husband was a good man and a respected warrior. He died a few months after our wedding."

There was no need to tell him any more—and certainly no need to mention Etonéto. She would never tell anyone about the night she had spent in the arms of the man who was now Ryan Tolliver.

"So you're a widow." Her explanation seemed to satisfy him.

"Yes. But I can't see that it's anyone else's business! Why should it matter?"

"Because I want you to enter respectable society, Molly," he said, his tone softening. "I'm hoping it's not too late for you to marry well and provide me with a few great-grandchildren in my old age."

Molly met his gaze across the table. In the depths of his light gray eyes she saw, for the first time, the fear that was driving Horace Mannington—the fear that he would die without leaving any part of himself behind.

It was fear, not love, that had brought her to St. Louis. Only through her unborn children could the Mannington bloodline continue. Only she could grant him the immortality he craved.

Molly felt a tremor pass through her body as the truth sank home. She was not a helpless prisoner in this house. Fate had given her the power and the means to get what she wanted. She could use that power to help her people.

Straightening in her chair, she regarded her grandfather across the table. "There are things I want you to understand," she said. "The Cheyenne were good to me. They raised me as one of their own, and there were many of them I grew to love."

Molly paused for a moment, gathering her resolve. Then, as simply and honestly as she could, she told him about her people's plight and her promise to find them a new home, away from the reservation.

He listened until she had finished, his shrewd eyes watching her carefully. "So that's why you agreed to come back here with Ryan," he said. "You wanted to get money to buy land for your Cheyenne."

"Yes." There was no reason for her to lie, or even to pretend that she loved this conniving old man.

Horace Mannington drew a cigar from his vest pocket and balanced it between his fingertips, but did not light it. "I think we understand each other, Molly," he said slowly. "But I don't have the kind of land you need, and right now I don't have the money to buy it. That's God's truth."

Her eyes widened. She bit back a moan of dismay.

"But I have a proposition to make you, girl," he continued. "One that, I believe, will get us both what we want. Hear me out."

Chapter Fifteen

Even after two months, Ryan's dislocated jaw was stiff and tender. While he was at rest, as he was now, he had fallen into the habit of rubbing the sore spot lightly with his fingertips. The hot spark of pain served as a reminder that a gross injustice had been done—an injustice to which he was about to return.

Ryan's pulse quickened as the train chugged through the outskirts of St. Louis. In his mind, he had rehearsed the confrontation with Horace Mannington a hundred times. But even now, he had no idea what he would do or say. He would, after all, be seeing Mannington on official ranch business, to make the final payment on a parcel of grazing land and see to the transfer of the deed. Until that was accomplished, he owed it to Morgan to keep a civil tongue in his head.

And then there was Molly, who had not been out of his thoughts since the moment Mannington had hustled her off that platform and led her to his waiting carriage. The desperation in her last backward glance had haunted him day and night. He had to know how she had fared and whether she was happy. Beyond that, Ryan yearned to hold her in his arms again. But he knew that would be impossible now. Even seeing her again would be a bad idea. Molly had a new life now. He had to let her live it.

But how could he not ask about her? How could he not try to see her if he could?

Ryan was still battling with himself as he paid the hack driver and mounted the front steps of the imposing red brick building that bore the sign Mannington and Company. His nerves shrieked as he opened the heavy brass-trimmed door and stepped across the threshold. The only thing he knew for certain about the next hour was that he would be relieved when it was over.

Phineas Carroll was nowhere in sight. But then the little toad would have known about Ryan's appointment and made himself scarce. Horace Mannington, however, emerged from his second-floor office and strode out onto the landing.

"Ryan! Good to see you, my boy! Come on up to my office, the papers are all ready!"

Prickling with distrust, Ryan mounted the stairs. Mannington's manner was too friendly, too jovial. Not a good sign.

Ryan's sources had confirmed that the company was indeed in dire financial straits. A vast tract of land Mannington had bought in Nevada had proved too dry and too alkaline for settlement, and there had been other bad investments as well. Recently a lawsuit from an important client had created further expense, draining away Mannington's available cash. It was easy enough to understand why the old man had defaulted on the reward for bringing Molly home. But nothing could justify the way his lackeys had treated Ryan.

There would be a reckoning, Ryan vowed as he reached the top of the staircase. He would not leave St. Louis without seeing some kind of justice done.

"Your brother's family is well, I take it." Mannington seized Ryan's hand, shook it and ushered him into his richly furnished office with a window overlooking the Mississippi River. "Such a charming, spirited woman, that little wife of his. What's her name, Clarissa?"

"Cassandra." Ryan was in no mood for chitchat. "Let's get those papers finalized. Then I'd like a private word with you."

"No need for that, Ryan." Mannington's expression was as bland as a child's as he motioned Ryan to a chair and seated himself behind the vast cherrywood desk. "I was anxious to see you again, so that I could apologize. What those brutes did to you was unthinkable, and expressly against my orders. When I heard about it, I dismissed them both."

"And Carroll?" Ryan's tone was flat and bitter.

"Mr. Carroll was authorized to pay your expenses and explain the circumstances. That, I believe, is exactly what he did. The two men who beat you were not acting on his orders.''

Then what were they doing there? Ryan wanted to ask, but he knew the question was pointless. If Mannington did not know the answer to the question, the oily old bastard would invent one.

''You earned every cent of that reward,'' Mannington said. ''And I fully intend to pay you as soon as my company recovers from this, uh, temporary setback. I should have told you that myself. Regretfully, I left the explaining to Mr. Carroll because I didn't want to subject Molly to any unpleasantness on her first day home.''

Molly. Even the sound of her name was like a stab in Ryan's gut. The dreams of loving her had continued unabated, as had his mental struggle to recall what had happened between them. Back on the ranch, with a thousand-mile distance between them, he'd felt insulated from the pain. Here, with her so near and yet so out of reach, the sudden longing almost made him groan aloud.

''How is Molly, by the way?'' he managed to ask.

''Oh, quite well.'' Mannington thrust the papers for the grazing land across the desk for Ryan to sign. ''The girl has truly blossomed in her time here. Why, you'd scarcely know her!''

Ryan felt a cold weight shift in the pit of his stomach as he perused the first paper and signed on the blank line at the bottom. Wisdom whispered that he should forget her. Clearly she had adjusted to her new life and was happy. But he could not help wondering what had happened to her dream of finding a homeland for her people. And he could not cool the burning need to see her again.

"Why don't you drop by the house tonight?" Mannington asked, and Ryan's pulse leaped. "We're having a little party. You'd be more than welcome. That way you can see for yourself how well she looks and how happy she is. That in itself should be a reward for you."

Ryan fought the temptation to grab Horace Mannington by his starched white collar and shake him until his teeth clattered out on the desk. "What's the occasion?" he asked, feigning disinterest. "Somebody's birthday? Should I bring a gift?"

Mannington smiled, clearly enjoying the moment. "There's no need for a gift," he said, "at least not yet. It's an engagement party. Molly is getting married next month."

Ryan almost didn't go to the party that evening. His first inclination was to purchase a bottle of whiskey, find a good-looking whore, and lose himself in a night of drink and debauchery.

In the end, however, his need to see Molly had won out. It would be for the last time, he told himself. And it would only be to say goodbye.

The strains of a waltz, the tingle of crystal glasses and the sounds of laughter floated on the cold night air as Ryan strode up the long front walk to the Mannington house. Judging from the number of carriages outside, this event was much more than a "little" party. Ryan had worn the suit he'd packed, but the people he glimpsed through the tall, narrow windows were dressed in formal evening clothes. He would look out of place. But never mind that, he told himself, marching up the steps. He had only come to see one person, and he didn't plan to be here long. Maybe after he left, there'd still be time for the whiskey and the whore.

Two women, one middle-aged and the other looking like a younger relative, were entering the foyer ahead of him. Lost in conversation, they were moving so slowly that Ryan had to pause to keep from crowding them. He could not avoid overhearing what they said.

"I say Horace should have locked her up," the older woman sniffed. "After living with those savages for so many years, and doing heaven knows what with them, there's no way she'll ever be fit for decent society!"

The younger woman, a gaunt, red-haired creature whose ruby necklace only enhanced her plainness, laughed wryly. "She's Horace Mannington's granddaughter. When the old man dies, she'll get everything! And in time, she'll have Winston's money, too! She'll be the richest woman in St. Louis. That should be enough to make her welcome in most social circles!"

The older woman shrank into her sable wrap. "But

my dear, just think of it! Her wallowing with those filthy, murdering savages! I've heard they have no morals at all! Can you imagine how many of them she's—''

''Excuse me.'' Ryan brushed past the two women, too heartsick to hear more. He had brought Molly back to St. Louis for his own selfish reasons, telling himself it was for her own good. Why hadn't he foreseen the viciousness she would have to endure?

He stalked into the brightly lit ballroom like a hawk into a bevy of bejeweled peacocks. It was a lavish party—much more lavish than Horace Mannington could afford if his claim was true. A long buffet table fronted one wall, laden with everything from oysters and champagne to roast lamb, truffles and exquisite little lemon tarts crowned with pastry wings. On a raised dais in the far corner of the room, a string quartet played a lilting polka. Glittering couples swirled around the dance floor in each other's arms. Ryan's sweeping glance confirmed that Molly was not among them.

Unmindful of everything except finding her, he pushed his way through the crowd. His eyes searched the ballroom anxiously, with the surety of knowing how much it would hurt when he saw her. He could only hope Molly was marrying a good man, strong and kind, a man who would cherish her and protect her from the kind of vicious lies he had heard tonight. If he knew that, maybe he could walk away, return to Wyoming and try to forget her.

Only when she turned around to face him did Ryan realize he'd been looking right at her. From behind, she had looked like a stranger. She had lost weight, and her glorious hair had been curled, twisted atop her head and adorned with butterflies fashioned from strings of tiny seed pearls. Her eyes were large, dark pools in a face that was too pale, too thin. Still, she looked beautiful. Her gown of pale apricot silk was cut low to show off her magnificent shoulders. Teardrop pearls dangled from fine gold wires in her newly pierced ears.

Her lips parted as she saw Ryan. She took a step toward him, then hesitated as if fearing disapproval. *Oh, Moon Hawk,* he thought, his heart contracting. *What have they done to you?*

As Ryan walked toward her through the crowd, it was as if someone had snatched a dark curtain from his mind. The memories struck him in full clarity now—the rescue from the snow, the warm darkness of the lodge, and their bittersweet night of love. He remembered the feel of her in his arms, her silken, pulsing wetness as their bodies joined. He remembered the scent of her, the taste of her…

"How kind of you to come, Ryan." Her taut voice, drained of emotion, penetrated his thoughts. He saw that she was standing beside an imperious-looking man whose thinning iron-gray hair was slicked back with pomade. His face was on a level with Ryan's own. Eyes the color of river ice, their whites bloodshot and slightly yellowed, glowered suspiciously from beneath thick black brows. Below them, a florid nose dominated a face whose receding chin was concealed by a freshly trimmed beard and mustache. In contrast with the cold eyes, his mouth was a satyr's mouth, Ryan thought, the lips too full, too loose, too red. There was something unsettling about the man.

"Molly speaks well of you, Mr. Tolliver. It's a pleasure to meet you in the flesh." His voice was deep and resonant, but his glacial expression belied his words. He glanced down at Molly, who flinched as if she'd been jabbed.

"Ryan," she said, her voice quivering, "I'd like you to meet Winston Galworthy…my fiancé."

Molly saw the horrified expression that flickered across Ryan's face. It was the expression she'd been dreading from the moment her grandfather had told her Ryan would be coming to the party tonight.

Why couldn't he have stayed away and spared them both? she thought, wanting to sink into the floor. Why couldn't he have taken his reward money and disappeared from her life forever? She would have chosen any kind of torture over facing Ryan tonight.

But now that he was here, she knew she owed him an explanation. She could not let him leave without answers to the questions that burned behind the fire in those golden eyes.

The musicians had struck up a waltz, one of the

tunes Molly had practiced with her dancing master. Turning toward Ryan, she seized his coat sleeve and hung on with a strength born of desperation. "I've been taking lessons!" she exclaimed with a brightness that fooled no one. "Let me show you—you'll be so proud of me, Ryan! My fiancé won't mind sparing me for a few minutes—will you Winston, dear?"

Without giving Galworthy a chance to react, she pulled Ryan into the swirling milieu of dancers. Picking up her cue, he caught her waist and swept her into the waltz. He danced superbly. Even Molly, awkward as she was on the dance floor, felt as if she were floating in his arms.

But she was not here to float. Ryan's stormy eyes reminded her of the unspoken question that thundered between them. *Why?*

"We need to talk," she said, forcing her face into a carefree smile.

"Do we? Would it make any difference, Molly?" His voice was cool and guarded. "I only came to give you my best wishes. Nothing else is asked or expected."

"Please." She had no pride left. "I can't get away now, but meet me later, after the party, in the summerhouse out back. There are things I need to tell you—things you need to know—"

She bit off her words as she saw the resistance in his face. "I'm sorry," she murmured, "I should have asked whether you had other plans. Do you?"

"I'd planned to get roaring drunk, pick a fight with the meanest bruiser in town and get myself beaten senseless," he muttered. "But since you've offered an easier way to accomplish the same thing—"

"Stop it!" she whispered, dismayed by the edge in his voice.

"Then stop playing games with me, Moon Hawk. You—" He broke off as he realized what he had just called her. Molly stared up at him, her heart pounding. It was all she could do to move her feet in a semblance of the waltz step.

"You remember," she whispered.

His eyes glittered like flints. "Yes, I remember everything. And right now I'm doing my damnedest to forget."

The waltz was ending in a swirl of music and color. But Molly's eyes saw only Ryan and heard nothing but the bitterness in his voice.

"Please," she said, "I have so many things to tell you."

She saw the hard line of his mouth, saw his head jerk in a barely perceptible nod. And then Winston Galworthy was striding onto the dance floor to claim her hand and lead her away.

He had been far more cruel to Molly than she deserved, Ryan chastised himself as he waited in the darkness of the summer house. None of what he'd said had been her fault. He had spoken to her from the black depths of his own loss, aching with the memory of how much he had loved her—and realizing how much he loved her still.

Whatever happens tomorrow and after that, never forget what I'm telling you now. I love you, Moon Hawk. And if fate is kind enough to let us to be together, I want to spend the rest of my life taking care of you and making you happy...

The words that had lain buried in his mind came back to Ryan with perfect clarity now. He had spoken them to Moon Hawk in the horse canyon on the morning before their battle with the bandits. At the time, he had meant them with all his heart. But now their memory only served to mock him. It was too late. He had lost her.

The late January night was cold, but for someone accustomed to Wyoming winters, it was bearable enough. Looking across the vast lawn, which was scattered with huge, bare elms and patches of melting snow, Ryan could see that the great, turreted stone house had fallen silent. Even the kitchen was dark now, as well as the servants' rooms. Holding his pocket watch at an angle to the waning moon, Ryan could see that it was nearly midnight. Maybe Molly hadn't been able to get away. Or maybe she had changed her mind.

He was standing in the doorway of the summer house, on the verge of leaving, when he saw a pale shape flitting across the lawn. In her long, white nightgown, covered simply with a shawl, she looked like a patch of melting snow. Only her movement gave her away. Ryan stepped back inside the summer house to wait for her in the shadows, in case she was being followed.

Moments later she flung herself through the open doorway. Wide-eyed and out of breath, she spun one way, then another, her gaze searching the dark summer house, the scattered leaves, the piles of stored wicker lawn furniture.

Only when Ryan stepped into a patch of moonlight did she see him. A little sob of relief broke from her throat, and Ryan knew that if he held out his arms, she would run to him. He willed his hands to remain at his sides.

"I was afraid you hadn't waited." She was still breathing hard. "I wanted to make sure they were all asleep—sometimes they check on me—I put the pillows in my bed—" She motioned with her hands to show how she'd arranged the pillows to mimic the shape of her sleeping body.

Nervous now, she took a step toward him, then, seeing his coldness, stopped an arm's length away. Her hair was loose, her face pale and haunted in the moonlight. She looked like a beautiful ghost, he thought, aching to hold her.

"How is my little spotted horse?" she asked, as if groping for words to fill the silence between them.

"Eating his fill in the corral. Johnny Chang thinks he has the makings of a good cow pony and wants to start training him this spring, unless, of course, you have other plans for him. He's still your horse."

Her fingers raked her hair back from her face. "Then I'd like you to turn him loose," she said. "Keep him until spring, when the new grass is on the mountains. Then take him up where the wild ones run, and let him go." Her voice broke in a ragged sigh. "It will make my life more bearable to think of him running free with his own kind." She rearranged her features into an artificial smile. "What about you? I thought you'd be off seeing the world by now."

"Your grandfather didn't tell you?" Ryan bit back a curse. Of course, Mannington wouldn't have told her, the old weasel.

"What?" She stared up at him.

"He didn't pay me," Ryan said. "According to the story, he didn't have the money. I was going to share the reward with you, to help you buy the land you wanted—not that it makes much difference now. All I got for my troubles was a beating and a free ride back to Laramie."

She stared at the floor, struggling to keep her emotions in check. Ryan fought the urgent need to gather her into his arms. That would only complicate things between them, he reminded himself. She belonged to someone else now. He had no right to touch her.

"Why, Molly?" he asked softly. "Why are you marrying that man? He looks old enough to be your father. And any fool can see that he doesn't make you happy."

The eyes she raised to him were pools of misery.

"Happiness, I've learned, is a very selfish emotion,"
she said. "My grandfather told you the truth about
his needing money. He doesn't have enough to buy
land for my people. Winston does. And he's willing
to purchase the land as the price for my becoming
his wife. The morning after the wedding he'll sign
the money over to me, and I'll start working with
my grandfather's agents."

Ryan stared down at her, dumbfounded. "Molly,
this is 1883! Women don't have to subject themselves to being bought and sold like—"

"Listen to me, Ryan." Her voice carried a note of
sad resignation. "A woman past marriageable age,
especially one who's spent most of her life with Indians, is no prize in this society. Oh, I've heard the
talk. I know what some of those women, and probably the men, too, were saying about me tonight.
Nothing I can do will ever make them accept me.

"But Winston doesn't care. He was in love with
my mother. When she ran off with my father, he was
so heartbroken that he never married. Now, for him,
it's as if he had a second chance."

"Molly, this is insane!" Ryan exploded, unable to
contain himself any longer.

"Winston's going to become my grandfather's
business partner," she continued as if he hadn't spoken. "His money will pay off grandfather's debts,
and I'll have the land for my people, and…I'll even
make sure your reward for finding me is paid, so you

can go traveling. Everyone will have what they want most. Isn't that fair?''

Ryan seized her shoulders, wanting to shake some sense into her. But the feel of her, so thin and tense through the woolen shawl, completely undid him. Lord, how had he gotten her into this mess? How could he talk her out of it?

''It's not that simple, Molly!'' His voice rasped with emotion. ''Once Galworthy has what he wants, there'll be nothing to keep him from breaking his word. And even if he buys the land, how are you going to move your people off the reservation and all the way to Canada when you're a thousand miles away from them?''

''I'll be there if I can.'' Her voice was calm. Too calm, Ryan thought. ''But even if I can't, there are men and women on the reservation who'll help, maybe even some who'll want to go along. All I have to do is get them a map.'' Her eyes closed briefly, as if she felt dizzied by all that lay ahead. ''I made my people a promise,'' she said, lifting her face. ''They're depending on me to keep that promise. Don't ask me to turn my back on them, Ryan. I won't do it.''

''But you don't love him!'' Ryan felt as if the earth were cracking open beneath his feet. ''I've never seen a woman look less in love than you do!''

She reached up and brushed his mouth with the tip of her finger. ''Being in love isn't everything. Like happiness, it's a selfish emotion. I was married to one man I didn't love, and I endured it. I can endure it again.''

She slipped out of his clasp and took a step backward as if she needed some distance to say what came next. In the silence, Ryan could hear the soft moan of the wind through the towering elms and the light rubbing of a branch against the roof of the summer house. When Molly spoke at last, her voice was so low that he could barely hear her.

''I know what it's like to be in love,'' she said. ''I was in love once, with a man called Etonéto, and it was the most glorious experience of my life. The memory of that time will be part of me to keep forever. But you, my dearest Ryan, must go away and not think of me again. Find someone else you can love…with all the strength of your generous heart.''

As she finished in a broken whisper, she began to tremble, then to shake, as if an arctic wind had blasted through the walls of the summerhouse to suck the heat out of her body.

Alarmed, Ryan yanked off his thick coat and flung it around her, pulling her close to keep her warm. She shivered in his arms like a half-frozen bird, her breath coming in gasps.

Ryan felt the wetness against his shirt and realized that, for the first time since he'd known her, she was crying.

Chapter Sixteen

Ryan clasped her hard against his chest, feeling the convulsive jerk of her body as she sobbed in his arms. "Oh, Lord, Molly, don't do this thing," he whispered, kissing her damp hair, her eyelids, her cheeks. "Come back with me now, to the ranch. We won't be rich, but we can have a good life there."

She pulled back a little, staring up at him with wet, bewildered eyes.

"I'm asking you to marry me, Molly," he said, knowing it was what he'd wanted from the day he met her. "A man called Etonéto promised that he would always love you, and that he'd spend the rest of his life making you happy. I want to keep that promise for him—and for me."

For an instant her radiance seemed to light up the shadows. Then her expression sobered and she shook her head. "Don't say such things," she murmured. "You have other plans for your life. And you know I can't turn my back on my people. If I do, I'll never forgive myself. My guilt will make us both miserable.''

''I understand. But there has to be a way to make things right.'' He cupped her beautiful, stricken face between his palms, desperate to salvage her happiness and his own. ''Will you give me an honest answer to one question?''

She nodded, swallowing hard.

''Do you love me?''

He felt a quiver pass through her taut body. ''Yes,'' she whispered with a passion that erased all doubt. ''I've loved you from the moment I found you half-dead in the snow. I will love you until the last breath of my life, Ryan. But that doesn't help us now.''

He kissed her then, a lingering kiss, as wild and tender as the love he felt for her. For the space of a heartbeat she hesitated. Then her arms went around him, and she responded with all the strength of her body and spirit. They clung together in the swirling darkness, desperate and hungry, dizzied by their need for each other.

He drank her into his senses—the taste of her mouth, the petal softness of her clinging lips and the musky woman smell of her aroused sex emanating through the soft flannel nightgown. Ryan felt the urgent hardening of his own body. He burned to take her here and now, with her back against the wall of the summerhouse, her breath coming in sharp gasps as she spread her legs and arched her hips to meet his thrusts.

But this was neither the time nor the place. The night was too cold, the danger of discovery too great. And both of them knew that it would not be enough. Nothing short of forever would be enough.

With a sigh he cradled her in his arms. "Let me buy the land for you," he said, knowing that, as far-fetched as the idea sounded, it was the only way. "Once it's yours, you'll have no obligation to Winston Galworthy or to your grandfather, and I'll hold you to nothing. You'll be free to go wherever you choose."

He felt her shake her head. "You don't have the money, Ryan. If you did, you'd be on the far side of the world by now."

"I'm hardly a pauper." Thoughts churned desperately in Ryan's mind. He had little in the way of cash, but his share of the ranch was valuable enough to make him a rich man. "It's likely to take some time—weeks, even months. Will you give me time? Will you have faith in me—enough to break your engagement?"

She nodded, but he could sense the doubt in her. He was asking her to exchange a bird in the hand for a very wild one in the bush. Mannington and Galworthy would be putting a good deal of pressure on her as well. The weeks ahead would be a trial for them both. Somehow, he had to make her believe in him.

His arms tightened around her. "Will you trust me, Molly? Will you wait for me?"

As her lips parted to answer, Ryan glimpsed a movement on the far side of the lawn—a raccoon, most likely, or a fox. From their kennel behind the house, a pair of hounds broke into furious barking. Molly stiffened in alarm and pulled away.

"You have to go. The dogs are chained and won't attack you, but someone will be coming out to check on them."

As she spoke, a lantern flickered in a downstairs window. "Can you get back into the house without being caught?" Ryan asked, more afraid for her than for himself.

"Yes—I know a way. Don't worry about me. Just go."

"I'll write to you," he said. "You won't be able to reach me because I may be traveling, but I'll send letters as often as I can. Trust me, Molly."

He squeezed her hand hard, praying she would be safe. An instant later, she was racing across the lawn. Ryan slipped out the back of the summerhouse and headed for the wooded strip at the rear of Mannington's property. There he paused long enough to watch the white flutter that was Molly's nightgown vanish into a side entrance of the house. No sooner had she disappeared than the glow of a lantern flooded the back porch.

Turning, Ryan broke into a run that carried him

through the trees and onto the road. When he looked back at the house, it was dark once more.

Thrusting his hands into his pockets, he began the long trek to the Union Pacific depot, where he had already checked his baggage and bought a ticket on the early-morning train. Leaving Molly at the mercy of those two old schemers would be one of the hardest things he had ever done. But if he was to get the land that would set her free, there was no time to lose.

He could only hope she would wait for him.

"You want to *what?*" Morgan Tolliver stared at Ryan over the back of the mule he had just finished shoeing. "Say that again, so I'll know it wasn't what I thought I heard!"

"I want to sell half my share in the ranch. For cash. To you." Ryan had expected this reaction from his brother, and he wasn't surprised. But that didn't make the words any easier to say.

All the way back from St. Louis, Ryan had weighed his options. Wilderness land in Canada was cheap enough. But Molly's Cheyenne would need enough room to hunt and roam, and to move their camp from one spot to another when food grew scarce. They would need water and rugged canyons where they could hide from enemies like the Crow, who had no regard for boundaries. The amount of land they required would be measured not in acres but in square miles.

He would have to buy Molly a mountain.

"Owning more of the ranch would be a good thing for your family in the long run," Ryan told Morgan. "Our father's will left a one-fifth share to Rachel. That leaves two-fifths for you and two fifths for me."

"Which sounds fair enough." Morgan's eyes narrowed suspiciously. Clearly he believed Ryan had taken leave of his senses.

"You've got two boys," Ryan persisted. "As things stand, the shares you leave them will be the same as Rachel's. But what if you have more children? It stands to reason you'd want a bigger piece of the pie."

"That part of your argument makes sense." Morgan replaced the hammer and tongs on the tool rack and turned to lead the mule back across the snowy yard to the corral. "It's the rest of your story that bothers me—the part about buying land in Canada for Molly's Cheyenne." He gave the mule's haunch a slap to get the stubborn animal moving. "It's crazy, Ryan, throwing half your birthright away for a woman who could turn her back on you when it's done. And from what you've told me, I'd say those poor people would be better off on the reservation. At least they'd be safe there. They'd have clothes on their backs and food in their bellies, and nothing to fear from the army."

"Try telling that to Molly." Ryan unfastened the corral gate and opened it wide enough for Morgan to shoo the mule inside. "She's determined to get the land any way she can, even if it means marrying a rich old bastard who was jilted by her mother!''

"And you're just as determined to save her." Morgan shook his head. "You realize you sound like a lunatic, don't you? If I do what you're asking, it could lead to the biggest mistake of your life. You could end up hating me for it!" Morgan bolted the corral gate. His long, brown hands were scarred and callused from the years of work he'd put into the ranch. "Besides," he said, "I can't just pull money out of thin air. I'd have to borrow it from the bank in Laramie. And then I'd have to pay it back. You know I'm a tight man with a nickel. You've joked about it often enough."

"But then you'd own twenty percent more of the ranch!" Ryan caught his brother's sleeve as Morgan turned toward the house. "Let me ask you just one question, Morgan. If your answer's an honest no, I'll go away and stop badgering you. If it's yes—"

"Little brother, you could worry the hide off a grizzly bear," Morgan growled impatiently. "Just ask your question and be done with it!"

"An honest answer now—promise me," Ryan persisted, gambling everything on this, his last card.

Morgan swore under his breath, then promised.

Ryan paused long enough for a deep breath and a silent prayer. "What if you were about to lose Cassandra, and you could only save her by buying her a mountain," he asked. "Would you do it?"

* * *

Molly stared out of her upstairs window at the budding leaves on the dogwood tree. By the white man's calendar, it was early March, and already the sun was warm enough to coax the green shoots of spring flowers out of the earth. Soon the bees would be foraging, and the air would quiver with the songs of returning birds.

At any other time she would have been happy for these signs of awakening spring. Now they only reminded her that her promise to her people remained unfulfilled.

Where her Tse Tse Stus lived, the land would still be deep in winter snow. But she knew her people would already be watching for her, counting the days until Moon Hawk would return and show them the way to their new home.

But she had no home to give them, and the fault was all her own. She had trusted a promise made by moonlight; and like the moonlight, the words so passionately spoken had faded away to nothing.

Looking down from her window, Molly saw the vulturine figure of Mrs. Hoffman hurry down the sidewalk to meet the mail wagon, as she always did. During the first few weeks of Ryan's absence, Molly had waited eagerly for the mail to come. She had met Mrs. Hoffman in the front hall every day to ask if there might be a letter for her. But the housekeeper always shook her stern gray head. By now Molly had stopped asking. There would be no letters from

Ryan. It was clear enough that he had already abandoned her.

Molly curled into the window seat, pulling her knees against her chest as she gazed around the bedroom that had once been her mother's. Once, no doubt, the ruffled rose-pink satin coverlet and lace canopy that adorned the bed would have been pretty and bright, as would the ivory lace curtains at the window and the richly patterned Turkish carpets on the floor. But now an air of faded neglect hung over the room, as if nothing had been freshened or replaced in the twenty-five years since young Florence Mannington had lived within these walls. Molly had asked for this bedroom in the hope that being here might bring her closer to the spirit of her mother. But there was only sadness here, and she understood at last how unhappy young Florence must have been in this house, and how the gentle love of John Ivins, the schoolmaster, had set her free.

Molly's head swung around at the sound of her grandfather's knock. At her murmured "Come in," he entered, still dressed for the office in a natty dark gray business suit. Molly's heart sank at the prospect of another lecture from the old man. Their relationship had been tolerable, even pleasant, until Molly had broken her engagement to Winston Galworthy. Since that day, almost two months ago, the tension between the two of them had reached a near screaming pitch. Molly had weighed the idea of running away. But where would she go? To leave would be to abandon all hope of buying land for her people, as well as any hope that Ryan might still come back and find her.

"I spoke with Winston today," her grandfather announced. Molly sighed, recognizing the diatribe she had heard so many times before. "He's still willing to marry you, Molly, but he won't wait forever. There are other women from good families, younger than you and just as pretty, who've set their caps for him. Why should he waste time pining for a woman who's rutted with savages and lived like a wild animal?"

Weeks ago, Molly would have flown at him for such a remark. By now she had heard it so many times that her only response was to close her ears and will the cruel words to flow off her like water. Her grandfather was an insensitive old man who understood nothing of her life or her people. She could not allow his thoughtlessness to crush her spirit.

But he was wearing her down, day by day, and Molly could not help longing for this standoff to end. This gloomy house had become her prison, her grandfather and Mrs. Hoffman her jailers. The thought of spending years of her life in these grim circumstances was more than she could bear.

"You're being selfish, you know," the old man continued as if following a memorized script. "All you'd need to do is marry Winston, and all our troubles would be over. You'd have his promise to buy land for your Indians and I'd have the partnership I need to save my business. Mannington and Company can't hang on much longer, Molly. Weeks from now we could lose it all, even this house. We're on the verge of bankruptcy, and it's your fault. What is it you want, girl—the moon and the stars? Winston is handsome and wealthy, and he'll treat you like a princess. He seemed to suit you well enough when you agreed to marry him. What changed your mind? Can't you at least tell me that?''

Molly looked down at her hands, choosing silence over a lie. She knew better than to bring up Ryan's name, especially now that he had vanished from her life.

For a long moment her grandfather's eyes seemed to bore into her, drilling for secrets she wanted to hide. At last, with a snort of disgust, he turned on his heel and stalked toward the door—his usual manner of leaving after these one-sided exchanges. This time, however, he suddenly paused in the doorway and turned back to face her.

"I almost forgot to tell you," he said, suddenly affable. "Today at the office I got a letter from Morgan Tolliver, wanting to know the price of some land."

"Oh?" Molly felt her pulse jump. Hiding the surge of emotion, she feigned mild interest. "Did he happen to say how Cassandra and the children were doing? They were so kind to me when I stayed at their ranch."

He fingered one muttonchop whisker, as if trying

to remember. "I don't recall anything about Morgan's wife and children. But he did mention that Ryan was married now."

Molly felt her heart lurch into her throat, stopping her breath, strangling her like a fish jerked out of water onto dry land.

"How…nice." She choked out the words, forcing her face into a smile. "Do you think it's too late for us to send them a wedding gift?"

Her grandfather shook his head. "Save yourself the trouble. According to Morgan, the new bride and groom are honeymooning in Europe right now. Her parents gave them the trip as a wedding present. Morgan didn't tell me her father's business, but I get the impression they're quite well off."

"Ryan always wanted to see the world." Molly could feel herself drowning in a tide of hopelessness. It swept over her, sucking her down, cutting off air and light.

"So I understand." He turned back toward the doorway, then paused once more. "By the way, I invited Winston to come to dinner tonight. I hope you'll put on a pretty dress and be pleasant to him."

Molly nodded mutely, knowing he would not leave until she acknowledged his wishes. As her grandfather's retreating footsteps echoed down the hall, she felt herself begin to die, crushed beneath the awful weight of what had happened—and what *would* happen. It made sense now, that she'd heard nothing from Ryan. He had found a woman who could give him everything he wanted, and he had acted in his own interests. Ryan had been the love of her life and her last, best hope of helping her people. But his promises had been as ephemeral as melting snowflakes—all lies.

Too proud to cry, Molly stared out the window at the distant river, its waters brown and swollen from the runoff of a thousand streams. She could feel the pull of her life, carrying her like a twig in a current, sweeping her helplessly along in its power.

There was no more reason to resist. With Ryan lost to her, only one way remained to help her beloved Tse Tse Stus.

For a long moment she stared westward, picturing each of their faces in her mind—She-Bear, Broken Elk, Bright Wing, Crane Flying, and the others. She had made them a promise, these beloved ones, and she could not fail them now.

Turning away from the window she moved like a sleepwalker across the room to the mahogany-paneled wardrobe where her gowns hung. It would serve her purpose to look her best tonight.

Ryan stepped off the train, feeling as if he'd just ended a journey of ten thousand miles. The glaring sunlight of an April afternoon dazzled his travel-weary eyes. The soles of his feet held the memory of the rattling railroad car, so that the solid wooden platform seemed to tremble beneath his boots when he walked. His jaw was rough with stubble, and he was in serious need of a bath and a change of clothes.

But none of that mattered now. The deed to the rugged, magnificent land he had named Molly's Mountain was in his pocket. He had reached St. Louis with his mission accomplished. Now all that remained was to find Molly and give her the good news.

It had taken nearly three months to get the money and buy the land. While Morgan wrangled with bankers in Laramie, Ryan had traveled north in the dead of winter to scout for land along the Canadian border. Finding the right parcel had taken weeks— weeks of camping in the bitter cold, weeks of following obscure trails and haggling with greedy land agents—before he'd found the triangle of wild country at the fork of two rivers, scarred by deep, sheltered canyons, dotted with alpine meadows that would be beautiful in summer, and crowned by a single snow-crested peak above a deep tarn of crystal water. Ryan had first seen the small glacial lake at sunset, when the fiery glow of the sky had turned the water to a deep violet-blue that exactly matched the color of Molly's eyes. That was when he had named the place Molly's Mountain.

The price had been dear, so dear that Ryan had been forced to sell an even larger share of his interest in the ranch than he'd planned. Morgan had grumbled and called him a fool, but he'd gone back to Laramie in bad weather to arrange for the additional funds. Nothing would do but that Molly should have her mountain. And have it she would. Her name alone was on the deed.

Putting the land in Molly's name had been an act of reckless faith on Ryan's part. But he had felt an exhilarating sense of freedom as he signed the papers that would make him a poor man. As the adored younger brother of the Tolliver family, he had grown up spoiled, self-centered and materialistic. This surrender of his false values had been surprisingly sweet—and also surprisingly heady, like diving off a high cliff and sprouting wings on his way to earth. Strangely, Ryan had not experienced so much as a twinge of regret.

He had promised Molly that he would hold her to nothing. Still, as he strode across the platform, he could not help imagining the two of them together, living on her mountain in a beautiful cabin of log and stone he had built with his own hands. Her Cheyenne would be nearby, where she could look after them, and Morgan's family would come to visit them every year. Once he had hungered to see the far corners of the world, and perhaps someday that would happen. But the only world he really wanted was on Molly's Mountain, in Molly's arms.

Burning to see her again, he all but sprinted out to the curb where the hacks lined up for passengers. To his frustration, there were no empty conveyances in sight. Too impatient to wait, he headed for the livery stable. Ryan was hard put to explain the sense of urgency that had come over him. He only knew that he was aching to hold Molly in his arms and make her his own, and that every minute they spent apart would be time lost forever.

There were delays, too, at the livery stable. The first horse brought out for him proved to have a missing shoe. Ryan stewed and paced while they transferred the saddle and bridle to a tall bay gelding that proved to be as skittish as it was handsome. It fought the cinch and the bit, wasting a small eternity before Ryan was finally mounted and on his way.

Horace Mannington's property lay on the far side of town. Rather than risk the nervous horse to noisy traffic, Ryan took the back roads to the Mannington home. The afternoon was warm, the sunlight so brilliant that Ryan had to squint to see his way. Tulips, daffodils and tiny blue hyacinths bloomed in dooryards, overhung by clouds of wisteria and flowering plum. Blackbirds sang and scolded in the treetops. When he'd boarded the Union Pacific in Laramie, the plains and mountains of Wyoming had been locked in winter. Here on the banks of the great river, it was already spring.

He thought of Molly and wondered how she'd fared in this strange new world. If she'd received his last letter, she would know he was coming, and she would be waiting for him. He had written to her at least half a dozen times in the past three months. A few of the letters had been mailed from such remote spots that he'd had serious doubts about their safe arrival. But surely some of them had made it to St. Louis, especially the ones he'd sent from big towns.

When writing to Molly, Ryan had taken care to keep the tone of his letters polite and friendly, their contents obscurely phrased. Much as he had wanted to pour out his heart, he had been wary of prying eyes. But Molly, he knew, would read between the lines and understand. She would know how much he loved her.

Ryan's heart leaped as he rounded a bend in the road and saw, at its far end, the open wrought-iron gateway that led to the Mannington mansion. Unable to hold back his impatience, he urged the bay to a trot.

As he rode up the long drive, he realized that the place looked much busier than he'd expected. Plank tables covered with white cloths had been set up on the lawn. Servants were dashing back and forth, carrying chairs, stacks of dishes and cutlery and platters of food, which a butler was arranging on a buffet table that stood near the house. He had clearly arrived just in time for some kind of party. But the fact that he didn't know the reason for it gave him a twinge of uneasiness. He could see no sign of Molly or her grandfather, and even most of the servants were strangers to him.

As he neared the house, he caught the eye of a gangly young black girl who looked to be about fifteen. Her dark gray dress was covered by a spotless white apron, and her hair was plaited into a dozen miniature pigtails, each one tied with a white bow.

She flashed Ryan a broad smile as he dismounted and approached her. "Y'all be early, Sir. The party won't be startin' till folks get back from the church."

"I didn't come for the party," Ryan said. "I'm looking for Miss Molly Ivins. Is she here?"

The girl's grin broadened as she shook her head. "Miss Molly, she be at Trinity Church for the weddin' now."

"The wedding?" Ryan's heart seemed to drop into the pit of his stomach. "Who—"

The girl's saucy giggle interrupted him. "You just fall out of the sky, mister? It be Miss Molly's weddin' day! She be marryin' Mr. Winston Galworthy!"

Chapter Seventeen

Ryan wheeled the bay and thundered back down the drive, leaving the pigtailed girl speechless in her tracks. Questions shrilled in his mind. How could this have happened? Didn't Molly love him? Hadn't she promised—or at least agreed—to wait for him?

Pain, desperation and fury clashed inside him as he pushed into the crowded roadway, taking the horse as fast as he dared. He had to get to the church. He had to find a way to stop the wedding.

But then—the question almost caused him to lose heart—what if Molly had no wish for the wedding to be stopped? What if she had chosen Winston Galworthy of her own free will and had even grown to care for the man?

The thought of her loving Galworthy twisted like cold steel in Ryan's innards. If that was truly the case, he would have no choice except to walk away and leave her in peace.

But how would he know? And what would he do with the deed to Molly's Mountain?

Trinity Church was not far from the center of town. By the time the familiar steeple loomed into sight, the task of navigating the crowded streets on a horse that spooked at every shadow had taken on a nightmarish quality. Ryan's progress was agonizingly slow, and time had become a quicksilver thing that fled past him at blinding speed. He even prayed, as he had not prayed since he was nine years old and his mother lay dying in childbirth. But God had not listened to him then. Why should he listen now?

Ryan had finally reached the churchyard and was about to dismount when the double doors of the church swung open to a joyous burst of organ music. Seconds later, crowds of people began spilling out through the doorway and down the long, broad flight of steps. In their midst, a pale, willowy figure, dressed in a plain ivory satin gown with a veil of Spanish lace, descended from the chapel. Her hand rested on the arm of a graying, weak-chinned man who looked more like her father than her husband.

Ryan had arrived too late.

Still mounted, and too numb to feel, he waited at the foot of the steps, holding the horse in tight check lest it rear and injure someone in the crowd. Molly's gaze appeared to be fixed on the hem of her gown. Was she hiding her emotions or merely watching her step? Heartsick, Ryan watched her glide toward him like an angel coming down from heaven. She had grown alarmingly thin, but she was still beautiful. Whatever had brought her to this day, Ryan knew he would never stop loving her. But she was Mrs. Winston Galworthy now. He could not let himself forget that.

Only when she had nearly reached the foot of the steps did she glance up and see him. And only then did the desolation in her face strike him like a blow. Molly looked as if she had not slept in weeks. Her violet eyes were laced with red and surrounded by shadows so deep and so blue that they resembled bruises. Her cheeks were colorless, and when she put up a hand to push aside the edge of her veil he saw that her fingernails had been bitten to the quick.

Her dry lips parted as she recognized him. In that moment, as their gazes locked and held, Ryan understood that something must have gone terribly wrong to force her into this marriage. But it was to late to try and change her mind. As things stood, there was but one last thing he could do for her.

Aching with love, he slid the deed to Molly's Mountain out of his vest pocket and thrust it into her hand.

"A wedding gift for you, Mrs. Galworthy," he said in his most formal manner. Then, choking on his own emotions, Ryan turned and rode away through the crowd.

Molly stared after him, clutching the folded paper. She had never expected to see Ryan again, and now the sight of him, rumpled, unshaven and exhausted, had left her thunderstruck. What was he doing here? Where was his wealthy bride?

"Well, what is it?" Winston demanded, keeping a firm grip on her arm. "Give me that paper at once, Molly. You're my wife and you promised to obey me. I won't tolerate secrets between us."

"He said it was for me, and I want to see it first." She clutched the paper against her ribs so that he could not snatch it away. Winston's mouth went hard, and Molly knew she would pay for her defiance later, but right now there was nothing he could do without creating a scene.

"Such an elegant groom you are, Winston!" A white-haired matron, draped in pearls, clutched at his sleeve with a lace-gloved hand. "And such a beautiful bride! Where are you taking her on your honeymoon, or is that a secret, you sly old fox?"

Molly seized on the distraction to slip out of his grasp and lose herself among the wedding guests. Her hands shook as she unfolded the paper and skimmed what was written on it. She had no experience with legal documents, but there was no mistaking the nature of Ryan's gift. He had just placed her dream in her hands.

For a moment she forgot to breathe. Her knees wobbled beneath her skirts, so that only the press of the crowd kept her from collapsing to the ground. From somewhere behind her, she could hear Winston muttering as he pushed his way to her side. He would be furious with her. But that no longer mattered.

Ryan had almost reached the street. Molly could see him above the throng of wedding guests as he maneuvered his horse through the tightly packed crowd. He was already beyond her reach. Seconds from now he would be gone.

Desperate, she plunged toward him. "Stop him!" she screamed. "That man on the horse! He's a thief! *Stop him!*"

As she fought her way forward, she saw the crowd close around Ryan. Hands caught the bridle of the stamping, whinnying bay. Other hands seized him and dragged him out of the saddle. By the time she reached him, he was struggling in the grip of three strong men. The angry red welt on one fellow's jaw showed that Ryan had not gone down without a fight.

A lock of tangled hair had fallen over his face. From behind it, Ryan's golden eyes blazed with helpless fury. "Molly, what in hell's name—"

Her hand flew to her mouth in a pretense of shock. "Oh, dear, I've made a terrible mistake!" she gasped. "Please let the poor man go!"

The restraining hands fell away. Ryan stood free, trembling with defiant rage. They faced each other an arm's length apart, surrounded by a mob of curious onlookers. This was not the best place to talk, but Molly knew it would be her only chance.

Her grandfather had found her in the crowd. "This is outrageous, Molly!" he hissed in her ear. "You're a married woman now! You've no business even talking to this man!''

Molly ignored him. Her eyes were riveted on Ryan's haggard face.

Ryan spoke first, his voice raw with strain. ''Speak your piece, Mrs. Galworthy. Then I'll be on my way.''

She willed herself to say the words. ''I heard that you were married, Ryan. Where is your wife?''

He stared at her as if he'd just been blasted in the chest with a shotgun. ''My wife? What the devil are you talking about? Didn't you get my letters? I told you I'd found the land. I said I was coming back for you.''

It was Molly's turn to be shocked. Dazed, she shook her head, thinking of all the times she'd watched Mrs. Hoffman greet the postman at the gate and take the mail directly from his hand. Now Molly knew why.

''You lied to me!'' She turned on her grandfather like an avenging angel. ''You hid Ryan's letters from me! You told me he was married! You—''

''That's enough, Molly!'' Winston's deep voice growled behind her. He seized her arms, his grip bruising her flesh through the fine white satin as he jerked her backward. Ryan started to her aid, but a swift shake of her head warned him back.

''You're making a scene in front of all these fine people.'' Winston's breathing was harsh in her ear.

"You're mine now, and you're coming with me this minute. That's an order."

"No." Catching him with a sharp elbow to the solar plexus, Molly twisted away and spun back to face him. "You don't own me, and I'm not going anywhere, Winston. Not until I've had a chance to say a proper goodbye to the man who rescued me."

Winston's features were contorted with pain and rage. His complexion had turned a pasty white, and Molly knew that, in defying him before his peers, she had done the unforgivable. There could be no staying her course now. She could only hope Ryan would understand what she was about to do.

When she turned to face Ryan again, she saw that he had not moved. His stoic features revealed nothing, but when their eyes met, she saw the kindred spark there. Slowly and deliberately she held out the deed to her land.

"Kindly put this back in your pocket for safekeeping, Mr. Tolliver," she said.

Keeping his gaze locked with hers, Ryan did as she'd asked, refolding the paper and sliding it into his vest pocket.

"Get back on your horse," she said.

Ryan eased himself into the saddle without a word and sat holding the horse in check, waiting. Molly's legs tensed beneath her petticoats, gathering strength.

"Now…go!"

With a flying leap that would have done credit to any Cheyenne warrior, she sprang up onto the horse's rump. Ryan caught her arm and swung her into place behind him as the startled bay reared, scattering the crowd and clearing their way. Molly clung like a burr to Ryan's back, her skirts bunched over her knees, her lace veil streaming behind her as they rocketed out of the churchyard.

As they cleared the gate, a small, shiny object struck the stones with a metallic clink. A curious guest picked it up, recognized it and presented it to a stunned Winston Galworthy.

It was Molly's wedding ring.

Two weeks later, with early spring greening the high meadows, Ryan and Molly crossed the boundaries of the Cheyenne reservation on the Tongue River in southern Montana.

Their journey together had been the sweetest time of Molly's life. On the train from St. Louis, they had traveled in their own private compartment—an extravagance on Ryan's part now that he was no longer wealthy. They had spent their time alone, gazing at each other in silent wonder, holding, touching, making tender, exquisite love, and talking endlessly, in soft murmurs, as they nestled in each other's arms.

Ryan had described every detail of the place he had named Molly's Mountain. Now when she closed her eyes, she could almost see the glistening peak with the deep glacial lake at its base. She could imagine herself bounding like a doe across meadows dotted with lupine and Indian paintbrush, or slipping through the deep shadows with her bow drawn and ready.

She could picture her people around her, the dear ones she loved so much. They would live in the old way, this time without fear or want. And Ryan would be there to share it all, for as many years as life allowed them to be together. How could her heart contain so much happiness?

In Laramie they had paid a discreet visit to a lawyer and set in motion the process of annulling Molly's marriage to Winston Galworthy. They had hoped Winston would spare them the trouble by filing an annulment himself. But, as Ryan pointed out, if the erstwhile bridegroom had an eye to becoming Horace Mannington's heir through Molly, he might want to leave the marriage intact. In any case, they'd agreed they could take no chances.

From Laramie they had taken the stage to Fort Caspar, then traveled by horse to the Tolliver ranch. The welcome given to Molly had left no doubt that she was now a part of Ryan's lively, loving family.

On the morning of their departure for the Cheyenne reservation, Molly had donned her beloved buckskins, which Cassandra had cleaned and put away for her. The feel of the baby-soft tanned leather against her skin was sheer bliss. If she had her way, she thought, she would never dress like a white woman again in her life!

Now her pulse quickened as they descended the last line of foothills and dropped down into the valley of the Tongue River. The land that lay before them was sparsely wooded, with rolling hills and flat valleys as far as the eye could see. The wind that blew steadily across it rippled the short spring grass in undulating waves.

"It's not such a bad place, Molly," Ryan said, pulling his mount up alongside hers, close enough for their hands to touch.

"And not such a good place, either." She nudged her spotted mustang, and they led the packhorses down into a broad meadow fed by a gurgling spring. They had agreed earlier that they would not visit the agency at Lame Deer, even though Ryan had friends there. The less conspicuous they could make their presence here, the better.

"How do you expect find your people?" he asked her as they unloaded the horses in the lee of a rock-strewn bluff. "The reservation covers more miles than I want to even think about. We could search for weeks and still miss them."

Molly flashed him a mysterious smile. "Then we'll have to stay here and wait for them to find us. It shouldn't take long."

They erected their cozy canvas tent, gathered wood for a fire and settled down to wait. After the long, arduous journey it was pleasant to relax. For three glorious days they slept, fished, explored, feasted and made slow, tender, unhurried love. "I know my people," Molly told Ryan when at last he began to grow restless. "Give them time. They will come."

On the afternoon of the fourth day, a solitary mounted figure appeared on the horizon. Molly gave a little cry of joy as she recognized Broken Elk.

Only as he rode into their camp did she realize how much the youth had changed. His shoulders seemed broader, his face more resolute, and when he greeted her, she heard the voice of a man.

"Little Brother, my heart is happy!" she said. "How are the others? Are they well? Where can I find She-Bear?"

He took the time to dismount, using a stout crutch to catch his weight, before he replied.

"Most of us are well, Moon Hawk. But She-Bear is with her husband beyond the four rivers."

Molly felt the earth drop from beneath her feet. "When?"

"She died on the journey here. It was her time. We buried her with honor in the mountains."

Molly felt Ryan's quiet presence behind her. His strength gave her the courage to speak again. "Come and sit down. I want to tell you about the beautiful new home Etonéto has found for our people, beyond the line where the bluecoats will not go. I have a map—you can show it to the others and tell them to get ready!"

Something flickered in his narrow, dark eyes—a resistance that puzzled and dismayed her. He took a long, deep breath, then fixed his gaze on her face.

"Moon Hawk, our people sent me to speak for them," he said. "Bird Woman and Spotted Fawn have found husbands and will soon have new babies. Strong Hand is living with her sister's family and is soon to be married. Buffalo Calf has found her lost daughter and her three grandchildren. Crane Flying has become a healer to all the people, and they need her…" His voice trailed off as he saw her stricken face.

"And you?" she said, reeling under the impact of his words and the unthinkable truth that loomed behind them.

"I have become the maker of ropes and the teller of Crow Feather's stories," he said with a little smile. "I ride from camp to camp and take his stories to all the people so the children will remember them. And—" The color deepened in his young face. "I have met a girl, Moon Hawk, a girl as beautiful as the sunrise, and I think she likes me."

Molly fumbled for Ryan's hand and felt his strong fingers close around hers. She held on tightly, as if he were her only anchor to the earth.

"All of our people send you their love," Broken Elk said. "While we lived in the canyons, you were our mother, and you cared for us all. But your children have grown up, Moon Hawk. Now we care for others as you cared for us. The old ways are needed here. *We* are needed here."

All night, in the warm darkness of the tent, Molly lay in Ryan's arms. She did not weep, but she knew that he was aware of her pain. He cradled her tenderly, as if he were keeping the shattered pieces of her spirit from falling apart and blowing away on the wind.

Molly was grateful that he did not try to offer empty words of condolence. There were no words for what she was feeling. After all her hopes and dreams, and even after Ryan's unbelievable sacrifice, no one wanted their gift. Her people had turned their backs on her to live their own lives. She sensed the rightness in what had happened. But even that could not lessen the sting.

"If there had been one of them who'd wanted to come," she whispered against his shoulder, "even one, I would have been so happy…"

"Hush, love," he whispered, his lips nuzzling her hairline and her forehead. "Get some sleep. We can pack up and leave in the morning."

By the time the sun's first rays streaked the eastern sky, Molly and Ryan had struck their tent, rolled up their clothes and blankets and loaded everything onto the two packhorses. They were having a last minute bite of breakfast when a moving figure appeared in the west, riding along the same trail Broken Elk had taken.

"Can you see who it is?" Ryan moved to stand beside her, his rifle nearby in case of trouble.

"It isn't Broken Elk." Moon Hawk strained to make out the features of the approaching rider, who was squat, broadly built and mounted on a sturdy mule. "It's a woman! It's Crane Flying!"

Crane Flying rode into the camp a few minutes later. She, too, had changed since the day Moon Hawk had bid her farewell in the canyon. The weight she had put on lent her an air of imposing dignity. She was no longer dressed in buckskins but in a long calico blouse and a dark blue cotton skirt. A string of red and yellow trade beads dangled over her ample chest.

"Little Sister." She returned Molly's greeting from the back of her mule. Although her eyes were warm, she did not smile. But then, Crane Flying had almost never smiled, even in the old days.

"I have brought someone with me," she said. "Someone who tells me every day that you made her a promise and would come back for her."

Only then did Molly realize that Crane Flying had not come alone. Her heart contracted as Bright Wing wriggled loose from her seat on the mule's broad rump and slid lightly to the ground. In the next instant the little girl was racing across the grass toward her.

Molly opened her arms just in time to catch the full force of Bright Wing's joyous attack. Almost weeping with delight, she caught the child close. How sweet it felt, the weight of the solid little body in her arms, the pull of the small, wiry arms around her neck.

Suddenly everything became as clear as the crys-

talline water of the tarn on Molly's Mountain. It was
Bright Wing who had kept her promise alive. And it
was Bright Wing who had brought her back to her
people.

"Etonéto!" Tearing herself loose from Molly's
embrace, Bright Wing launched herself at Ryan. He
caught her beneath her arms and swung her off her
feet, lifting her higher until she collapsed, giggling,
against his shoulder.

Above her dark head, Ryan's eyes met Molly's. In
their golden depths she saw nothing but love, understanding and acceptance. The final decision, she
knew, was hers to make.

"I brought her things." Crane Flying held out a
small, leather-wrapped bundle. Bright Wing had
fallen silent, as if sensing that something momentous
was about to happen.

Molly tried to speak, but her throat was so choked
with emotion that no words would come. As if per-
forming a sacred ceremony, she reached up and took
Bright Wing's bundle from Crane Flying's hands.
Only then did the older woman's face break into a
rare and radiant smile.

"Now things are as they should be," she said.
"*Nestaévahósevóomatse, hemeho.* Goodbye, little
sister, until we meet again." With that, she turned
her mule and rode back the way she had come.

Ryan swung Bright Wing onto the pommel of his
saddle. "It seems we have a daughter," he said,
catching Molly in a quick, fierce hug.

"I think this makes us a family," Molly whispered, loving him.

"Then let's go home," Ryan said. "Home to our mountain."

Epilogue

The rambling log house on Molly's Mountain lay bathed in summer twilight. A cool evening breeze fluttered the aspen leaves and carried the scent of pine down from the higher slopes. The gurgle of a clear spring mingled with the sounds of the coming night.

Molly Ivins Tolliver sat on the front porch, gliding back and forth in the swing her husband had fashioned with his own hands. Ryan had built the house and almost everything in it with a fine attention to every detail. From the high windows with a view of the far mountains, to the bookshelves in the library, to the wide four-poster bed in their bedroom, every inch of their home was a labor of love.

They had abandoned the idea of building at the tarn in favor of a rich, green meadow, lower down on the sheltered side of the mountain. Here there was room for a barn and corrals and a garden, room for a family to work and play and grow.

As Molly gazed out over the porch railing, she could see the flicker of a campfire in the canyon below. The smell of roasting venison drifted upward to her nostrils. Molly's Mountain was no longer a lonely place. It had become a refuge for those among the Tse Tse Stus who were in need or in trouble or wanted something better for their children than reservation life. A dozen Cheyenne families had already settled in the lower canyons. Molly often took the horse and went to visit them, with nine-year-old Bright Wing tagging along on her own pony and young John, named for her father, strapped to Molly's saddle in his cradleboard.

Molly's black-haired boy had been an unexpected gift. She had longed to give Ryan more children, but that one blessing had been denied her. Then, last year, she had opened her door to a grief-stricken young Cheyenne brave whose wife had died in childbirth. He had placed his newborn baby in Molly's arms and gone, never to be seen on the mountain again. Now Bright Wing had a baby brother, and Ryan had a son to raise. They had long since agreed on how their children would be educated. Ryan would teach them reading, writing, mathematics, history and literature. Molly would teach them the way of the Cheyenne, so that when they grew up, they would be at home in either world.

"They're asleep, both of them." Ryan slipped out onto the porch and settled himself beside Molly in the swing. She nestled against him with a sigh, utterly contented.

"Have you thought any more about the money?" he asked her. "It's yours, Molly."

"It's ours," she said, wishing he would change the subject. Two weeks ago, through Morgan, Molly had received word that her grandfather, Horace Mannington, had died of a heart attack. Much of his vast wealth had been lost, but after the payment of debts and the sale of the house, a comfortable sum remained in a St. Louis bank. Molly was his only heir.

"I have no use for my grandfather's money," she said. "Everything I need is right here. But you—you gave up your own inheritance and your chance to see the world."

"With no regrets," he said, his arm tightening around her. "My world is here, Molly. My world is you." His eyes followed the path of a falling star. "But maybe in a few years, when the children are older, we can all see the world together."

"Or we can save the money for our children's education."

"Or we can forget it for now and go to bed." He drew her close, his kiss leaving no doubt as to his plans for the night. Molly melted into his arms, and they lost themselves in loving.

* * * * *

Stay tuned for
WYOMING WOMAN,
the final book in Elizabeth Lane's
Wyoming trilogy!
Available only from Harlequin Historicals.

Your opinion is important to us! Please take a few moments to share your thoughts with us about your experiences with Harlequin and Silhouette books. Your comments will be very useful in ensuring that we deliver books you love to read.
Please take a few minutes to complete the questionnaire, then send it to us at the address below.

Send your completed questionnaires to:
Harlequin/Silhouette Reader Survey, P.O. Box 9046, Buffalo, NY 14269-9046

1. As you may know, there are many different lines under the Harlequin and Silhouette brands. Each of the lines is listed below. Please check the box that most represents your reading habit for each line.

Line	Currently read this line	Do not read this line	Not sure if I read this line
Harlequin American Romance	❑	❑	❑
Harlequin Duets	❑	❑	❑
Harlequin Romance	❑	❑	❑
Harlequin Historicals ·	❑	❑	❑
Harlequin Superromance	❑	❑	❑
Harlequin Intrigue	❑	❑	❑
Harlequin Presents	❑	❑	❑
Harlequin Temptation	❑	❑	❑
Harlequin Blaze	❑	❑	❑
Silhouette Special Edition	❑	❑	❑
Silhouette Romance	❑	❑	❑
Silhouette Intimate Moments	❑	❑	❑
Silhouette Desire	❑	❑	❑

2. Which of the following best describes why you bought *this book?* One answer only, please.

the picture on the cover	❑	the title	❑
the author	❑	the line is one I read often	❑
part of a miniseries	❑	saw an ad in another book	❑
saw an ad in a magazine/newsletter	❑	a friend told me about it	❑
I borrowed/was given this book	❑	other: _____	❑

3. Where did you buy *this book?* One answer only, please.

at Barnes & Noble	❑	at a grocery store	❑
at Waldenbooks	❑	at a drugstore	❑
at Borders	❑	on eHarlequin.com Web site	❑
at another bookstore	❑	from another Web site	❑
at Wal-Mart	❑	Harlequin/Silhouette Reader	❑
at Target	❑	Service/through the mail	
at Kmart	❑	used books from anywhere	❑
at another department store or mass merchandiser	❑	I borrowed/was given this book	❑

4. On average, how many Harlequin and Silhouette books do you buy at one time?

I buy _____ books at one time ❑

I rarely buy a book ❑

MRQ403HH-1A

5. How many times per month do you shop for any *Harlequin and/or Silhouette* books?
One answer only, please.

1 or more times a week	❑	a few times per year	❑
1 to 3 times per month	❑	less often than once a year	❑
1 to 2 times every 3 months	❑	never	❑

6. When you think of your ideal heroine, which *one* statement describes her the best?
One answer only, please.

She's a woman who is strong-willed		She's a desirable woman	❑
She's a woman who is needed by others	❑	She's a powerful woman	❑
She's a woman who is taken care of	❑	She's a passionate woman	❑
She's an adventurous woman	❑	She's a sensitive woman	❑

7. The following statements describe types or genres of books that you may be
interested in reading. Pick *up to 2 types* of books that you are most interested in.

I like to read about truly romantic relationships	❑
I like to read stories that are sexy romances	❑
I like to read romantic comedies	❑
I like to read a romantic mystery/suspense	❑
I like to read about romantic adventures	❑
I like to read romance stories that involve family	❑
I like to read about a romance in times or places that I have never seen	❑
Other: _____	❑

*The following questions help us to group your answers with those readers who are
similar to you. Your answers will remain confidential.*

8. Please record your year of birth below.

   19 _____

9. What is your marital status?

   single ❑   married ❑   common-law ❑   widowed ❑
   divorced/separated ❑

10. Do you have children 18 years of age or younger currently living at home?

   yes ❑   no ❑

11. Which of the following best describes your employment status?

   employed full-time or part-time ❑   homemaker ❑   student ❑
   retired ❑   unemployed ❑

12. Do you have access to the Internet from either home or work?

   yes ❑   no ❑

13. Have you ever visited eHarlequin.com?

   yes ❑   no ❑

14. What state do you live in?

   _____

15. Are you a member of Harlequin/Silhouette Reader Service?

   yes ❑   Account # _____   no ❑   MRQ403HH-1B

eHARLEQUIN.com

The eHarlequin.com online community is *the* place to share opinions, thoughts and feelings!

- Joining the community is easy, fun and **FREE!**

- Connect with **other romance fans** on our message boards.

- Meet your **favorite authors** without leaving home!

- **Share opinions** on books, movies, celebrities…and *more!*

Here's what our members say:

"I love the friendly and helpful atmosphere filled with support and humor."
—Texanna (eHarlequin.com member)

"Is this the place for me, or what? There is nothing I love more than 'talking' books, especially with fellow readers who are reading the same ones I am."
—Jo Ann (eHarlequin.com member)

Join today by visiting www.eHarlequin.com!

HHMED3

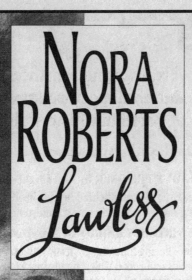
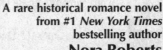
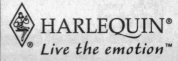